GW00374614

TALLET

Simon Cooper

Simon Cooper

Copyright © 2021 Simon Cooper

All rights reserved

The characters and events portrayed in this book are fictitious. Any similarity to real persons, living or dead, is coincidental and not intended by the author.

No part of this book may be reproduced, or stored in a retrieval system, or transmitted in any form or by any means, electronic, mechanical, photocopying, recording, or otherwise, without express written permission of the publisher.

Cover design by: Lucy Cooper
Library of Congress Control Number: 2018675309
Printed in the United States of America

'Th'ye Good Saylors' Advyce's '1407'

"a sumwat barrid and darkend navyge'shum', having roks and sands at its opening, dark and steep syded rivers that you may fynd if you sail into it … and about'e a good mil'e within the mouth of thyr'e haven … byond its wynds and layke is "Dittshum", a Fisshar Towne, a fair settle - with smugglers and villain's".. "You will fynd' no profy'ts there."

TALLET

"The only person that is not rowing, has the
time to rock the boat?, Stop talking!"

As far back as far as the late 17th century, the Cornish Pilot Gig was one of the first shore-based lifeboats that went to vessels in distress, it is a fixed seat, six-oared rowing boat. It is rowed by six rowers and helmed (steered) by a Cox, The Gig is built of Cornish narrow leafed elm and measures 32 feet long with a beam of 4 feet 10 inches.

The original purpose of the Cornish pilot Gig was as a general work boat and was used for taking pilots out to incoming vessels off the coast.

In those days, the race would be on to get their pilot on board a vessel (often those about to run aground on rocks) before any other coastal villages pilot got the job, and hence a payment.

Today, pilot gigs are used primarily for sport, with around 100 clubs across the globe. The main concentration is within Cornwall and the Isles of Scilly in the UK; however, clubs exist in Somerset, Devon, Dorset, Wales and London.

All modern racing gigs are based on the "Treffry "built in 1838 by William Peters of St. Mawes, she is still owned and raced today.
The sport is a way of life for some coastal village people and offers the chance to take part in an aggressive, fast, intense, rowing sport where the century old traditions remain, and where the comradery is still deeply ingrained in the sport of Gig rowing.

"Tallet" is a homage to these exciting hard worked racing boats, Tallet is identical to these much loved boats, she is sleek and loved and cherished by its owners and her dedicated rowers, Posh Henry, Blaggs, Tommo, Fish, Jake and Jools who skilfully power her through the cool waters of the south coast under the coxswains'ship of Coxy.

The only thing about Tallet which is different to approximately 400 other Cornish Pilot Racing Gigs worldwide, is that she "is" an imagination, perhaps a fantasy, "as" are the events in a quiet Devon riverside village in a September, just a short time ago.

TALLET

fierce, the look on the crew faces was pain, shear pain red faces breathless, Cox needed more, "now for me boys come on boys dig in, dig in" louder and louder his request became. "Come on lads I don't give a fuck where you get it from just get it and get it now Puuuuull!"

"Now boys, now boys, do it boys come on", and give me 40, the other boat was now 5 yards behind and 6 yards apart and closing, closing steady and fast. The finish line was now 60 yards away, the opposing Cox was closing in, "come on lads don't let then have it! come on aaaaand pull! come on!".

The other boats crew were grunting hard their Cox was screaming at the top of his voice, "hard, hard, hard, come on stroke it Stoke!"

Both boats lined up right angles on the end of the jetty where the waiting official was waiting, wearing his blazer and white plimsoles, a cravat finished his ensemble and as far as Cox was concerned a stupid cheap captain's cap, with his stopwatch and a pad, a few others on lookers were standing with phones and cameras filming the final few yards. As they passed the Ham it was lined with holidaymakers and onlookers watching this testosterone infused spectacle.

The two boats raced in an arc past the deep moorings at High Gurrow the wakes from the two boats bobbed the smaller yachts and the riggings sounded off clink, clink, clink, this added the clatter and noise of the gigs as got closer to the end as the rushing of the water and the 12 big men grunting and being goaded by two little coxswains approached, "a hell of a noise", It was close, it was furious the river water was being churned and the wakes from each boat now reaching out behind across the river and across the stern of each boat.

As they got to the line; Stoke was 3 yards behind and only 12 yards left in the race, "come on come"
on Cox shouted for the Dittisham boat "they are going
to get you" shouted Cox, Stoke were closing still; their
men, breathing deeply in chests almost ready to burst,
red faces shoulders aching and thighs burning hot as they
rush towards the line - Dittisham across by just 2 yards,
the Stoke boat riding Tallets stern wave as the Dittisham
boat upped oars and the crew leant back into each other's
laps coasting downstream.

Victory was theirs; they were closely followed by
Stoke with oars up; all the crews were exhausted.

The Tallet was crewed by Cox, Tommo, Jake, Posh
Henry, Blaggs, Fish and Jools (Joolie). They turned the gig
around with 2 oarsmen and gently made their way back
to the Jetty, to be met by applause from locals and holiday onlookers, it may have been war to Cox and the crew,
but it was also a great end of the summer spectacle to be
viewed from the benches along the Ham.

The crew of the Stoke boat were on their way back
fighting the flow of the turning tide, they looked shattered. As they clambered out of the boat on the side of
the jetty, standing up looked like an effort. The six winning crew members formed a line and clapped the Stoke
crew through to the quayside and the seating area outside the Ferry Boat Inn.

Chapter 2

Twelve men flopped, sweaty and wet, with a mixture of perspiration and salty brackish river water. Jools went into the pub and organised a pre ordered and very welcome round of iced cider for everyone, the conversation was good spirited and banter gaining volume as each compared blister on the palms of their hands and the level of pain in legs thighs and lower backs, three more trays of cider arrived soon after.

Traditionally the losing team would get the food organised, however the Ditto crew were in their local and as such they oversaw the flow of beers from the bar. Three large trays of sandwiches and savouries and bowls of chips arrived as the second round of beer arrived on three wet trays.

Posh Henry stood up and opened his toast to the losing team "you came, you tried, and you are very trying all of you, and you failed, bad luck Stoke Angels we will see you again, oh sorry, I meant see you off again", Boos came from the Stoke team as their Cox Quentin stood up. I would like to hand you over to our new captain Spanner.

"Spanner" the biggest team stoke member stood up with a half empty pint, the glass almost lost in his enormous hands" Eerm, Thank you Posh Henry for those kind and cruel and eloquent words" a cheer went up, "I'd like to respond by saying thanks to the Ditto Crew for a great fight today, you beat us by a couple of feet of fresh air which as you know in this weather is next to nothing, more cheers drowned out it his attempt to continue.

"It has been a good fight this year and we still have one more to go, I see that for next year and in order to beat you fairly, "another cheer went up" you fat bastards!, a roar went up from crew Ditto yeah; yeah! whatever you lot need to put some more weight on and slow that boat down for next year's battle, so eat all those chips up and drink up, the beer is on us, seriously guys thanks to you all" A good win.

Clapping and cheering went on for a while, another tray of beers arrived, the glasses were removed from the tray rapidly being replaced by empty glasses making their way into the pub kitchen for a clean and refill. The Pub was ideally placed, right on the quayside of this quaint old Fishing village, hidden 2 miles upriver away and sheltered from the sea. The area was densely wooded, steep tree covered hills surrounded the village, the weather was calm and gave a balmy evening for this celebration.

The tray of food was already looking sparse, Jools went into the bar to ask Sue for some more food, "oh bloody hell Jools's where do you think im going to get that from?" Sue the landlady was already starting to stress out about the noise and volume of beer being drank. "Well Sue its either you or the Agra Tiffin for a ruby". Jools said, Sue scowled at him and growled "get out!"

Jools stepped outside and called to his team and the Stoke Angels," "hey guys Cox, Tommo, Jake, Posh Henry, Blaggs, Fish it looks like we need to call the Agra!" Yeaaaah! The cry went out, "give Jas a call and book a session" replied Fish, "are you guys coming? he called over to the Stoke team, "hey guys we are booking a table at the Agra are you up for it? in about an hour?" who's up for a ruby?

Three of the Stoke crew said they were going home to a hot bath.

Blaggs stood up and said "no you don't", why? said Fish, "We need to get the gig off the water before the tide drops any more" said Blaggs," oh fuck it, I forgot ok, me Jake and Tommo will pull it up", a similar small team were put together for the Stoke crew too so they could get their boat off the water.

The Six made their way to the Quay and onto the Jetty, they manoeuvred the boat on to the trailer and pulled it up the slipway with Cox's old Land Rover as a commiseration gesture, Tommo pulled the Stoke crew's boat on their trailer to the Quayside alongside the Tallet crew's boat.

Jools still went and booked a table for 10, the guy on the phone at the Agra said, "who is dis booking for Please?" "Tallet crew thanks mate" Jools replied, "Oh my god hold on wait he said, I go check with the boss we came back after a minute, "ok mate in 1 hour ok. "Ok" Jools said smiling, he knew is was going to be a good night.

When Joolie got back to the two-crews sat round the tables the sun was getting low and beers were still flowing the banter was bold and getting bolder. The pub landlady arrived from out of the small black studded door of the Ferry Inn, "ok lads I can do Fish and chips 12 times and pie and chips twice who wants some?" "Ooohwaaaahr"! the roar went up again "yeah bring it over here Sue ill have some"! Sue looked directly at Blaggs who shouted it, "dirty bugger" she mumbled," " ok Sue we are off to the Agra for a curry", Posh Henry said "thanks all the same, "ok well that's fine!" then Sue turned and stomped off into the pub, "Barstard's" was the shout from inside the pub.

The boat crews had been coming to the ham and the ferry boat in to launch the boats for 50 or more years, this last two years Sue and her son Dave had bought the pub and were making improvements and changes some in the village didn't like, Posh Henry was always very vocal about Sue and her "grandiose plans" and the changes to the character of the place, for the other crew members they used the pub on boat training nights and races but lived outside the village, so Sue wasn't such a familiar face.

Sue was no slim chicken mid 40's's ruddy complexion, she was volatile and easily provoked especially by the rugby boys and the boat crews, who loved to take the piss with the banter.

One or two other locals were considered by Sue to be PITA's (Peters = Pain In the asses) often calling last orders, she would shout from behind the bar "can all the Peters please go home and thank you" most are in her good books are or tourists were oblivious to her little private joke.

The Stoke team's 4x4 had arrived to two the gig on the trailer back the 10-mile route across the river via the upper car ferry, if they didn't get a move on the car ferry would close and it would be the morning before they could get across or a 26-mile round trip up to Totnes to make it back.

Tony Hansom was the driver he was the local copper the lads called him an ugly defective from Stoke a real Gabriel man, he had been on the beat over there for many years and knew all the locals and made his job to know all the locals.

He was a trusted copper, a "detective Constable and he knew who the people were who made it their business to attract his attention. His office was in Dart, but he worked mainly from home.

He was known locally in Ditsham and Stoke as "Ugly", in the main, due to his name, but a few, very few of the local criminal community always even to his face would call him Ugly.

Tony used to be part of the Stoke crew but was injured in a hit and run car accident and now has a painful recurring shoulder injury which was the factor that encouraged to do so by his wife Beth, to give it up and become more involved in running the club.

Boat crime had been a big problem in the area for years but some of the bigger marina's that had grown up over at Brixham had taken some of the focus off the river moorings and more on the bigger crime scene further along the coat and across the water to Northern France.

Chapter 3

Cox had said goodbye to the Stoke team, bang on time some of the Stoke crew's wives had turned up to pick up the stragglers, Cox was making his walk up the hillside home, waving at the cars as they passed him he didn't drink like the others and probably hence why he all his life had remained slim and slight. The walking he did was also a factor. He was a plasterer by trade and was always busy and kept himself physically fit through work.

He also didn't particularly enjoy the raucous banter in the curry house or the curry for that matter. It just wasn't his thing. But the Ditto team know he is a bloody good Cox and had been loyal to the team for years as a Ditto resident.

As he Passed the church the old land rover chugged up the hill behind him, it was loaded up with the main core of the team, "Come on Coxy come for a vindaloo butty, the Land Rover stopped come on Coxy the front passenger seat had 2 six foot guys, Tommo and Jake sat together, Posh Henry was driving, "Nah lads thanks but I've got to work in the morning so I need an early on, good effort today though."

"Have a good time", he tapped on the roof and Posh Henry took off as the over loaded Land Rover juddered up the hill. Bellowing smoke from the rear, the boat trailer still attached Cox shouted, "you've still got the boat on you morons", Blaggs shouted from the rear "yeh we know were dropping it off at my place".
Blaggs had a bigger than normal garden at the end of the narrow lane leading up to the top of the village.

nice Cox. let's see how the weather turns out, June looked across gazing to 3 miles away and the dim mist covered twinkle of lights in Stoke through the lounge window.

June said again in a soft voice," Poor Mary, "she's only young you know? I do hope she is alright Coxy, its sounds like they just wanted to deal with it alone, I hope Mary has someone to talk to other than Quent. "

Chapter 4

At the local Indian restaurant, the Agra Palace the atmosphere was rowdy very loud, and the clear Indian cobra beer was flowing well. The winning crew were in full song so were the three guys from Stoke who were brave enough to join the Ditto celebrations. *"She Wore, She Wore, Wore a yellow ribbon She wore a yellow ribbon in the merry month of May and when I asked her why she wore that ribbon She said it's for the Ditshum boys who rowed you off today, off today......* Tommo and Fish were still eating, wiping up the last of the rich curry sauces, they had eaten all the pickle and all the chutney, the waiters standing around the edge of the room with arms folded.

They were being much more than gracious and smiling whenever a member of the ditto team caught their eye. The windows were steamed up, but Jake wiped the window and saw the rear lights on Posh Henry's Land rover, he stood up and shouted Henry your car is being nicked! All the crew ran out of the restaurant into the car park and there ticking over in the corner was Posh Henry's land rover still running, he hadn't turned off the ignition when they arrived.

Blaggs couldn't stop laughing what a total tosser, "fuck off" said Posh Henry "to much bloody noise made me forget" what a piss poor excuse Posh. The others went back inside Posh Henry turned the car off and Blaggs and him walked towards the restaurant, Blaggs said "tell you what Posh, do you want to earn a few plied, "well you will if you smell the old kippers" Posh shouted," Fuck off" Fish replied. raising two fingers as he made his way into the dark lane.

Posh Henry said to Blaggs as they walked the last few yards to Posh Henry's Flat above the old chemist shop, "were you serious about a bit of work Blaggs?" "deadly serious, yes mate come down to the workshop om the foreshore near the Ham on Monday I'll give you the stuff, you will need your Landy and the use of your boat", "So, what am I doing?" asked Posh Henry, "I'll explain it Monday" Blaggs said. "It's easy but you will need a good breakfast inside you, bring me a bacon roll too." "Cheeky bugger" said Posh Henry "I've not started yet and already promoted to head of catering", they both laughed, see you Monday bright and early" said Posh Henry. "Yeah, see ya mate" replied Blaggs.

Blaggs lived in back lane it was a long lane running alongside the back of the park, the moon was up high and his footsteps heeded by small pot holes and broken branches from a storm a few days prior, as he approached the gate where he lived there was a car parked next to the gig and trailer.

The car flashed its lights, Blaggs stopped and held his hand to shield his eyes, he recognised the guy as the house manager from the new house development, Blaggs approached as the window on the driver's side dropped,

"Bit late for you to be out isn't it" Said Blaggs, "My mother will not be concerned" said the driver", "How can I help?" said Blaggs, "there will be a boat come into the marina tomorrow", the man was talking slowly and calmly, he drew on his cigarette, there is a box and a package to be recovered from it, but do not approach the boat until I tell you, the package will be in a plastic bag to don't get it wet and do not open the package, bring to me at the new house".

"I will be there on Monday, "So, what's in the package?" Blaggs enquired, "being nosey isn't an elegant virtue" said the guy," but as you ask it is for the new house a new camera system is being fitted, we need this, understood?".

"OK said Blaggs, "the other work will continue Monday I have some help so it should be easier", "Some help? "said the dark figure in the car? Who is this help"? "It's ok" said Blaggs he is a close friend of mine, I've not given him any detail, he will deliver the fuel as directed and has a 4x4 and a boat so extra useful"?

"Mr Blaggs, I cannot emphasise to you enough, that in all respects trust is at the base of everything we do, do not let me down," the man's eastern European accent was pronounced and had an edge of threatening in it, "I won't let you down" said Blaggs the man's face was silhouetted out as he drew again on his cigarette "wait for my call before you go to the boat" "what is the boat called?" said Blaggs , after a few second the man said quietly " The Makonde " he flicked his nub end across the parking area, The man wound up the window and started the car up, it silently drew away. "and good night to you too Uri" said Blaggs under his breath. He opened the gate and went into the house.

Chapter 5

Saturday morning was drizzling with misty rain, the air was warm "greasy air" Cox called it, the view from Coxy's big window as grey mist and wet everywhere. It was 7 am and Cox was getting ready to start at the house and finish off the last two walls of plastering. He finished his cup of tea and slid his plastered covered coat on and made his way out of the door.

Posh Henry was walking back up the hill with a thumb out and hoody up in the drizzle trying to grab a lift back to the Indian restaurant to collect the Land Rover. As he passed Cox's door it opened and Coxy stepped out, "Christ Posh, you look rough", "yeah, I feel like shit inside, I've been on the bog all night, Tommo puked up too", "well par for the course then, he always does" laughed Coxy,

"Where you off?", Coxy asked, Posh Henry said, "I got to get my Landy back its up at the top at the Agra", Cox said "that's a half hour walk for you then Posh" " Yeah don't I know it, are you going my way? Yeah? any chance of a lift?", Coxy put some buckets and towel's in the van and said, "come on ill nip you up there you poor waif" Cox smirked at him, he said "God loves a tryer Posh and you are very trying!"

Posh waited until coxy reversed his little white van off the drive, Coxy unlocked the passenger door and Posh jumped in, "thanks for this Cox, I appreciate it cheers" Posh thanked Cox "No worries im a little early anyway with this weather todays plastering is going to be fun, fun, fun"! Coxy said.

After a few hundred yards Coxy said "good god Posh what have you been eating your breath stinks", "oh I was sick in the night", "oh how romantic" Cox chuckled. Cox wound his window down to let a rush of air into the van phew Cox exclaimed waving his hand in front of his face, Posh laughed is it that bad?", "too right it is" said Coxy, "are you sure you should be driving?" Posh said Im not driving you are! And laughed yeah im ok id had a few last night but not as bad as Tommo and Blaggs, those two were cankered"!, C ox said "a good night then? "oh yea, as usual Coxy you know we always try to keep up standards".

"Mind you it was a good night for me I've picked up a bit of work with Blaggs, so bonus night. Oh yeah said Coxy what's that scallywag got you doing?" "it's a mystery job Coxy, "I don't fucking know yet".

"So you don't know what Blaggs has got planned for you? "No other than im taking the breakfast", "Ha that's Blaggs all over" said Cox, "just mind you're not pearl diving or oyster harvesting or barnacle scraping", Posh laughed, as they came to the tee junction at the top of the hill, "here you go then Posh".

Hope your old beast start up for you. "She will" said Posh Henry, he got out of the van, Coxy turned the van around and papped his car horn and wound the window down, "Posh, just a word to the wise, Blaggs is a great guy, but sometimes sails very close to the wind, you mind what you're doing and stay safe", "I will old mother Coxy, I will" Posh retorted with a smile. Cox shook his head and made off down the hill back to Dittisham.

Posh arrived at the Agra and there was his Old

white shirt and dark blue silk tie, he was wearing what June would say were 'significant shoes' he was sat at a desk reading some documents in a foreign language, "yes Cox have you finished? house manager didn't look up.

"The plastering is finished, but the painting will be done tomorrow, I have a some help in the morning, who is this help the house manager looked up," he is from the rowing club, he is a good lad," Cox said, "You trust him"?, the manager asked, "er well yes I suppose I do" replied Cox ,

"you suppose? You don't sound sure Cox", The manager looked up again, "yes, I do trust him", good Said the Manager as he closed his document wallet "if you trust him Cox, I will allow him in the building, I personally will let him come in.

OK So where can I get the paint from, " ah yes the paint of course, the Manager slung his jacket across his shoulders and marched off to a downstairs storeroom, there were large tins of paint, The manager said it's a pale blue a special mix, there, take two tins now, I will bring how many Cox? "I would think another 5 or 6 will do it", said Cox.

"Very good I will make sure they are in the room tonight". "Ok good said Cox, "do you have any heaters, fan heaters?" "why are you cold Cox its September not January!" "To help dry off the plaster, just gently overnight, "ok Cox I bring you one before you go" "Thanks", said Cox.

Cox went back up with the two tins of paint, he was clearing his buckets and trowels away and sweeping up the loose plaster from the floor when the manager came in, "Cox here is a heater, ok thanks, Cox said "can I ask you a question?" "well maybe" said the Manager, "what is your name?" Cox asked, "my name?" said the Manager, Seriously?" "yes", Cox said "we have never been formally introduced."

"The manager thought for a couple of seconds then leant forward tapping some gold rimmed glasses on his chin, he said "well Mr Cox my name is no concern of yours", the manager looked him in the eye in a menacing way for just that little bit too long making Cox feel uncomfortable.

"Oh, ok then said Cox I'll be off then". Cox thought to himself "fuck you Mr Charisma". Coxy collected his buckets and tools and levels loaded them in the van he didn't look at the manager but was aware he was watching Cox closely; he got in the van and reversed the van off the property.

As he dd the enormous gates close silently their dark battleship grey exterior towering above Cox's little van. A shiver went down Cox's spine as he drove away. "Something not right there" he mumbled.

Cox arrived at home some minutes later, he locked the van up and walked up the few steps to the house, "Hi June im home," the house was cool, the kettle was cold, he guessed she was out.

Having not eaten all day he filled the kettle and found the biscuit tin, he crunched into a couple then as the tea was brewing, he heard Junes key in the front door, as she came in Cox asked if she wanted a tea, "not bothered" she said, "ok then" he said, he poured himself a mug of tea dunking in several biscuits.

June came into the kitchen and slapped his hands off the biscuits, "you're not the only one in this house". "I've had nothing to eat today!" Cox said, June turned to lently. Cox left his van outside the gates on the roadside. "Come on Posh just watch your mouth in here they are funny lot and don't touch anything", "Ok, ok" said Posh Henry.

As they entered the lobby the house manager appeared "ah Cox you are early, "well we occasionally catch the odd worm said Cox, "worm?" replied the house manager "what worm? "an old English saying" said Cox, "and this is your trusted helper for today? "yes said Cox, this is Posh Henry" Cox introduced Posh, "I see said the house manager, looking Posh up and down. "well, I will leave you and your helper to the job the things you requested have been done" "ok Thanks" Cox said Come on Posh follow me."

They arrived in the large room, Posh went to the window, "blimey look at that view Coxy, something else eh Henry" Coxy replied. "This must one of the highest points in the village, said Posh, well it is with this outlook Coxy confirmed. I bet this house is going to be worth a packet eh, look you can see over to the lake and over there look to Gurrow Point, "Yes Posh all good but we are not here for a geography lesson I need to get two coats on this wall by 12 sharp", Coxy was insistent they make a start.

"Should be no problem," said Posh Henry stood there looking at the three tall and wide walls "well come on then" Cox said, "get your hands out of your pockets and lets crack on". Posh Henry sauntered over to the paint pots, how are we mixing this said Posh Henry, "we are not I am" said cox, "we do a wash coat first then another coat, hopefully that should so it. Here put these dust sheets down and poke then into the corners."

Posh Henry was spreading out the old dust sheets

he had just about covered the floor area Cox had mixed the paint and made a thinner wash coat as the plaster walls looked dry but he still wasn't happy, "are you ok, you look stressed Coxy is everything ok", "fucking well will be when im done here, these guys give me the creeps!"

Posh was putting the dust sheets down "oh there's a mystery afoot Coxy tell me more! "said Posh Henry with a smile on his face, "Posh keep your voice down man ok? honestly Posh you are a cracking lad I've seen you come up through the ranks in the rowing club, I knew your Dad well and do some brilliant rowing, but sometimes you are such a twat," Posh Laughed "ok im getting the picture here Cox but I've been called worse than that, "well a fucking twat then Posh , Come on mate im really under the hammer and I just want to finish up and get lost".

"You want this done fast and light Coxy? "Yes Posh, yes Posh just yes please Posh! "Ok Coxy watch me go", The duo had rollers and paint brushed in hand and made a start, as they worked the were oblivious to the regular check that were being made by the house manager, he would walk into the doorway behind the backs of the two painters and look for a few seconds then walk away, he was dressed down today, an open neck white crisp shirt folded at the sleeves, slacks and his aviator sunglasses rested on his head. The house manager was constantly looking this watch, a huge gold timepiece on his dark wrists, he seemed preoccupied with the impending visitor tomorrow.

Posh Henry and Cox spent the best part of an hour getting the "first wash on, "time for a fag" said Posh Henry, I didn't know you smoked Posh? Said Cox in a concerned way, "No I don't but in the absence of food im going to eat one, "I'm fuckin starving." Cox pointed over to his lunch box, "Here Posh, he reached for the box and handed it to Posh Henry "June put a bacon sandwich up and a drink help yourself".

"Oh spot on chap" said Posh Henry, as Posh Henry tucked in to a thick cut Bacon and tomato sandwich, the house manager appeared, "how is you progress Cox?" He asked in a direct address to Cox, he didn't take his eyes off Cox or look around the room he just stared into Cox's eyes.

Cox said, "that's the first coat on, the second will look better, then if it needs another coat then it will get one before we go today at lunch time".

"It needs about an hour between coats, explained Cox, So, we are having a sandwich then we will start again." "OK Cox, but today you must finish" the tall house manager said slowly as his gaze moved from Cox to Posh Henry who was mid bite on his sandwich, he slowly looked Posh Henry up and down.

"Yes, we have had this conversation yesterday" said Cox, "your memory is not diminished by the paint fumes then? Good that's good Cox, today than it is understood". The house manager turned on his heels and walked out and down the stairs.

"Arrogant twat" Posh said with a mouthful of bacon roll and tomato, "I think another coat should sort this one said Cox", as he surveyed the wall, "but the paint is thicker this time around", Coxy aimed the fan heater at the wall, he needed the wash coat to go off.

Right quick bite to eat the……. where's my sandwich?   "Arrgh sorry Cox Posh looked sheepish and slowed his chewing down, "I thought when you offered them you didn't want one! If it's any consolation Cox they were lovely," he burst out laughing as Cox poured himself a tea, "only joking old fellah here's your sandwich", Posh Henry had put one sandwich on the side for Cox, Cox looked at him and said, "Bloody Peter." "Posh Peter now eh Cox?".

"Cox said "come on while this paint dries off a bit, I need a fag", they made their way down the glass panelled staircase and out into the garden, there groundsmen and landscapers were building rock gardens and lawns being laid, bushes being planted it was all going on, "A bit of last-minute tidy up here?" said Posh Henry, "Yes looks a hell of a lot better than it did a week ago."

"It was a bomb site then; it looks half decent now". Cox drew on his cigarette and looked across to Stoke, the mist form earlier has cleared, and it looked like it might be a bright afternoon.

"Come on Posh Lad lets crack on and make this coat the last one, you cut in and I'll do the central bit", Posh said "I'll do the central bit and you cut in", "you're better on those stilts than I am and that means we will finish quicker", "ok Cox said "that's the first sensible thing to come out of your mouth today, well this week, or this year for that matter."

The two men carried on, no interruption and they worked as a team in unison, this was good work Cox thought, it probably came about from working together on the boat, part of a team and they knew what each other was doing, it was working well.

An hour in and Cox said we just got one more wall to do then we can do one and have a few hours chilling on the water. "What are you up to this afternoon then Cox?"

"Im taking June over to Stoke In Busty Belle, the new engine is in and she's purring at the minute", "who?, June is? joked Posh Henry "ha, ha I'll tell her you said that" said Cox, "yeah Im so scared" replied Posh with a laugh.

Posh was reaching up to finish the edges of the last bit of the last wall "what was up with Quent on Friday he was a bit moody wasn't he", "well I think he has a lot on his plate" said Cox, were popping in for a cuppa and Quent wants to see the new engine layout in Belle so well leave the girls chatting whilst we potter about in the boat. Make an afternoon of it".

It was 11.45 and they finished the 3 walls, Cox said "right let's clear this lot up and get off home, come to the house with me and I'll give you some cash, great thanks Coxy nice mornings toil".

There was no sign of the house manager, Cox and Posh loaded the van up and cleared the floor upstairs, all was clean and tidy, the walls looked ok, Cox just hoped the two coats would settle down and the colour would dry in time for Mr Charisma to do whatever he needed to do.

Just as they walked through the front door to make their way to the van the house manager appeared, "All done Cox?" his voice echoing across the lobby, "yes it's all done, the paint will dry in a few hours, then it's all good to go" "Thank you Cox". the house manager said holding his hands palms together and smiling, Cox thought bloody hell a compliment, "No worries said Cox, "I would like my bill settling tomorrow" "Tuesday Cox I pay you Tuesday" the house manager waved his hands in dismissal "Er ok Tuesday" Cox replied.

"Now! Mr Posssshhh" said the house manager, "I need

these chairs bringing upstairs will you do it? Before Posh could answer the tall man shouted Good bring two with you now" the house manager picked up 2 of the 12 carver chairs wrapped in a protective film, "I'll get off then Posh" see you later Cox "

Come, Come Mr Posssshhh repeated the manager. The house manager continued to give his instructions, "When they are here on this landing you will remove the packing and dispose of it in the dumpster downstairs make sure you put something heavy on the top so my new garden isn't destroyed by the wind blowing this rubbish around the garden, then the men from the garden will help you move the table upstairs, you will see it is in two parts, make sure this part is placed on the far end closest to the window. Do you understand?"

Okaaaay, So have we agreed an hourly rate for my assistance said Posh Henry, the house manager stopped in his tracks, his back straight and his shoulder held high, he held the two chairs one in each hand like they were made of matchwood and not heavy south American mahogany, he turned and looked Posh Henry right in the eye .

"Mr Posssshhh you will learn that in order to aspire in the world you have to first carefully and thoughtfully, he hesitated for a second or two, this strange man knew the power of the pause, ….. "Envisage", then he paused again …. "Enhance" then, "Exceed" and then Evolve Mr Posssshhh"

He licked his bottom lip and took a step back towards Posh Henry then continued he looked Posh harder then paused again, Posh didn't know where to look.

" In order to start on that long process you have to

impress, you can't impress if you are not moving these chairs and that table on to my mezzanine floor quickly and with the minimum of attention to the grubby subject of moneaaay! Mr Posssshhh!"

Posh Henry picked up a chair and selected another, he caught up with the house manager the tall man looked at Posh Henry, Posh Henry looked back directly, and said " I like your style Mr" Follow me", Posh took the lead as they climbed the stairs.

The house manager opened a window and shouted downstairs in s foreign language, "Hey! *Vasilis, pryvit, vy, troye cholovikiv, zupynit' sya tam, yaki znimayut' vash cherevyk I zakhodyat' dopomohty zi stolom, pro yakyy ya vam rozpovidav Qvikly*!!!

The house manager opened the door the 3 big Ukrainian men walked in, "alright chaps" said Posh as he picked his sixth and seventh chair up, he ran up the stairs with them in each hand, Posh Henry was obviously fit and a big guy these chairs were a good workout as an oarsman. The house manager said to the 3 gardeners *dopomohty' ts'omu durnyu, shchob zakinchyty sad, u nas menshe 24 hodyn.*

The three men grabbed the table, lifted it up, Posh joined them and they manoeuvred it to the top of the landing, there they rested it and went down for the second piece, they assembled the two parts and placed the table next to the window as instructed.

The 3 men returned to the garden in silence. Posh Henry picked the last two chairs up and arranged the table Posh found a dusting cloth and cleaning the tabletop to a mirror finish, he went around the chairs again re arranging them so the gaps between were exactly right.

Unknown to Posh he was being watched by the house manager; he was leant against the doorway. "Mr Posssshhh you have an eye for some detail I see that is commendable". "as you know, I like to Impress" said Posh in a sarcastic tone. "Ha good, do you have time to help me one more time?" " I do, but I need to get off shortly", said Posh Henry, "Yes of course please come help me now.

They walked quickly out into a courtyard, it was hidden at the side of the house, from the side entrance it looked like a garden but was a circular courtyard cobbled and planted with ferns overhead.

There parked was a jet black BMW M50 spotlessly clean as the house manager opened the boot, the smell of new leather wafted out of the warm interior, "Nice wheels" said posh, the house manager said "it's a tool Mr Posssshhh", "nice tool" said Posh, no, it is for A to B Mr Posssshhh that is all."

In the boot were 2 solid looking suitcases, "you take one I take one but hurry" "ok" said Posh, "follow me" said the house manager, the case was heavy and solid, this didn't have weekend holiday cloths on or suits. The manager leads him into an office, the walls were blood red and the desk.

The artwork on the wall was almost pornographic two naked bodies entwined; the ornaments of Nubian figures were in a glass cabinet. "Pleases put this case down here", Posh put the cases on the office floor, next to a cabinet made from stainless steel. There were four masks on the back wall they looked old and looked African. "Are those African masks?" Posh enquired, "Madagascar death masks" replied the house manager.

So, Mr Posssshhh your fee for today is here, the

house manager held out his hand and in his fingers was a neatly folded wad of notes, "I thank you Mr Posssshhh you helped me today".

Posh took it and said "thanks if you need me I only live down the hill", "thank you Mr Posshhh I know where to find you yes?" "Ok cheers" said Posh, he walked out into the lobby opened the big black doors and made his way out into the driveway, the side gate was unlatched from the inside, he made it onto Hill street.

As he stepped out into the road Cox and June were driving in the van down the lane, "Posh, Posh" called Cox out of the van window "there you are mate, Cox held out some money, "cheers mate thanks for your help" thanks Coxy, "don't mention it Cox I just had a bit of shifting to do with Mr Cheerful so no worries", "have a good afternoon", June said "Hiya Posh love how are you keeping, im good thanks June," I hope you have a good afternoon on Lusty Belle enjoy yourselves its Busty Belle Posh!" corrected Cox.

Posh just smiled at Cox and gave him a wink, he waved them off as they turned towards the Pub and the jetty just beyond, Posh took the wad out of his pocket and added the £50 to it from Cox, he then leafed through it and there was £150, Bloody hell thought Posh, happy days good work there posh.

"Time for a pint or three" he said to himself the Ferryman Inn was just 20 yards away. Posh gravitated toward its open doors. As he entered the landlady Sue shouted, "look who the dog dragged in", "ok ok can we stop now posh called to her, "Your prince charming is here, so pour me a pint wench; whist I take my place on my throne next to the window".

Posh Henry sat down, and Sue bought over his pint of Bayard's best, are we eating today Sir? Sue said in her best patronising tone, curtsying before him and handing him a menu, yes, I will said Posh I'm famished Susan and I need sustenance.

Excellent Sir what may I get you? "I think Landlady will go for an all-day breakfast with extra fried bread, chips and beans please". "Not the Sunday roast then Posh? We have got a kitchen full of the best Sunday roast for 10 miles and you want a bloody fry up", "it's a free country" said Posh.

"You bloody peters make me blood boil", Sue exclaimed. "I tell ya what" Posh said "put me a side order of roast spuds with that".

Posh Henry sipped his pint and leant back watching Cox and June unhitch the Busty Belle from the pontoon, June was sitting in the cuddy with a head scarf on and Cox was in his trademark khaki shorts Posh chuckled to himself as Cox had a streak of blue paint still down the back of his leg.

As Cox turned the engine over it jumped into life, it started up and puffing grey black smoke from its exhaust just on the water line, spurting cooling water from the polished copper exhaust pipe, as Cox sat down at the rear of Belle the exhaust note changed as it bubbled as it went below the water line.

Bubbling and burbling Cox pushed off the stern and put the little white motorboat into reverse and then forwards and on to the lake to make a trip to Stoke Gabriel.

"Nice works" Posh muttered to himself as he watched them cruise away "nice work Coxy".

mate!", "you are, I am yea ok,

"Ok subject closed, I've got cans of cold Guinness and some Bayard's which do you want?", "I'll have a Guinness" said Quent "here you are Cox tossed him a can and smiled, well get her through this, we are the coxswains in this race, and we are going to win it", "Right on" said Quent, right on? So Quent So You're a frikkin hippy now? "you know what I mean Cox," cheers buddy.

The girls arrived all freshened up and new makeup applied, Cox held the girl hand as they climbed aboard Cox pinched Marys bottom as she boarded, "oiy that was a bit cheeky" Mary said as she gave Cox a kiss on the cheek, "well I am captain of my ship and it is my prerogative madam," June stepped aboard and tweaked Cox's nose and said "oiy you dirty bugger hands off my friends you!" Cox said "I'll tweak yours for you later!".

Quentin pushed the boat back and untied the bow rope, Cox started the engine and the Belle burst into a low powerful burble from the newly refurbished engine, "you take the helm" Cox said to Quentin, everyone comfortable?", "aye, aye Captain" came the unified call to get the trip under way, with one stride Cox leaped aboard Quentin put the Belle into drive and off they set.

"Where are we off to?" said Quentin, "Boat house at Greenways" said Cox "ok captain". "I thought it might be cooler than this, so head there, and it is sheltered a bit" Cox said as he sat down and poured a glass of beer, Quentin took a swig of his Guinness from the can and they set off.

June handed Cox an ice-cold bottle of Prosecco and Cox soon had the cork popping off the back of the boat, "hurray" the girls shouted, June held up two glasses and Cox filled them up to the top, "Cheers Mary June called, the" boys followed with a "cheers Mary", "yeah thanks guys, up yours" said Mary," That's the spirit said Cox as he put his sunglasses on.

The little boat burbled gently across the water, the sun was high, and the warm breeze helped relax everyone on board. The Girls were chatting in the front and as Cox and Quentin enjoyed the Boat all chatted about boats and boobs.
"Which way?" said Quentin, "the long bloody way" said Cox. That was a signal to take a route around, it didn't matter, as long as they had time, why not fill it with a boaty afternoon.

The Boat house at Greenways was a quiet spot but on the inside cusp of the bend across from Pighole a deep part of the river navigation, it was a favourite spot to anchor up and watch the world go by, its backdrop of woodland and high trees made it ideal to hide out and do a spot of Fishing and here, the Fishing was good and had been since Quentin and Cox were young and Fished this spot with their fathers some 40 years earlier.

It has been said many times by various pundits who comment on the Ditsham and Gabriel races that the two best gig Coxswains were in the play at this time the last 5 years has seen two talents of Cox and Quentin who know this part of the river like few other men.

Their relationship is unique and unfathomable to some, they are supposed to hate each other according to some when they are in a boat, but these two childhood friendships are made of more than rowing and getting the gig across the line first. Both the Gabriel and Ditsham boats would end up in the final. The races were always close, close by feet or even inches and splits of seconds, or the width of an oar blade.

good time to discuss the Busty Belle which was Quentin suggestion for its name as in his opinion and only shared between the two friend June had the best chest and as such Quentin suggested "Busty Belle" the two friends never discussed it with the wives, it was a bit of a contentious issue as if either of the wives had found out both of them would be in for a roasting.

As busty Belle and the four friends crossed the ferry line there 500 yards in front of them was the Old Castle ruins and the entrance to Greenways little creek leading to the boat house. Quentin looked far ahead to the turn in the river where the marina on the outside turn was full of 30-foot yachts and sailing boats their tall masts like an aluminium forest of clinking in the breeze.

Chapter 6

"Bloody hell Cox look at that!", in front of them moving very slowly under power was a 50 ft sleek modern yacht, 3 mast big wheel house twin Diesel engines roaring along.

"Where is he going to turn that?" said Cox "not up here" said Quentin.

Quentin turned to Mary and said "Love have you got your phone with you?", "yes, she said here", she passed the mobile to Quent, "what are you doing?" said Cox, "Im calling Harbourmaster Dave, that will not turn up here and the tide is swinging in two hours." "Oh, come on mate we are having a day out not playing harbour coppers", Quent handed the tiller over to Cox and shuffled forward.

This Is Quentin Morris can I speak to David please? There was a short delay whilst the harbourmasters office found Dave and put him on the phone "Hi Quentin What's up how can I help??

"Hi Dave, Hi Quent how is it going?" "Good thanks, look Dave there is a masted wide beamed 50-footer on its way up to Ditsham and the lake nearly at Pighole on the wrong side of the up-tide buoy, what is he doing this far up.?"

Dave the harbourmaster said, "No room for him at Bramble or Ravenshaw marinas so I've put him up on the lake, he's only here for two days then he'll be off across to Roscoff in France again, again said Quentin, yeah, he was in Brix last month, but they have the regatta on, so he's come here, how's Mary?" Quentin said, "she's fine thanks", Cox nudged Quentin to stop the call, "Ok Dave got to go, just checking if you know about it, Cheers mate".

Cox said, "what did he say, it's a rich bugger who was at Brix last month, he's a regular visitor Dave recon", "ok can you stop worrying now?" Coxy quipped. "We'll see said Quentin". Quentin handed the phone back to Mary who was still in deep conversation with June.

Cox turned the belle in to the rounded inlet next to the boat house a disused part of the Greenways Estate made from Local Sandstone it had been looked after by the National Trust but still held its own along the river as a pretty and peaceful place to be.

Quentin stood up and used a boat hook to catch a low branch on the overhanging trees, this one said Quent "ideal said Cox, then Quent threw a rope over the tree branch and pulled the boat in a little being able to tie of the long end. The rear of the boat slowly turned around its stern facing out of the inlet, the boat became stable and the flow of water under the boat kept its position perfectly.

Coxy cut the engine, it was quiet, the only thing to be herd was the chitter chatter of two grown up women, look at these two chopsin said Cox, the two men sat with their arms folded, eyebrows raised whilst the girls talked about new shoes, eerghum! said Cox, nothing the Girls carried on, eerghum said Cox again.

June looked around, she looked at Quentin and Mary looked at Cox, "eerghum!!" Mary said "Mr Captain my glass seems to be empty OK said Quentin we are starving where the tucker? I'll get it said June, she had a hamper under one of the front seats, she has it all set out plates napkins forks, and under all of this there was cold chicken, bread rolls filled with prawns' crab and salad dressed with mayo Marys favourite, June would always put on a good spread.

The four friends set up and started to enjoy the picnic, several minutes into the first bite Cox nudged Quentin, Look he said, Silently the 50 ft yacht cruised past them, 15 feet away, in the main cabin he could see a smart woman at the helm stood to the left of her Cox could see another man, his back was to him so he couldn't make him out, as the boat just cleared the end of the ferry and the floating pontoon, another man got out of the cabin at the front and stood over the bow with a boat hook.

"I still don't think that is going to turn in the next two hours Coxy, the tide will turn at 4.23 pm today and by 4.30 that beast will be causing havoc, said Quentin. The impressive boat rumbled past, as the stern passed the cove where Busty Belle and the friends were moored up, the transom displayed the name of the boat "Makonde" underneath the name of the registered port was "Monaco".

Cox turned to Quentin and said" not so Local then!!", "maybe not" said Quentin "look there if my eyes don't deceive me, I've seen that guy before", Cox looked, the tall man on the bridge of the boat turned he put on his sunglasses and looked over to the back of the yacht it was the house manager. "well, well, well look who it isn't" said Cox.

From where the busty Belle was moored up it would have been difficult to see them enjoying their picnic, from the "Makonde's helm but nevertheless Cox kept his head down until it was past the end of the battlement outcrop.

Cox said to Quentin, "there's mighty dollars there, real money, the cash they have spent on the new development must be £100's of £1000's" it feels like an endless flow, "stick another nought on your invoice" said Quentin. "Not likely" replied Cox "I just want out of there".

The four friends continued with the picnic the prosecco flowed and the beer was almost gone. June announced, "who is up for a slice of cake" Oh June no not for me, I do need a wee pretty soon though," Mary said giggling.

Cox said "it is going to get a bit cooler on the way back to Stoke so why don't we potter back and call it a day , its gone 4 o'clock and we've had a nice day," "We have" said Mary "I've really enjoyed having a catch up" she said, "come on Coxy get me to a loo and step on it" June instructed Coxy, "See what I have to put up with Quent", "Me too"! he replied ,aye, aye m' lady Cox saluted and started the engine. Quent cast off the rope across the tree branch and they reverse into the main channel. The Busty Belle turned so gracefully, Quent and Cox stood up as it powered ahead into the mainstream.

Further on beyond the ferry they could see the chaos ahead, the "Makonde" had drifted into the main channel and was attempting to turn, "He'll never do it" Cox said, "nope that looks like a mess" Quent observed. As they approach the floundering "Makonde in all its great glory was attempting to turn and be pointing down river, but at 50ft long it was struggling to move back and forth and because the tide was still on the rise, they were fighting against the 3-knot flow.

Cox and Quent and the two friends in the front looked on as the drama unfolded, the girl on the helm was clearly not in control of this big boat. All the house managers was doing was shouting in his native tongue at the top of his voice, *"Nazad, nazad, nazad, nazad, povernit' yoho povernit' yoho ne v inshyy bik povernit' yoho."*!!

The girl was frantically turning the big wheel nearly as tall as she was. After a little time, the house manager desperately grabbed the wheel himself and pushed the girl aside like a rag doll. He took control, the sound of it big labouring engines roared and echoed around the river valley. Oh, dear oh dear said Cox not so funny now are you Mr Charisma.

As the 50 feet of yacht slowly turned the flow of the water caught the front end rapidly forcing it round faster the bow caught the ferry pontoon it ripped some of the matting and the wooden facing from the top, the pontoon swayed violently as the yacht moved forwards again, I told you she wouldn't fit here said Quentin, not wrong there said Cox, the yacht swung backwards and the back end crunched into another sail boat moored on the off side of the landing stage by the steps leading down to the ferry point.

Cox reversed the Belle backwards and held off, Quent said "if you can drop me off by those steps I will try and get aboard and sort this fool out". Cox moved the Belle close, Quent hopped off, Mary shouted Quent where are you going? Cox said "Don't worry Mary, he's going to help that idiot move the boat",

The "Makonde" was not able to swing round the house manager was looking more and more lost.

Quent came to the back of the Yacht and shouted to the tall man "hey let me aboard I can help you the house manager looked him up and down ok quicky Come he called",

Quent leapt on to the rear wooden stand way of

the boat and went directly up to the helm, he shut down the engines, the roar of the engine sound continued to echo, the house manager stood back and watched the expertise of Quent as he turned another key on the control desk.

You have a 3 bladed folding propeller on this boat, great for cruising forward but next to useless reversing with any surety, so we shut down the engines and run off your VIP 140 Duo Max Power bow thruster.

On the control panel there was another control that the girl and the house manager obviously didn't know existed, Quentin calmly took the wheel and spun it to midships, he pressed two red buttons and a smaller throttle controller, back and forth he switched between the two red buttons as he did the boat began to edge round on the bow thruster., the boat was moving in the other direction against the flow of the rising tide, it was nearly high tide so the maximum amount of height for this big monstrous boat was available.

Quentin asked for quiet as he listened and guided the boat its bow pointing back down river. The House Manager gave Quentin a thumbs up, Quentin called to him "do you know where you are to a be moored or are you just turning around?" "Here! Here!" the house manager shouted pointing his long finger downwards "Makonde stay here!

"No I don't think so Quentin advised, it would be better if you were opposite the Ham rear facing, "where is this?" the house manager demanded to know "why do you say this".

"I'll explain when we have it moved, but right now we need to move this and get out the way of the ferry, further north, off Stoke Gabriel, the main channel runs close to the eastern shore can you see? and there look are three visitor buoys, but they are often occupied, I can see one empty one look! Quent pointed across the lake.

Quentin continued to explain, "the harbour authority usually discourages yachts from anchoring near them because excursion boats run up and down the channel, but being an experienced yacht Ocean master, you and your crew would know this from your charts?" Quent looked for a reaction from the house manager, a comment, or words of agreement, some demonstration of some knowledge, there was no reaction, no comment just a hard dark stare. Quent sensed this guy was clueless.

"You can't moor here it is a busy lane with pleasure craft and which in turn interferes with the running of the ferry. "Are you a professional"? asked the tall moody looking house manager, "let's just say im an inshore pilot enthusiast with 40 years' experience, but it is a good job im not a pro, they would take this boat off you in a blink of an eye."

Quent looked for Cox in Busty Belle, He leant over the side of "Makonde" and shouted to Cox "guide me back im moving on thrusters so I'll be slow, but I have the tide with me but only for a few minutes ok?" "ok" shouted Cox.

The two men worked as boat and pilot slowly they moved "Makonde" back up the river a quarter of a mile, one of the crew hooked a buoy as the tall Makonde 's masts rotated on the river, the tide had started to turn as the huge sailing boat slowly turned with it swinging with the bow into the flow. Quentin made it look so easy and he was in control.

Quentin shut the engines and thrusters down, he

put the wheel back to midships, Busty Belle was circling waiting for Quent to give the signal to disembark from the stern end.

The house manager approached Quent," I must thank you, that was impressive how do you know this boat so well, it is very new?" "I don't said Quentin but what I do know is you need to learn how to sail this boat, "Oh I assure you".. the house manager started.

"You can assure me of nothing" interrupted Quent, "get some lessons , learn and quickly; that goes for your lady friend back there pointing at the young lady stood at the back of the boat"

"you put people's lives in danger today on that ferry back there and crunched your bow in the process, which by the way will need a repair before you set out on any long ocean or open sea trip the damage is above the waterline but only just.

Quent put his hat back on and continued, "so good afternoon, enjoy the rest of your day, I need to go now", "no wait please" said the house manager, he tapped Quentin on the shoulder with his finger outstretched, "I could use a good man like you", "no thanks" said Quentin you could desperately need some sailing lessons understood and before you kill someone, we call your sort of sailors "atgani" which is Devonshire for something else, im sure you can work it out?"

Quent signalled to Cox he was ready, Cox was still circling but trying not to get too close "June love pass me you hat" Cox said as he moved closer the Makonde, "why…, what?" June asked, "just please give me your hat" She passed over her big blue flowery and wide brimmed floppy hat to Cox he put it on immediately,

Quentin beckoned him closer, Cox kept his head

down, Quent stepped to the transom stage on the rear of Makonde, Cox moved in and Quent stepped aboard Busty Belle like he had done it 50 times a day. "Nice hat" said Quent to Cox, as he sat down, "I don't want that nutcase to recognise me."

Busty Belle powered off in the direction of Stoke as they got 50 or so yards away Quent asked Mary for the mobile phone, "who you are calling" "im not said Quent "im taking some pictures holiday snaps if you like".

Quent took the mobile phone from Mary, he took 20 photos in succession, "she's a whopper said Quentin, Cox said "for such a modern boat she didn't move easily for a 50-footer" , "mmm might have been the fact the water there is deeper in the middle channel, I felt it had grounded out front and rear. She seemed sluggish that's for sure and low in the water.

"Oh, Quent you are a hero "called the girls giggling and blowing kisses from the front of the boat, "what about me" said Cox, "with a hat like that naaahh" all laughed out loud.

As they cruised closer to Stoke, Quentin did report to Dave the harbour river master, he told him about the chaos, the damage to the pontoon and ferry terminal and the damage to the "Makonde which on Quent's opinion should be looked at by a specialist repairer before being seaworthy "ok Dave said it sounds like you have had a bit of an afternoon?", "yeah you could say that Dave catch up with you soon". Quentin ended the call, Cox said "be careful mate, who you speak to about all this, it looks like trouble just rode into town," You might be right there.

The little boat arrived at the landing jetty near the dam in Stoke, a familiar face was waiting for them Oh look girls "it's Ugly Tony" Cox laughed "hello folks" said tony. "Busty belle looks fabulous Cox wow look at her". "Yeah, I've finished all the upgrades im pleased with her", "you should be" said Tony.

The girls were standing up and Tony held his hand out to welcome them back to dry land, as soon as the girls were out of the boat they moved off quickly to find the nearby ladies toilets. Got to dash were busting! They both giggles as they made off.

Tony was off duty and wearing shorts tee shirt and around his neck was a pair of binoculars, bird watching Tony asked Cox, ha you could say that, or watching oversize boat across the lake, yes a bloody foreign idiot with no idea, or as I told him all the gear and no fucking idea!" Cox turned and looked across the 2 mile stretch of water Quent said "I gave him a strip; he needs to learn some basic skills and then learn how to captain that beauty".

Tony asked "it would be interesting to find out who the owner is? You might ask who the owner is? said Quent "well you won't believe it Tone," Cox interrupted", but it's the same guy who I was going that big plastering job for", "ah so" said Tony, Mr Mystery "oh yes said Cox an ignorant tyrant at that too I'd say." What's the name of the boat asked Tony "Makonde " replied Cox, "Monaco" "really" said Tony.

He took another look at the boat through his binoculars, the tall man could be seen talking to someone further inside the boat's cabin door on the helm. "How many on board Quent? "Three as far as I could make out a guy up the from young chap a girl clueless helmsman and godzilla"

"What is his business, do you know Cox"? "Art and antiques I think, African stuff in crates all over the place, It's all very nice" Cox said but just inside seems a little odd, you know no women, yet the place needs the woman touch".

The ladies re appeared still giggling, "So, guys, nice to see you but I must be off, Tony started to walk along the pontoon towards his home," Ok Tony take care mate Cox shook his hand and Quent patted Tony on the shoulder. "Bye Ladies he said as he made his way up the jetty".

Cox June Mary and Quent all got together for a last drink at the riverside café, coffee all round I think ordered June from the waitress.

"What and action-packed afternoon eh Girls", "Mary said "I've had the best time, I loved our picnic Coxy, thank you darling, and you June lovely food as usual",

Quent turned to Cox "thanks mate I appreciate this today, I'll see you on Wednesday for training night? "yep, you will, the crew had better be ready" replied Cox. "They need to be "Quent said giving a knowing smile and a wink to Cox. They might be close friends off the water but on the water in a race these two are adversaries of the worst type.

The four friends finished up their coffee and made their way down the jetty to Busty Belle, they all hugged and kissed a goodbye, smiles all around, Cox and June jumped in the Belle, the engine rumbled into life, Quent gave Cox the thumbs up let off the bow, Cox slowly reversed the boat around gracefully it powered off into the lowering sun which was alighting the lake with an orange yellow glow, "that looks so romantic doesn't it Quent" Mary said as she held his arm, "yes it does" replied Quent admiring the lines of Belle.

Cox and June were waving good bye, June blowing kisses

too as they rumbled off across Ditsham Lake.

Chapter 7

Monday Morning came far too quickly as it always does, Posh Henry was up and weary eyed after a long afternoon session in the Ferryman's Inn, he too had witnessed to the Makonde incident, he was walking down to the garden to pick up his Land Rover, he stepped in clearing the cabin of spider's webs, and turned the key, slowly and with grinding slow turning the engine caught and fired into life.

He made his way to the small shop next to the only other pub in the village, he ordered 2 bacon rolls and 2 machine coffees, he grabbed a handful of sugars and put it all in the Landy. It was only a few minutes to the hard next to the foresaw on the Ham, this is where Blaggs had his boat workshop. It's far too bright he thought to himself.

Posh Henry made his way onto the foreshore, he slowed and looked onto the water the vista was dominated by the enormous sailing boat Makonde, the lake was mirror still, the reflections offered a spectacular view of the surrounding hills and the green reflections making a colourful pallet before Posh Henry's eyes. Blaggs wasn't there yet so Henry got out and sat on the bonnet of the car. It was quiet there no one around other than a dog walker some distance away.

The sun was warm, the air was cool the bacon roll was as good as the coffee, ok Posh thought it's out of a machine.

Half an hour had passed and still no sign of Blaggs, so Posh got his phone out and called him, Blaggs phone rang out for a long time then he answered, "Ok Posh?"

Blaggs said are you there yet, "Hey I've been here for 30 minutes where are you mate?" "Im coming I'll be there in 3 minutes". "see ya" said Posh Henry.

Henry kicked back and took in the view, the Makonde was moored a way offshore, it looked motionless, its massive beam planted it like it was paced on a mirror, it was sleek, low in the water, a very impressive ocean-going bus. A couple more minutes saw Blaggs arrived in his pickup truck, he parked directly outside his old workshop.

He unlocked the big double wooden doors and swung them wide open letting the morning sun stream inside the disorganised workshop, he wedged each door open with a brick and a old drum of oil. The sun shone in the workshop bringing it to life in an instant.

Blaggs filled the kettle from an old tap at the back of the workshop and clicked it on, hey I bought you a coffee said Posh, oh good said Blaggs, I prefer a tea this time of the morning. Blaggs pulled up a couple of stools, come here sit down, Posh bought over Blaggs bacon roll, "oh is that for me? Cheers Posh lad top apprentice of the week, Good weekend?" I spent the afternoon in the ferryman's, said Posh, Sue was on form so I spent the afternoon being a Peter.

So, you will have seen the drama on the ferry route then, yeah, it's that big boat there isn't it. Yeah, that's the one. It belongs to a good friend of mine, really!? said Posh who's that then? Don't be nosey said Blaggs.

Blaggs and Posh ate bacon rolls and chatted about nothing, So Posh said im here and on the payroll what do you want me to do. Right said Blaggs, the deal is this, every day there is a sack or two maybe three to collect from the Big boat moored over yonder, which one said

Posh Henry, that one which fucking one? That one Blaggs pointed towards the Makonde the new one, Yes said Blaggs, all you have to do is go over, drop them some diesel off in these tubs, he pointed to some yellowing clear plastic drums.

So, who pays for the diesel Blaggs?" don't worry Andrews Ferrers farm has a diesel pump, its red diesel so can't use it for cars and trucks, but you can fill a boat up with it, Are you sure? Yep we've been doing it for years. "have you?" said Posh, "where"? "over in Brixham" replied Blaggs tapping the side of his nose, "really?" said Posh.

"So, what the deal is Posh, you go to Ferrers farm fill these two up, bring them back, load them onto your boat, then motor over to Makonde, then load them onto the back, and wait. One of his guys picks the diesel up and leaves either and this is where you need your thinking head on wurzel, there will be a returning drum it will be round and heavy and marked up farm fuel".

"Ok, but there may be bags of coffee beans", "Coffee? Yes, it smells good, but not our coffee so don't get robbing any for your percolator at home.
They are very strict on weights and measures with this Posh so no fucking about, who are? asked Posh, I told you not to be nosey these are very private people. "why are they making farm fuel from a boat?" Posh was frowning and asking again, "Posh I really must get it through to you not to ask questions, it really upsets them, so please don't!. its good business I've been on this for a few years now and I don't want to lose out".

Ok! ok! ok! said Posh "but is this all legit and above board?" "of course, we are just let's say the logistics department, they provide the goods we just move them and as there is an element of wetness between the us and the boat it's up to locals like us to facilitate a solution where all benefit from the kind and generous payment s received in lieu of this service". Blaggs waffled on.

Bloody hell Blags you almost convinced me this is legit, it is Posh honest it is, they just don't want to attract attention so shush is the watch word, understood?", yeah I think so, so how many trips a day? "Blaggs looked at the Makonde and said, "it's only 1 or possibly 2 that's all". "And where do I take them? Posh sought clarification, "for the first few trips, you bring them to me either here or at my house. Not anywhere else understood and never ever leave them in the Land rover you only have to blow that thing a kiss and its open." "Hey, that's my land rover you're talking about" Posh laughed.

Posh Henry was having a tough time understanding this scheme, "ok and how much do I get from the deal for using my boat and wheels? enquired Posh, £60 quid a day and £80 for an evening trip, "wha?" Said Posh "evening trip?" no Blaggs"! "im not doing evenings; it gets dark at 7.30 Christ sake Blaggs im not humping in the dark ... excuse me" Posh Henry protested.

"no, no! said Blaggs "if you want this job it may be an occasional evening trip", It's an occasional one, im sure they get short of space and will need just more one picking up".

So, £60 quid plus £80 if I pick up in the evening, who will let me know if they need a pickup? I will be said Blaggs and its £60 or £80 !! there not that much money in it".

There is one thing though, Blaggs cautioned Henry," what's that"? asked Posh Henry. "You must not discuss this job with anyone other than me and me alone, not a word elsewhere, Blaggs was tapping the side of his nose "why"? Said Posh Henry, "Blaggs raised his voice "BECUASE ITS FUCKING CONFIDENTIAL"!!! Alright keep your hair on Blaggs!! come on then let's get going".

"I need to find my boat" said Posh, " well hurry up Posh let's get a lick on!!"said Blaggs. Posh set off across the foreshore in front of the Ham green park, he left his Land Rover at Blaggs workshop.

Posh located his boat on the jetty outside the Ferry-man's Inn. Sue was outside cleaning the windows "oh hello sailor" shouted Sue "love the wellies" She joked, "it's all just for you Sue just for you" as he grabbed his crotch through his overalls. "Dirty bugger" said Sue "ahh you love it" retorted Posh Henry. He continued onto the floating jetty.

Posh's boat is a 15 ft rower converted to take an outboard the paint work isn't brilliant, it is painted dull grey and a red bottom, but it was a well-balanced boat easy to row and was Posh's training boat for many years before they started using the gym in the village hall. It was his father's boat for many years but Posh eventually took it on.

He pulled her from her berth and placed the oars inside and pushed her off as he stepped in, the ripples scattered across the stillness of the lake. He dropped the oars into the rowlocks and started to pull on one side turning the boat towards the foreshore in front of his land rover. He started to row his strokes were deep and hard, he let out a little grunt as he got into the stride, the little craft flew across the surface, the 6 foot 2 inch Posh Henry made light of the distance.

Blaggs was waiting, what the fuck are you doing Posh? What? said Posh, Where's your outboard? I don't need it said posh "im only moving stuff from there to that boat enit?" "Yes mate" Blaggs said "but it would be a lot quicker," Blaggs said, "you didn't say it had to be quick Blaggs, this way I attract less attention than a boat tripping back and forth doesn't it?" quiet?, un hurried?" "yeah, I suppose, but in the evening trips you might need that extra bit of grunt to get you across the tide markers." "Im the top rower not you", "you're so funny" said Blaggs"," I'll go and get the diesel first, Blaggs loaded the diesel drums into the back of Posh Henry's Land Rover, Blaggs closed the tailgate and said I've spoken to Andrew at the Farm, he is expecting you".

Posh got in and set off up the hill. His Land Rover with the body work creaking and squeaking the exhaust popping and banging as it went up the ramp. "So much for being quiet" Blaggs shook his head.

Blaggs called the house manager, the phone rang 6 times then there was a click, "Yes Mr Blagg", "hello my guy is getting the diesel he will be at the boat within the hour" Blaggs said. "Very good, I will let the boat know." The phone clicked again Blaggs put his phone in his top pocket, he then went inside for another cup of tea before starting on an engine fix in the workshop.

Posh arrived at the farm, Andrew was working in the main barn and saw him arrive through his farmyard, he walked out from behind the corner of the barn spying Posh Henry as he arrived through the slats of the doorway, wiping oil of his wrench with a dirty looking rag, "Hello lad, he paused then asked, "who are you?" Andrew stared as Posh pulled up next to the fuel pump, "they call me Posh Henry I'm here from Blaggs to fill these two drums up," "Ok lad do you know how to use this?" Andrew pointed at the fuel pump bolted to the wall next to a huge black tank.

"Yes, I can manage it" said Posh Henry. Is there any paperwork, "no not likely, no lad I sort all that out." "Ahh alright then, - Ok" said Henry as he started to fill up the first drum, "Im new to all this", Andrew turned and said "No Shit Lad, he stared for a few seconds at Posh, this made Posh Henry feel a little uncomfortable, it wasn't a friendly sort of stare.

Posh Henry felt like he was being looked at as if he was an idiot, Andrew was looking round the Land Rover circling it, "be careful these drums are not as stable as you think Lad, if you are standing them up in the back of this old lady, so use these straps, do not spill it!" "Ok thanks" said Posh. "Is this thing roadworthy lad, Posh Henry smiled, "well it's on the road and its mine and I see worth in it so" ......" alright, alright!" Andrew interrupted Posh Henry muttering under his breath "Posh git I don't need a fucking lecture."

Andrew placed some old dusty red strapping on the back of Posh Henry's Land Rover. Andrew had emphasised the not spilling of the diesel, Posh Henry wondered why he was so insistent it wasn't spilt. It came across like not a spot will be spilt like Posh's life depended on it. As he filled the first one, he put that in the back of the Landy, then went back and started to fill another, Andrew had returned to the barn and continued his work.

Posh had filled the second drum and secured the lid, he lifted it up and put it in the back of the Landy sliding it in fully next to the first drum swinging the back door closed with a bang, Andrew reappeared, Posh started the truck up and started to move off, He ignored the gesticulations from Andrew as the barn filled with grey black smoke, Posh looked at him and drove away.

Posh drove out of the farmyard down the drive and onto Steep Lane, ten minutes later he was back on the foreshore, "Some fucking friendly people you hang out with" Blaggs Posh shouted across the Foreshore, Blaggs came to the doorway of his workshop, come here he beckoned Posh over.

"A couple of things Henry mate one, don't shout things on this job, just be a little discreet it's important to the employers, private people, you know what I mean?" "we have spoken about this, two is this land rover mot'd,? yes said Posh, three don't fucking spill the red diesel we don't want the VOSA turning up, ok ?" "Ok Posh?" "Yes Blaggs OK!" Replied Posh.   "Now get those two barrels over to Makonde they are waiting, and you have three returns, I'll tell you where they go when you get back".
Blaggs turned around with his back to Posh, Posh was already getting pissed off.

Posh Henry loaded the two drums from the rear of the Land Rover to the Boat, he moved the Land Rover above the tide mark locked it up and pushed the boat off it was difficult as the weight of the drums made the boat ground out. Posh pushed it in to float and jumped in wetting one foot as he did "oh shit" posh exclaimed.

As the little boat drifted off the shoreline, he sat down organised his oars and rowed three strokes staring at Blaggs as he did. Five strokes in and he was approaching the Makonde, waiting for him on the rear of the boat was a suntanned stocky man with dark glasses, Posh said "alright then mate", the man didn't say a word. Posh tried to lift the first drum, his little rowing boat moved away as he lifted the drum up and rocked the little boat.

Unsteady on his feet Posh struggled to maintain a balance, but managed to grab the Handrail on the Makonde, the man said "you no touch boat no touch hand off" in broken English. Posh Henry said "Jesus man can't you help?" The stocky man said, "put oil here", he pointed to a spot at his feet, "here!"

Posh managed to drop the drum near but cussing as he did, the man reached round to his own back pocket and produced a pair of black rubber gloves, he slowly put them on watching Posh Henry as he snapped his hands into them.

Posh tried to lift drum number 2, again the small boat moved out when Posh Henry tried to lift the heavy drum and place it on the transom platform of the boat, the man lifted the first drum like it was empty, "fucking show off "muttered Posh Henry.

The stocky little man came for drum number 2 lifting it again like it was no weight. Posh waited, the man came back he removed the gloves and stood watching Posh Henry, the two of them stared at each other for a few seconds then the man said "you go now", Posh's usual sarcastic retort automatically come in to play " no chance of a coffee and a danish then Yuri?" the man turned around and went down through the cabin doorway, in a few seconds he arrived back with two drums one in each hand again he seemed to be using no effort to carry them.

He placed them close to the edge, "for you" said the man, ok said Posh Henry he went to lift the drum bloody hell it was heavy it was white clean with green and blue writing on the front "Eco-Kleene Bio Fuels" the man disappeared and come back with a third drum "this for you also" grunted the man, "oooh Yuri you shouldn't have thanks mate" Posh's funny remark made no difference to the dead pan look on the stocky man's face.

Posh Henry loaded the last of the three drums into the boat spacing them out along the bottom of the boat, Posh sat down in his little boat, set his oars up and drifted off the back of the Makonde. The man picked up a mop and bucket and started to clean the transom mopping it furiously back and forth soap suds falling into the water as he did Posh watched closely, "he's a bloody good mopper Posh quietly said to himself.

When the man had finished mopping the rear deck, he gently removed his gloves finger by finger and folded them carefully and replaced them in his back pocket, he folded his hands in front of him stood with his legs apart as if as ease on a parade ground and watched Posh Henry as he drifted off.

Posh tried to stare back, the sunshine reflecting from the water was ultra-bright and made Posh squint, his oars rested on top of the water slowly dragging the boat around. "see ya later Yuri" said Posh to the man, as he slowly rowed a few strokes the man disappeared inside the boat "that's it, Yuri get the kettle on old son, make YOURSELF a coffee".

Posh Henry rowed the 150 or so yards back to the shoreline, he put some effort into the last few strokes, he knew the boat was loaded up and didn't want another wet leg. The boat graunched to a halt on the muddy beach. He picked up the first drum and took it across to Blaggs. "So, how did it go Blaggs said not looking up at Posh Henry, "well you have some miserable friends Blaggs" where do you want these? "For fuck sake Posh don't bring it in here put it straight in your truck!"

"What? said Posh Henry for fuck sake Blaggs im not a mind reader".

Posh stormed off, he left the drum and went to get the Land Rover, he reversed it up at some speed to the boat and loaded the two drums into the back, then making the point he was pissed off by slamming the rear door.

He then reversed the car back to the workshop doors and loaded the 3rd drum in, slamming the door again, "Blaggs said can't you make less noise?", Posh said "I'll make some fucking noise if you want Blaggs!", Posh's tone of voice had changed from mildly pissed off to angry pissed off! "Oiy" Blaggs said "wind your neck in".
"Here this is where these three drums need to go". Blaggs held out a piece of paper Posh took it for granted there would be something akin to an address on the note which he crunched up and put in his pocket, "Yes capitano" said Posh "Then what?" Posh waited for an answer, "Blaggs what is next?", "that's it all done" said Blaggs, "for today, same again tomorrow, but tomorrow have a fucking smile on your face"

Posh drove off the Land Rover still creaking and whining as it climbed up Steep Hill, the three drums were rolling back and forth in the back, Posh had made his mind up and cared little. He had the address of the drop off as *Makonde Farm Holdings Ltd* Just outside Tuckenhay so not far, he found the lane leading to the farm, "Gallows Lane", it was narrow darkened, over hanging tree branches called for careful progress.

He arrived at a gated road, on a rough sign of old peeling paint it said, "Gallows Farm Dairy This Way", Posh Opened the gate and entered the driveway. He drove along to the entrance of the yard, out of the corner of his eye he could see movement, he went to the back of the

Landy, he hauled out two of the drums and then placed the third on top, he slammed the Landy rear door and marched towards the Farmhouse and barn.

There he was met on the other side of the old run-down farmyard, by a middle-aged man with a very smart tweed suit his trousers were tucked into this socks, and long boots on his head he wore an expensive looking fedora tilted slightly to one side.

"Im Posh Henry" he announced. "good morning Yeass I knooow who you are" the man said in a slow well-spoken English, modulated, deep voice and calm reply, the man lit a cigarette slow drawing on it letting the smoke curl around his broad brim of his hat. "and your late", "am I Posh asked "why?" "why what? the man said, "why am I late?" "well, I really don't know old boy and I really don't care much, the man winked at Posh, he continued" but don't be late again", "no, I asked you why am I late? Posh reared up, "no one gave me a time or told me to hurry up, so how the fuck can I be late?

"I suppose the fact that Mr Blaggs let us know you were on your way might colour the water old boy, so next time you are sent up here with a delivery you will jolly it along a little pull your fucking little finger out and get here quickly and without that appalling attitude."

The man walked towards the drums, come on I'll show you where these goes, bring that truck here, Posh grabbed a sack truck on the fence, the man loaded 2 drums on to the sack truck, you bring that one, follow me, Posh followed the man to a ramp in the corner of the farmyard. "never come here unaccompanied ok" the man said to Posh, "ok" said Posh. The ramp had a large door which as they approached opened vertically, inside it was warm Posh felt the rise in temperature immediately.

He followed the man around into another large factory space, there were rows of benches with one person at each bench. Each person had a drum in front of them, they were all just standing there looking down at the bench.

As Posh Henry and the man passed through the people looked up and carried on with whatever they were doing before Posh and the man walked through.

The man was marching at a pace as he moved into the third room, In there was a conveyor belt, the man pointed to posh to place his drum on the belt, the man loaded on one more and Posh picked up the third and paced it on the blet behind the others.

The man removed his hat to reveal a badly scared bald head, and a scar above his right eye, Wow you've been in the wars mate said Posh, the man just stared at him, "sorry, sorry "Posh apologised none of my business "Cocky fucker aren't you? the man said, "not really I just had a shit morning". "We all we all have those Mr Posh, or should I call you Christopher?" Posh Henry looked at him, "how do you know my name?" "well Mr Posh im a keen fan of rowing, I asked a pretty barmaid at the Ferryman's Inn if she knew you".

The man led Posh into an office, he moved around the opposite side of a desk. A simple angle poise lamp was the only thing on the desk apart from a pen and a pad, "I think her name was Susan, sweet lady, she obviously knows you Mr Posh, she said you were opinionated, loud, brash and stuck up, she obviously a particularly good judge of character, she told me your real name isn't Mr Posh and in our line of business it is very important we can trust our employees".

So, Mr Posh a coffee? "er ok yeah please, black

three sugars thanks," Posh responded in a surprised tone, the man prepared a cafetiere, the smell of rich coffee permeated the office. He reached for two mugs, Posh was looking around, "So Mr Posh, I guess you will ask me what we do here?", "no, Posh said I was going to ask you your name, I don't like drinking coffee with strangers". "My name is Devlin, "is it Mr Devlin or just Devlin?" How nice said Devlin an element of respect, I like that"

"I prefer just Devlin but please, Mr Posh never call my name we only speak one to one either here or on the Makonde . Never anywhere else, this all might seem a little Jonny secrets society to you Mr Posh, But I assure you it is for all our benefit that we respect the wishes of our employers, so to you and everyone in our employ "schtum" is the name of the game".

Devlin finished pouring two steaming hot coffees, here, Mr Posh, I look forward to working with you, from what I know you're a good chap with potential, he handed Posh a mug. "I like that," Devlin gestured to Posh to sit down.

So, posh started to ask, he sipped the hot coffee, "what do you do here?". "Devlin lit a cigarette he offered Posh one and nodded his head in encouragement, "er no thanks" said Posh, "wise Mr Posh very wise, so, this is our conversion operation here and distribution is next door, our expertise is in the conversion of certain materials from around the world into what we term a higher value commodity, we refine it and enhance its market value, then we simply distribute it to a network of distributors, in the UK and France and onwards into the greater markets of Europe". "Oils and that sort of thing?" Posh asked, "yes sometimes" Devlin replied, but the specialist oil operations are relatively lower value to the overall international operation, it's the commodity distribution that brings in the main income, in a sense though the oil is a critical part of what we do here".

"So how many work here, oh only 20 or so, they are not local people of course, they live here and are from overseas. "like seasonal workers? Posh asked, "Yeeas exactly" said Devlin, he stubbed the nub of his cigarette out on a plate on the side table next to the desk and rose to his feet.

"Tomorrow we will expect you a little earlier than today please Mr Posh, I'm sorry to request this but it is important to keep the line fed and the workers occupied, Im sure you understand this."
"Yep, I'll be here as soon as I can, I will be at the boat by 8.30 and hopefully be here by 9.45 will that fit" "It will fit perfectly Mr Posh", Devlin replaced his fedora hat and led Posh Henry out of the room into the main factory, as they entered all the workers stood still, stopped what they were doing and lowered their heads down, like dolls they stood there motionless.

"Bit strange isn't it? "said Posh" "what is strange old boy" said Devlin, "that they stand to attention like that", "oh that yes it's a work ethic they bought with them its like a respect thing, I just go along with it.

Erm before you go I wonder if I could ask you to drop these two sacks of coffee off with your oil delivery in the morning, Blimey said Posh that's a hell of a lot of cups of morning glory isn't it", "yes quite Replied Devlin, but would you? I would appreciate it", "Yea said posh no worries ill drop them in tomorrow first thing" "terrific old boy" said Devlin. "They will be expecting you."

"It has been a pleasure to meet you at last Mr Posh, I hope you find your way back, I look forward to seeing you tomorrow have a good day", as Devlin walked away across the farmyard he called to Posh Henry, "Please liaise with Mr Blaggs "Er Will do" replied Posh.

Posh get into the Land Rover and started to move towards the gate, the gate automatically opened the gate slowly swinging sideways to let Posh and the Land Rover out into the dark lanes.

Posh returned to the Ham foreshore, there was no sign of Blaggs, Posh Henry parked up his Land Rover next to the recycling station, and walked over to the Ferryman's Inn, "Hey Sue, he called as he entered, Hello Poshy babes alright then?" Sue was putting beer glasses on the shelf above the bar, "Yeah im fine, can I get a coffee please, bit early for a beer." Posh sat down on one of the tall stools at the bar. "Here you go", Sue slid a large cup of coffee and an Italian biscuit, "Sugar?" Sue enquired. "Yeah only 3 or 4!" he laughed "you know me Sue, not sweet enough". "yep, sour old bugger you are" retorted Sue.

"So, what have you been up to Poshy in your gorgeous wellies?" "well Susan, I've a new part time job", "Oh Yeah", said Sue "who's that for?" Posh pulled the stool closer the bar, "a local distribution outfit at Tuckenhay way "Posh sounded quite proud of himself, "well done Poshy congratulations." Cheers Suzie" "Posh opened the biscuit, Sue, Posh started as he bit into the biscuit, "has there been anyone asking around for me, you know like asking who, or where I am or live anything like that?" "No, Posh not that I can remember."

The only time I spoke about you was when a cyclist asked who you were, like you were an unidentified rock star!" "oh yeah what did he look like? "tall ish guy scar on his face, too well-spoken for round here id say" "and what about his head? did he have a scar or burn on his head," "wouldn't know love, he had a beanie hat on but I'd say he was bald but he was just a cyclist passing through I guess".

"When was that then Sue?" Posh was now thinking this seems a little uncomfortable, "oh recently the night of the boat race when you beat Stoke?" "Ah ok", "why said Sue are you being stalked" she laughed and came to the bar she put her head on her hands and looked at Posh, "you know if you were not! so bloody annoying you could be a good catch for someone", "Your puerile fantasies Sue are just too much to contemplate", "don't flatter yourself sonny" Sue replied.

"Thanks for the coffee, Posh bid Sue his usual banter filled cheerio "catch you later you old tart" made for the car and then home.

Chapter 8

Tommo, sat on the edge of his windowsill looking out across the river at the bright day, he was feeling sick again, the previous night he had eaten an Indian take-away it was only a day old. His mobile buzzed as a text message came in, he opened it, it was Fish " Hi M8 are you coming out for a pint" Tommo thought it would be a good idea as it was training night at the gym but the cool beer might make his guts feel a little better so he text back, " ok M8 When an where? In a few seconds Fish texted back "Ferryman 12"

Tommo texted a "thumbs up" and got in the shower, he put his favourite jeans on and a fresh shirt, after getting ready he put his gym kit in the bag and locked the door behind him, the Ferryman's arms were 100 yards down the steep hill, Fish was waiting for him half way down, he was nosing at the new development, the big grey gates started to open, a big black BMW pulled out, in a powerful turn it entered the steep hill and waited, the rear windows were blacked out and a curtain covered the back window, following the car walking out of the building was a smartly dressed lady sunglasses, high heels clicking as she marched toward the car, she wore a tight red top, Fish followed her delicious scent, as she turned to get in the car she looked towards Fish and gave a smile.

She closed the door, the grey gates closed slowly, the Black car moved off as the gates closed. "Makonde" Fish mouthed and whispered", "What did you say?" said Tommo, "Hi mate " Makonde , look on the side wall next to the gates was a brass plaque and on in was engraved " Makonde " Fish pointed it out. Tommo said, "what does that mean Fish?" I don't know, Fish replied I was watching her, did you see that? not the sign sounding as if he was not caring, the two rowing crew mates continues to the Ferryman, the doors were open and Sue was waiting behind the bar,

      "Hey Sue two pints please" "Hi guys coming right up" , "oh don't say that Sue Love, said Tommo "I've not been well the last few days, since our win over Stoke I've been right off my grub",

      Fish said its your own fault eating shit that doesn't agrees with you, yeah could be right said Tommo, So how is tricks? Still working at eh garage, yeah, we are busy right now, So, what are you doing off asked Fish, "Im entitled to a day off now and then" "ok, ok" said Fish keep your hair on.

      "Sue arrived with two menus in her hands, right you two the scampi is off, and the soup of the day is Parsnip and French onion, fresh crusty bread and lots of it, "we'll have two scampi's then Sue please" Said Tommo Joking, "you and Posh Henry went to the same funny bugger school then Tommo?" "Ha of course mind you he got better laugh because he's ugly too! Said Tommo, "Talking of which" Fish said, outside the pub from the jetty Fish pointed out Tony Handsome from Stoke Gabriel "wonder what he wants?".

      Tommo went to the window and looked, Tony was standing there leant against the corner of the wall, he was looking through a big pair of binoculars he kept dropping them down and putting them back up, it looked as if he had spotted a rare bird, out of his jacket he pulled a notebook and was scribbling something down looking at his watch and making more notes.

"It's ok's he's bird watching or something on the Ham shoreline has his attention, he's not spying on our game tactics for the next race in a couple of weeks then? Fish laughed "what sitting in the pub on training day nah were just putting him off the scent." Tommo said.

Sue arrived with her order pad at the ready, made your minds up boys, "1 Soup and 1 cheese burger, no cheese no relish ordered Tommo, "Sue looked quizzical that's just a plain burger isn't it Tommo?" "Er yes but can I have cheese and relish on mine", "funny bugger" said Sue.

So, what are you up to the week after the race Tommo?" "nothing much why?", "I have a 36 foot available for a long week end skint over to France", "I wondered if you were up for crewing with me?", "what just the two of us?, well how about Jake and Posh too?" "ok great, im up for that, they will be at training tonight so we can butter them up for a lad's weekend".

Sue arrived with the food a steaming hot bowl of Parsnip and Onion soup for Fish and a plain Burger no cheese no relish with a side of cheese and relish, "that is spot on Sue you got it right", yes it is right said Sue "but I've had to charge you for he side orders, Side orders Said Tommo? Yes, Sue said "the cheese and the relish". "Ha ha Tommo laughed "you are so funny Sue, you should be on the stage............sweeping it."

Tommo and Fish were chatting whilst they ate at the bar discussing plans for the forthcoming boat trip, "whose boat is it Fish? It's my dad's brothers he has had it for about 5 years but uses it only now and then, he works in London and finds it hard to get home at the weekend and then get the energy to go for a trip, I was talking to my Dad sand he suggested I take it for a spin now and then and sort of look after it for him", "Happy Days" said Tommo, just then someone tapped Tommo and Fish on the shoulder, standing directly behind them was Cox,

"Hi Coxy mate how are you,?" Fish said, Cox leant forward and said in a quiet voice, " what the fuck are you to slackers doing in a pub on training day"? "See me tonight" said Cox pointing at the two of them, Cox left the pub and went to stand with Tony Handsome outside.

Sue came and stood in front of Tommo and Fish "Oh boys, or should I say little boys, she fluttered her eye lashes, "you've been told off by that nasty Coxy, you both had better order a pudding to give you two ickle lambs some energy tonight , it sounded like Mr Coxy is going to make to work for it tonight." " Have you started to sweep that stage, yet Sue" joked Tommo?

The two crew mates chatted over coffee and an inevitable sticky pudding served by Sue with lashings of hot custard, Fish said he was in heaven, Tommo didn't think it was such a good idea to eat too much, his guts were still giving him some trouble.
They left the pub at 3.00 ish, Cox and Tony were still bird watching, making notes and discussing something in detail," why do bird watchers get so passionate about feathers, I don't know tommo said but the short fat one is going to whoop our asses to night, Fish agreed "Not wrong there Tommo".

Chapter 9

Training nights were held at a local Gym made up in the Village Hall, it was financed partly by the sponsors of the gig in Dittisham and is mainly for the use of those in the village but was primarily for the boat crews of the gig the male team and the female team.

As Tommo and Fish arrived Jake and Jools were already using the exercise bike 13 minutes on then 13 minutes off , sit ups and spragg's or battling ropes are used for fitness training to increase full body strength and conditioning., spraggs was their own crew term for the heavy ropes which had to be lifted in each hand each rope was 15 feet long and 2" in diameter heavy and a dead weight, 30 spraggs was a killer on the upper arms but it did build strength and muscle.

This was the torture night, on the orders of Coxy "Inner core boys' inner core."

As he marched up and down the line in his old grey trainers and track suit. Cox was proud of his track suit be believed seriously that if it was ever washed it would wash the good luck out of it, June was never allowed to even fold it, on the front and back it displayed badges from over 10 years of competition wins across the south Hams coastal areas, wins in Teignmouth, Exmouth, Salcombe, Paignton, Torbay, Torquay, Totness, Brixham, Stoke Gabriel the impressive list was there for all to show that Coxy was an expert force to recon with.

"Tommo and Fish over here 20 press-ups and I want to see your snotty noses on that deck, get on with it" demanded Cox, Cox was walking up and down as Posh

Henry arrived, with Jools he was subjected to spraggs "Posh 30 spraggs off now come on, where's Blaggs? Cox called to the assembled" Cox blew the whistle, and everyone moved round one station to take up the next exercise, "Tommo 30 spraggs come on get on it!" "I've just done 30 said Tommo complaining well do 30 more then! "there was no compromise this was training night and Coxy liked to see the pain on their faces.,

"Where is Blaggs"? shouted Cox again, Jools, Jake, Posh Henry, Tommo and Fish all working hard, they had got the point where the sweat had started, Cox used this point as a gauge of effort within a few minutes he could smell the sweat, he clicked his stopwatch and gave them another 3 minutes.

As the countdown on his stopwatch came to zero, he shouted "And Stop!...... take 5 gents" He looked at the bunch of big men all puffing and panting, sweat stained tee shirts and red faces abounded, he stared at Tommo and Fish, "so you two fatties get down and give me 20!, "what?" said Tommo "again"?, I caught you two in the pub Lunchtime what the fuck are you thinking? So, 20!, Cox pointed at the floor he repeated the instruction,"20 both of you now!"

The two reluctantly got down and started a slow pump in the press-up, Cox reached for his Mobile phone and tapped at the screen, he raised the phone to his ear as the boys were gulping water from numerous water bottles.

Cox said into the mobile phone, "Were the hell are you Blaggs"? Cox raised his voice "you know its training night, we, "the crew" are 20 minutes in and getting ready for Friday, do you want a seat on Friday"? - "You do? Get your fucking lazy ass in here then" you have 15 minutes then in giving the seat away".

Cox hung up, "don't be too hard on him Coxy he's got a lot on" said Posh Henry. "this is not the first time he's not put in the effort. I'm sick of him letting you lot down, why should he get a rowing seat without putting the effort in?"

Right, I want Posh Henry, Fish Jake and Tommo in position on the floor, the crew sat in their positions as if they were in the boat on the floor. Right in thinking to moving you around, why said Fish, well the last race was close, we had only a few yards lead, the crew from Kingswear are a heavy team, I need to lighten our boat at the front, Kingswear are a strong team they are located on the east bank close to the river's mouth and opposite the small town of Dartmouth.

"We don't need to be digging the bow in so much, Blaggs and Tommo can sit stern end first then Jools and Fish then Tommo and Posh Henry" Coxy discussed with his team.

"Let's just move and see where it leaves us". The boys scuttled around on the floor and took up their new positions. Cox looked over the new layout scratching his chin and making some notes in his little blue book, "Ok said Cox can Fish and Posh Henry swap left to right? the two big men moved across, that might work said Cox, Ok Thursday 4.00 pm can everyone make a 3 mile row just to see if this might work,? Cox asked "Yeah ok" each man gave his pledge to be there. Tommo said "weather will be shit". "pardon Tommo? Said Cox, weather Thursday rain, squalls, windy is what I heard".

Cox said "is it going. be sunshine on Friday Tommo, er well I doubt it Coxy , but Saturday is looking good", "that's right so why we need to change the boat layout, give it a go on Thursday, then we take the pants off Kingswear on Friday, remember lads we are taking the boat closer to the river mouth entrance, the swell can be a bugger we are starting on the ferry side, so this side of the ferry but we have to cross the lower ferry line and make sure we hit the middle channel , so I want the Brixham style Strat Plan in place, speed from less strokes which means????" The crew said in unison "deeper strokes Cox". "ok so let's get another half hour in right now."

The door of the gym opened and in walked Blaggs, "Oh so nice of you to show up Blaggs", each of the crew having a little dig. Blaggs got changed then joined the crew in the main hall, Blaggs had a mark on his face under his left eye, "hey up who's been fighting?" Fish and Jools came over to Blaggs "who thumped you Blaggs?", "it's nothing Blaggs said, "fuck off I hurt myself at work."

Cox came over and looked at Blaggs face, Alright Blaggs? "Yeah" Blaggs replied, Cox said "can we have word before you go?" "Yeah ok" said Blaggs the others continued with the exercising the session lasted 45 minutes or so Cox relented as Fish and Jake finished their set and left Posh Henry and Tommo had come to the end of their cycling, Jools was changing and Blaggs finished the last of the Spraggs.

Cox went over to him and asked, "Are you ok?" "Yeah" he was wiping the sweat off his hands Cox noticed a swollen knuckle on his left hand, "yeah Coxy im fine, so what's up?" You tell me Blaggs? asked Cox, "nothing up what's with all the questions, well you turn up late with a belter under your eye and you're not your usual effervescent self,"

"I'm ok Cox honest I just had a disagreement

with a spanner", "was she worth it? Cox smiled, Blaggs looked left and said, "is that it?", "that's it" said Cox "see you Thursday, oh Blaggs, can you bring the boat down at 5.30?" "sure" said Blaggs "see you then" Blagg didn't bother getting changed he threw his kit into his bag and left.

Cox tidied up and Jools helped clear the floor, "what's up with Blaggs? Jools asked Cox, "beats me Cox replied, "but he'd better not let me down on Friday". Cox locked up the Village Hall building and Jools offered a lift, "Nah" said Cox "Thanks but the walk will do me some good."

Cox continued the walk down the Hill as he turned at the top of Steep hill, a Black BMW passed him, it slowed down near to the new development and the grey gates whined as they opened, from the left he could see Blaggs standing in the post office shop doorway, the window of the Black car wound down and the driver was pointing at Blaggs, the conversation was short, it ended the BMW shot off and turned into the new house. Cox waited a few minutes as Blaggs made his way along the lane toward his home looking far from happy.

Cox continued to his house, as he opened the door June called "hello love do you want a cup of tea, it's in the pot just fresh, Ok Love thanks" replied Cox. He went for a shower, June was talking on the phone to Mary, they were chatting about a shopping trip, June said she had some birthday cards for Mary and Quentin as their birthdays were close.

June suggested another boat trip on the Saturday, Just let me check Mary he's only just got in, "Coxy love can we nip across to Marys and Quent's on Saturday after-noon? "Er yes love no problem, I need a chat with Quentin anyway", "Yes Mary that's fine see you Saturday . June ended the call.

Cox came in showered and with a cup of tea in his hand. He sat down "That'll be nice" said June it's their birthdays next week, perhaps we could have a drink and come straight back "sounds good said Cox I want to catchup with Quentin".

Thursday evening arrived and the crew were gathering at the Dittisham jetty, the tide was slack and the water calm, Blaggs arrived with Tommo and Posh Henry in the land rover. All 6-crew helped to launch the gig, a crowd of onlookers had gathered. The boat slipped int to the water almost silently, it made hardly any disturbance on the water Posh Henry held the long rope and gently pulled the gig back to the jetty side. Each crew member took their oar and placed it over their shoulder, Posh Henry and Tommo held the bow and stern as the rest of the crew stepped aboard one by one, they sat down, almost like a military exercise each man knows his place and where to sit. Posh Henry and lastly Tommo Cox stepped aboard and let go, the ropes, Tommo pushed off the bow, Blaggs pushed off the stern, the gig floated off into the stream alongside the Jetty.

The 6 oars were upright pointing skywards, the boat moved off further off the jetty clearing it, the oars came down one by one, each crew placing the oars in the rowlock, Cox called to them "for'ard boys! The oars all moved back in an accurate synchronization, no one spoke, with one sweep of the oars came on contact with the water.

The boat lurched forward, "and again" Cox called, the crew repeated, the sweep of the broad blades dipped into the green water one sweep, the oars twisted and came up out of the water flowing past the white hull, the crew held their respective oars out of the water whilst Coxy steered the boat away from the ferry traffic area and out into deeper water, Give me one more called Cox, the oars without hesitation robotically moved back on a swept rearwards lurching to boat forward again.

Blades up! Cox requested of his crew, their eyes fixed on him like an orchestra conductor, the musicians awaiting the next instruction of when to strike up the music, Cox said to them we will have a warmup boys 20 beats 4 minutes, quietly whispering Cox looked at the crew almost as one, each man taking a gaze from the conductor "aaaaand Goh!

Immediately as if Cox had thrown a switch the blades dipped and the boat surged forwards, each man twisting the oars at the top of each stroke, the rhythm increased till they were at a beat of exactly 20 beats per minute, Cox could feel the immense power of 6 big men pulling a combined weight of half a ton, the boats slipped through the water.

Cox was steering with a minimum of effort on the tiny rudder fixed behind his head directed with a wire held by a wooden toggle in his left and right hands. each stroke of the six oars shocked Cox's neck muscles, his head nearly being snatched back as the blades made contact in the water and the force of the water drove the wooden Elm clinker hulled 133-year-old boat forwards.

After his estimate of 4 minutes Cox glanced at his stopwatch ordered "blades up lads" with the same immediacy and military accuracy as when they started the crew held the oars up.

The boat continued to coast forward, on the only sound was the rippling of the water behind the boat, Cox surveyed the crew, all were breathing well, a few beads of sweat on Tommo as he was one of the older crew members, Fish was the fittest of the crew a slighter man than the rest of the crew but him and Jools tended to look after themselves, and better than Blaggs, Tommo, Posh Henry and Jake.

"lads what we want tonight is to have a try with this new set up, as I spoke at the gym, we need a stronger starboard turn and we need to ride the rough water at river dart mouth, history tells us we can't do both, but we need to change history", "so we are going to do 3 turns in succession, im not going to call this out, or count it down to the turn, im going to give you one and a half strokes warning, so as I steer to the buoy, I will call turnabout on the bottom stroke, as the blades come up we will go straight in on the starboard side and dig in deep, we may get wet but we need to turn on a penny any questions?" There was a general shaking of heads everyone understood Cox's plan.

"Give me one boy's" said Cox, in a second the blades went in without a splash, the boat moved forwards, Cox shouted random turn here lads, the 3 men on the port side stopped rowing the boat with assistance from Cox's rudder made then boat swing into a turn with the starboard 3 dropping the blades in deeper, the boat tipped up and the turn was in place. "Ok Cox said "we need to do this on the point and now at speed ok lads, so, against a buoy, at speed, and in rough water, so a lot of pressure to come on".

"30 strokes at speed please" Cox growled, the boat shot forward each man pulling hard, the boat started to creak the oars pulling hard on the gunwale and pins, the creaking gave each man an audible confidence of how hard they were all pulling and again Cox called "and again" he repeated, and again his voice becoming a little raspier, "and one more for me" the boat was really moving now, each of the six oar's dipping twisting and breaching 6 perfect oar patterns off the stern the crew were really now in unison.

Cox had eyed an empty mooring buoy out in the channel, that was his target he looked all around to make sure they were clear of any other boats. The crew were pulling well, the boat was surfing along, "Cox called it "Turnabout"!, the oars came under the boat, the nose of the boat was aimed by Cox directly at the buoy, only 15 feet to go and the port side crew lifted their oars out the starboard crew dug in their blades the boar lurched to the right, Cox put full rudder on, the stern of the boat was underwater the water being help back only by the speed of the boat moving away from the rising mass wave created behind the boat ,"and pull" Cox grunted, all the oars men pulled on their blades and the boat levelled up, the 1st stroke they were pulling on accelerated the boat away from the turn.

"Good! good!" Cox called "that was good, we need it tighter boys. "and go!" the boat moved effortlessly through the water toward a second buoy 300 yards further out, the breeze was easy earlier on but now it was lifting the water's surface a little, Cox scanned the water a head , he spotted a patch of water off the White point headland , it was a little choppy where the breeze was now a constant blast from across the top of the point and the headland and tree line cut the breeze on to the water bringing it up a little cool and choppy looking, " perfect "Cox thought he headed for another smaller buoy.

This time he waited for the distance to be about

the same as the length of the gig, the boat was spinning through the water, the blades were deep under the boat, "Turnabout" Cox shouted, the starboard side dug their oars in, the port side team leant over to try and keep the boat flat, a rush of water came over the back of the boat soaking Cox, he held on as the boat dropped back level and the turn was successful. The boat felt as if it was sliding down its own wake as the crew picked up the rhythm and the beat of the strokes settled in again. Tommo and Blaggs shouted that was brilliant we should do a few more, Cox looked at his watch and called back "OK lads lets go again".

The pace picked up as the boat shot forward long strokes in the making, the boat doing its usual creaking and banging from the oars in their keeps, as the blades were lifted from the water the crew really getting a pull on and now accelerating the blade through the water creating a vortex behind the blade from where the blade was expertly extracted without disrupting the flow of the boat.

A regular pattern of 6 vortexes behind the boat is what Cox was looking for, "who is Ragging the leather?" Cox demanded to know, he could feel and see it in the pattern of the water – Jake your blade your pulling across your body and not in its arc come on Jake we have worked on this before; come on concentrate", Jools and Jake sort it out, in the arc please" Cox looked at Jools , he was tired and getting cold the soaking on the first practise turn had been chilling him off in the breeze, the weight of his blade was making him pull across the arc of the oar, Cox made for the midstream Buoy, as he approached from 20 yards he shouted "getting ready crew"

"Turning on my word", as the boat streamed towards the big white buoy, the blades disappeared for a full stroke, as the blades past Jakes mid position Cox bellowed "Turnabouts" the nose of the boat missed the buoy by only an inch, the starboard blades dug in deep and the port side crew leant out to stabilise the boat in the turn, the rear of the boat slide round the boat moved gracefully into and out of the turn, the blades on the port side slide into the water in perfect timing to the start of the stroke from the starboard side and off they set in perfect unison.

"Woah Lads! that was bloody perfect shouted Cox, all the crew knew it was good turn confidence was growing the lads were in good spirit and the boat was performing perfectly. "Ok Lads slow it down now just a cruise back to Ditty so we can have a chat, the crew slowed the pace and effort to a steady comfortable surface speed, Tallet looked and felt so graceful in the water each crew member felt it, without words it was the best feeling.

"So, good work tonight lads thank you, it's been a good work out", said Cox, I have a few pointers though these need to be sorted out before tomorrow. Jake and Jools your tired get some rest tonight and for all of you no drinking out tonight, rest up eat well pasta supper full breakfast eggs bacon bread, light lunch chicken pasta, snacks at 2 and 4 pm" you all know the crack, Jake, stop ragging the leather, same for you Jools keep your eye on it. A brilliant run lad's in fact they are the best I've ever done on Tallet".

The crew shouted "Valhalla"!
Cox waved his hands down to signal a slower approach to the jetty and the slipway, as they arrived the crew lifted the blades on the port side, all 3 oars stood vertical, as the boat nestled next to the jetty the oars on the other

side were hoisted up all six blades stood in the air like a guard of honour as Cox stepped off the boat.

He attached the rope to the front of the gig, he turned to the crew "So, let's all be here at the jetty tomorrow by 4.30, we are cruising to them tomorrow its 25 minutes so to be at Kingswear by 5 ish ready for the dash at 6.30, we might need to ride the tide for a bit of extra a practise, let's see what we find tomorrow. Ok you lubbers, that's all she wrote guys".

Cox made for the way home up the hill street and the crew organised the boat ready for tomorrows battle with Kingswear. Tommo Blaggs and Jools loaded oars into the Gig then the Boat on to its launching trailer then hooked it on to the back of the waiting Land Rover, Posh Henry and Jake guided the boat back to turn up the hill back to Blaggs home where it would be drained and covered for the night.

Tommo and Jools got together as they walked up the hill, behind the Landy. So, what time are we getting under way Saturday Tommo asked, 7 am said Jools, we need to stop and register at Dartmouth yacht Club that only take 10 minutes, then we can make our way off, can you get some food and something to drink, the water tanks are empty and full of crap, uncle hasn't used them for a year or so and im not going to have a dose of something, so we need bottled water".

Tommo said he would get the provisions first thing in the morning. Jools mentioned warm clothes a sleeping bag waterproof jackets and wellies. "Ok said Tommo I think I can put all of that together".

Chapter 10

Cox was marching towards home as he passed the New development the grey gates whirred into action and started to open, the tall figure of the house manager stepped out, "Hello Mr Cox, I wonder if you could spare me a few moments? Cox slowed to a stop as the house manager was blocking his path, "what for"? said Cox, "Mr Cox it seems we have some sub-standard work", "not from me you haven't" said Cox defensively, "Mr Cox the work you have done is not what we expected, the finish indeed is extremely poor and requires attention, could you spare me a few minutes to confirm this"?.

The house manager was playing with a pair of spectacles tapping them on his teeth offering Cox a determined stare. Cox took a look at this watch he looked up the street and down making sure no one would see him,

"Ok, said Cox "I don't have much time so please be quick", "Thank you so much" said the house manager, holding out a hand to point the way inside the building. "This way" said the house manager, Cox followed him up the double flight of stairs to the landing seating and dining area he finished a couple of weeks earlier with Posh Henry.

Show me Cox said where the problem is, right here the house manager pointed to a corner of the room where the plaster and the paint had blistered using his spectacles to outline the area he was complaining about, "here, Mr Cox this is far from what we would accept as a good finish", "Yes said Cox I agree with you". "It has turned out a bit of a problem isn't it?" Cox gave a short intake of breath. "Yes? Mr Cox what are you going to do about it.?" The house manager said.

The house manager stood in front of Cox, there was an awkward silent moment then Cox said as he shook his head in disbelief, "if you remember and I do remember clearly telling you that the plaster whilst still not fully dry would give rise to problems if painted too soon, but it seems you knew better and instructed me to paint it and in a rush two Saturdays ago, there was an urgency to get it finished you said you had your boss coming and it must be completed, I told you not to paint it you ignored my advice, so what do you want me to do now"?

Cox was clearly angry and frustrated the house manager had confronted him with this after Cox had told him this would happen.

"It is simple Mr Cox I want you to repair it or preferably re -work it to an extremely high standard indeed". I bet you do said Cox, well I will need a couple of days to consider my price for doing this work and I will come back to you". "No Mr Cox this work will be completed tomorrow and there will be no price for it also,"

Cox laughed out loud, "you're not only deaf to

my reasoning you are totally incapable of understanding why this job will take 10 hours at least to repair the plaster then a four day wait at least to let it" …..mid-sentence the two men were interrupted by another male voice "Vasyli" the voice called out, Cox looked around to see two people at the top of the stairs behind them.

A stocky man and behind him a woman, he was the same height as Cox but much heavier immaculately dressed the woman who stood behind him was smartly dressed a striped silk top and tight skirt, her hair was jet black her features eastern European.

The room fell silent, the house manager stood back, Cox stood and face the man approaching him across the landing, the woman stood in shadow behind him.

Please excuse my housekeeper, said the man in his broken and quiet rasping voice," I am Aleksander Karpov, and you are Mr Coss?" Cox said Cox correcting him "I am sorry sometimes the English names are difficult for me to pronounce,

Mr Cosx, I own this building it is beautiful Yeass?" "Yes but" Cox tried to interrupt, "I have asked my housekeeper to make perfect the building before my arrival in the last few days, I must say the work is excellent and I am for the main part happy with all the decoration, However, this is a problem and to make my whole world complete I need it to be made perfect. So, Mr Cosx can I rely on you to attend to this problem?"

Cox said "yea I will but this time it must be done as I say, no rushing it , the plaster and paint are to be supplied by you I will supply the expertise and labour, it will be at £30 pounds per hour , and I will insist on no time keeping or rushing the job, it will be done when it is done.

Is that understood and agreed?" "You are an exceptionally talented craftsman Mr Cosx I will of course respect your wishes and afford you access to complete the work. When can you start? asked the house manager."

Cox glared at him, "Im on a job for the next two weeks, he walked back to look at the wall again, he looked around the whole room comparing the blistered portion to the other perfect walls, but if I can have access to this part of the building I will be able to do the preparatory work and make a start, this is not going to be a repair, on this section," Cox pointed out the whole wall section "we will scratch it down to a key, recoat and repaint, it will be the only way I can get a finish like on the other walls". "and" Cox continued, "this furniture and those paintings need to be removed, the dust will play havoc with those and they look expensive, so move them out."

The house manager had turned around talking to the woman who was now down the bottom of the stairwell, she was giving him a hard time Cox thought as he couldn't understand a word she was saying.

Aleksander took Cox by the arm, Have a look at this Mr Cosx, they walked to the centre of the upstairs room the double sliding doors gave way to a small terrace, he slid back the doors and they stepped out, the sunset was in full form glorious reds and oranges strewn across the sky bouncing off the adjacent hills across the river made for a stunning picture , " you see" said Aleksander, "how beautiful is this mother earth in all her glory Mr Cosx", "yes I know this view well said Cox, "Oh really how is that , "I knew the people who lived here before you", "oh really I thought this place was abandoned" Aleksander enquired , "yes it was" said Cox, it was sold to a property developer 8 years ago nothing happened , several planning applications were put in and refused" "the village had waited for someone to come along and make it wonderful again. You have done a good job, bit big for my liking but a nicely finished off place". "So, Mr Cox I owe you a debt of gratitude, I must explain my housekeeper is a driven man, I apologise for his abruptness , and I drive him hard. "That's ok said Cox, I will make it good for you, but we must"... "yes, yes ok ok" Mr Cosx," interrupted Aleksander.

So, let me show you to the door, I am leaving town for a few weeks, but I hope to see the room finished on my return", "I will do my best said Cox, thank you, we now have an understanding, yes? replied Aleksander, they made their way down the stairs to be met by the black-haired woman, she smiled at Cox and asked, "are we all agreed now?" "Yes, said Aleksander, "Silvia this is Mr Cosx he very kindly said he will fix the wall for me here Silvia.

"Mr Cosx, this is Silvia, Silvia works for my Art business, she is a conservator of art and paintings and helps me with other things". Aleksander turned to Silvia, "please Silvia, I want to know you will pay Mr Cosx and his bill will be settled immediately, "I will of course" said Silvia she smiled and said, "come to me and I will settle it for you".

"And another thing Silvia, Aleksander continued to explain, Mr Cosx knows the view across the river very well", "oh Interesting", "how is that Mr Cox she asked her hair falling across her soft face.

"Mr Cosx knew the people who were here before" Aleksander continued, "ah" said Silvia some local social history then?, did you know them well?", "I did" said Cox, he waited a few seconds then said with a smile looking directly at Aleksander, "they were my parents, I was born here".

"Mr Cosx, Mr Cosx repeated Aleksander "I am so sorry I did not know; I do now truly hope you approve of the renovations,"? "they are very ...contemporary and I do approve it is nice and im happy you have done something with the old place, im sure my parents would approved too", "Thank you, Mr Cosx", Aleksander bowed his head and offered his handshake, Cox shook his hand.

Silvia said "Mr Cox you are welcome anytime here is my card, please call me when you need to come here, I will prepare things for you".

"Cheers thank you" said Cox and he left picking up his kit bags as he left, the grey gates under the glass canopy opened in their menacing whining. Cox stepped forward, to clear the gap in the gates, on the other side was Blaggs, "Christ Blaggs what are you doing here?", "hello Cox I could ask you the same question", "I've got some business left over with Vasyli, watch out mate he's had a bit of a rollocking from Silvia",

"So, you've met the lovely but vicious Silvia eh? Yeah", just now" said Cox turning around to look at the house, there in the doorway was the housekeeper Vasyli with his brown eyed 1000-yard stare. "You'd better go in said Cox it looks like Mr Charisma is wating for you. See you tomorrow said Blaggs yeah see you later" Cox said.

Cox made his way out of the driveway and up the hill to his home at the top of the Steep Hill.
Blaggs made his way to the door "Mr Blaggs" said Vasyli, "so pleased you could join us, inside please". Blaggs moved inside, he was met by Silvia and Aleksander, "is everything in order with your team" asked Aleksander, "yes said" Blaggs, "good!" said Aleksander "why the meet-

ing? Asked Blaggs, "all will become clear."

Aleksander sucked on a half lit Cuban cigar, struggling to light it Silvia took it from him and used a big marble table lighter from the golden surrounded coffee table in the reception area to re-ignite the huge cigar, she took a couple of long puffs on it, she inhaled the cloudy last puff, as she blew it out of her red lips, she looked at Blaggs, her dark brown eyes were smouldering, and the look for Blaggs was enticing. She handed it back to Aleksander, he glanced at her and said, "thank you my dear", "where is he?" Aleksander looking down at the gold watch on his broad wrist, Vasyli, said he is here, he is just coming."

Vasyli closed the door, Blaggs looked across to see one other guy going into the office, he sat down inside the door of the office. Vasyli and Silvia flanked Aleksander, the door buzzed, Vasyli stood up and walked over to the security panel on the wall next to the door, he pressed a button and the panel lit up blue, on the small screen Blaggs could make out a car arriving the bright head lights blotting out detail. The black BMW swept into the driveway and circled the round pond and water fountain. The doors of the car opened.

Aleksander said something in Russian to Silvia, she stood up and walked across the reception area her legs and tight skirt bringing Blaggs eyes to her high heels as the clicked across the marble floor.

As she got to the door, she pulled it open there stood in his country set Harris tweed gear was Devlin. He removed his hat revealing his badly scared head, he leant forward to accept three cheek kisses from Silvia, she took his hat and coat, he thanked her and marched across the marble reception area to join Vasyli, Aleksander and a nervous looking Blaggs.

"So, gentleman we have a problem?" said Aleksander, we are losing product somewhere. It must be stopped and now! Vasyli what do you have? Silvia spoke up "in the last month we have processed 113 kilos this has given us 111 kilos of finished product grade A,

Vasyli continued, but on shipping we have only 97 kilos accounted for, Devlin said "I have audited the works today I can account for the 113 in and the 111 out, we keep the second grade in the lock up and it is all there.

Aleksander turned to Blaggs. Mr Blaggs is your man able to account for deliveries to the Makonde, we only pick up and drop off barrels and drums plus coffee bags and the diesel oil," "2 kilos is not a full drum" said Devlin, and of course they are sealed.

Blaggs continued "All the drums are sealed we have no access to them, Posh Henry, the guy who is helping me is a good guy but isn't interested in what we are moving.

Aleksander paced up and down the echoing marble floor his leather shoes creaking as he paced. Ok said Aleksander, "listen to me, from now this minute I now trust no one, from now you trust no one, you and we will find the problem and remove it. I will be leaving for Monaco in a few days; I want an answer before I get back."

Aleksander scanned to room, "seal this down and quickly" Aleksander said, Silvia and Vasyli stared back at Aleksander, Blaggs looked at Devlin, Blaggs broke the silence and to Devlin said "I'll come to see you tomorrow I want to check out what Posh is doing, "It is not Posh Henry" said Devlin, "OK, I will see you at the farm". Devlin looked at the floor he said, "Call me before you get there".

Gentlemen and Lady I repeat seal this up quickly, Aleksander bellowed "the consequences are severe if we do not, we need to be inconspicuous under the radar and out of sight. Silent everywhere." He paced towards a table, on which Silvia had placed a large single malt whiskey.

Aleksander took a sip, he turned to the assembled in the reception and continued, he took another sip from the crystal cut whisky glass in his hand, "we do not need attention, that is why we are here and not in central fucking London".

Aleksander stared at Vasyli as he finished the Whisky, he then very carefully placed the edge of the whisky glass on the table tipping it back and forth, he moderated his voice and in a quiet low voice with his head down staring at the table and glass, said, "is that clear?" He slowly looked up.

His eyes stared at everyone in the room one by one. "Please understand me, however we deal with this will be under or own Ukrainian ways of doing business " "Is understood yes?

Aleksander's question was direct and to the point. "Understood" was the unified reply, Blaggs was sweating and feeling uncomfortable, he was sensing this was one pissed off Russian dude. Silvia took a nod from Vasyli as he shifted his brown eyes in Blaggs direction, she turned to Blaggs "good night Mr Blaggs" she said as she led him by the arm to the door.

Blaggs made his way, Silvia was close to him side by side as they walked, her hands and nails were immaculate her clothes swished as she walked, her heels clicked in unison with his pace as they walked, he could smell her perfume, it was heady, expensive delicious, something he never had smelt before.

She held his arm tight her fingernails pushing into his arm, he looked at her hand there was a tattoo on the back of her hand it looked like an octopus, He looked back as the door was opened by Silvia to see Aleksander staring at him with a 1000-yard stare. "good evening Mr Blaggs thank you" said Aleksander; almost ushering Blaggs out of the room with his eyes, "yeah see you soon" said Blaggs in a semi-automatic reply as he passed through the door.

As Silvia bid him goodnight from the door Blaggs could feel a dribble of cold sweat running down his back this chilled him as he walked the 200 or so yards to home. Blaggs locked the door behind him, he took his jacket off and cracked open a half-finished bottle of whisky, he poured a large glass and took a drink, he was thinking that he didn't want to think about what was said tonight across the road, it was best he didn't think. He needed to speak to Posh Henry and quickly.

An hour or so after he had arrived home he had fallen asleep in front of the tv, there was a rapid knocking at the door, he stumbled to his feet realising the whiskey had been too easy to drink, he opened the door there stood Silvia, "can I come in"? she asked, "yeh yeh come in this is a surprise", her perfume filled the room, she was wearing a black overcoat, "listen to me" Silvia said don't put the light on, just listen.

"The stuff is going missing Vasyli is at the bottom of this, I know it and I know him, he is dangerous Blaggs be incredibly careful what you say and careful where you say it. If they find out, we have spoken they will send Devlin to circle on you, then me".

This is down to Vasyli be careful, thanks for the

heads up said Blaggs, I don't know what to say, am I being set up?" "No but they -; Vasyli and the crew on Makonde are dangerous people, Blaggs was still in his shorts and sweat stained rowing vest, she looked him up and down, do you always sleep like this she asked? Blaggs being slightly aware he wasn't at his best "in a semi disgusted way" said "only when im not naked he laughed", "how can you English be so funny at a time like this".

She stepped closer to him, the only light in the room was coming from the tv, he stepped closer to her he could see the sheen off her jet-black hair, he could feel the heat off her face, he reached forward and kissed her, first on the cheek then on the lips, she responded her face so warm and eyes closed.

He held her in the small of her back bring her closer, her hands clasping at Blaggs arms, she was shaking, he wanted more but she pushed him away, "too dangerous" she said, a quiver was in her voice, she was breathless, "I like danger "said Blaggs flirting with her, "no you fucking do not this isn't a joke Blaggs," she was all of a sudden very serious a harsh look in her eyes and Blaggs felt it.

She turned and opened the door looking left and right, she stepped out and walked out of the lane into the street. Blaggs watched as she walked to the new house. She tapped in the numbers on the security gate and it opened the side gate, she passed through.

As she entered the reception it was in darkness, "ah Silvia" came a voice from behind the office door, "where have we been my dear" it was Vasyli "for a walk to clear my head get some cigarettes" and by the way Vasyli, none of your fucking business!".

Vasyli stepped back into the office, the door closed

slowly, a loud click from the latch echoed around the reception area. Silvia removed her shoes and went up the stairs to her room, as she walked in, she covered her face with her hand and burst into tears. She knelt on the bed repeating to herself "Oh my god, Oh my God".

Blaggs sat up for a while, 20 minutes had passed, he could still smell her in the room. There was another knock at the door, he immediately thought Silvia might have changed her mind and come back to finish off what she had started, Blaggs groomed his hair and removed his sweat ridden vest, he stepped onto the rug behind the door, he couldn't see her but opened the door, as the door swung open something hard and heavy struck him in the head, as he bent forward he received a heavy hard punch to the ribs, this winded him, he fell back over the arm of the sofa, the intruder came in for more Blaggs turned over and took another blow to the kidney on the left hand side, he managed to stand up a crack came to his left eye socket and another to the top of his lip the pain surged though his head, another fast crack came in under his breast bone cracking his ribs, Blaggs fell to the floor, curled up in the foetal position he tucked his head down as kick after kick reigned in.

As suddenly as it had started there was silence, Blaggs sensed the person was leaving the room, he looked and saw someone he didn't see a face just a knitted black hat. Blaggs was aware of warm blood pouring from his face, as he tried to get up the pain in his chest was excruciating.

Blaggs managed to slump towards the door, locking it and bolting it. He turned the tv off and looked from behind the curtains, he saw the man walk off down toward the jetty. He had no idea who it was or why he had been beaten. The words of Aleksander echoed in his head

"From now on I trust no one!

The next day Tommo was shopping for the up-coming Trip aboard Fish's uncles boat "Bacardi" Tommo picked up crisps and chocolate bars coffee and long-life milk, he picked some sandwiches and fruit cake, bananas, Tommo and Fish had worked out the trip to France from Dartmouth was approx. 10 hours maybe more if the wind isn't with them, however a 7am start would give them a good start. Fish had booked a stopover in Roscoff there was a choice of several overnight berths he preferred the main harbour moorings they were on deep water and well sheltered.

Roscoff was a good place for something to eat and several French bars offered plenty of opportunity to sample the local beer wine and nightlife. Fridays semi-final for the gig race was first and foremost, they needed this win to take the points, the final was not confirmed yet, but could be a serious contender.
The results would be out on Saturday lunchtime, Fish had said to Tommo that he hoped Cox would not be call-ing for his usual meeting Saturday afternoon to rabbit on about the final, Fish thought they all deserved a break and some chill time. A trip over to Roscoff would do the trick and help his uncle, two birds one stone.

Tommo walked back towards the harbour to find Fish, instead he found Posh Henry sitting outside the Ferry-man, Hi mate how's it going"? Im cool said Henry, where are go off too with all that grub, I got a trip to Roscoff tomorrow with Fish, you wanna come"?, "wish I could" replied Posh Henry "im working", "that the spirit, peace and wicked eh"? said Tommo, "yeah something like that", have you seen Fish? "nah mate",

So, what are you doing for work now Posh? "err well Tommo I work in logistics these days Tommo, oh yeah doing what?" we move high quality oil products" , "Oh yeah from where to where" ? "what?" said posh, confused, "where to where? repeated Tommo, "If you are in logistics?", "oh yeah eerm, from that boat to a farm and from that farm to aaah that boat.

"And who is we?" asked Tommo "Oh, well I don't really know" said Posh scratching his head, so it's you then? So, your odd jobbing Posh? "I suppose" said Posh, "That sounds a worthy career to me", said Tommo, "so excuse me James Onedin, I need to find Fish", "he will be at home" said Posh, "will he? asked Tommo "yeah of course, its Friday he'll be ironing his vest for tonight, he's so well domesticated you know? said Posh in a sarcastic voice. Very funny said Tommo.

Tommo made off towards Fish's bedsit along the front, Fish was in and he was ironing, Tommo knocked and let himself in "Fish here is the food for the weekend", ok put it in the box next to the sink, Fish called from the lounge." When Fish emerged, he was carrying a pile of clothes all crisp and freshly ironed, Oh Fish look at you said Tommo, you'll make someone a lovely husband one day,

"I've had a look at the weather and the maps we should be in for a quick ride across" said Tommo, yeah I saw a westerly 5-8 knot wind will do us fine", Fish pushed forward the latest print out from the met office and a map of the English channel up to Portland and down to Lands' End, do you want to trial her before or should we just go for it, let's go for it we can trial her as we go, said Fish.

"OK by me, is there anyone else coming?, "Nope I

have asked Blaggs and Posh Jake is away so Cox, "Cox said Tommo why Cox, he's bloody good on the helm said Fish and he's a good laugh when you get to know him" anyway I've asked all of the crew all are doing something else so its you and me.

Ok said Tommo I've got to be away, off to get a new vest. I'll see you jetty side at 4.15ish?? yeah fine mate remember to eat!" Fish commanded. "I will, I will" said Tommo as he left.

Posh Henry made his way across the Ham towards Blaggs workshop, Blaggs was already there, "Hey ho my friend" called Posh Henry as he approached the workshop doors, Posh I need a word, Blaggs stood up slowly "oh no Blaggs not a dear John word is it?", Maybe depends on your answer.

Blaggs turned to Posh Henry Fucking hell Blaggs what's happened to you, Blaggs was holding his side the had plasters over his eyebrow and his eye was pretty much closed up. I need a straight answer and I need you to be honest, because people might get hurt. Fuck me Blaggs you need the emergency room no no! Blaggs said just listen, "whoa" Blaggs cried out as he stood up. It's my ribs, fucking hell Blaggs your rowing later, you can't row like this "I can said Blaggs I need some bandages to wrap my ribs up, hold on said Posh, I'll be back in a couple stay there don't move.

A few minutes later Posh Henrys Land Rover pulled up outside the workshop. Come on get in, get in he was insistent! Posh drove off the Land Rover climbing the steep hill toward Posh Henrys small house, what are we doing here? Blags groaned, "I can fix you up but you need to go to A and E get this x-rayed" "No fucking way" said Blaggs, "too many questions", Posh Henry pulled up at the little house he rented, here Blaggs put his arms over Henrys shoulders, he slid him out of the car, Posh opened the door keys jangling in a furious attempt to open the stiff lock.

He pushed the door open and Blaggs lay down on the sofa, let's have a look at his eye, Posh retrieved a bag of peas from the freezer, here he placed them in a tea towel and placed then on Blaggs eye socket it was black and blue.

"OK Blaggs what have you done now? "Posh stop with the talking, have you picked anything up from the farm that you shouldn't have? boxes or packages anything? are you just collecting the green drums?," "yes Blaggs only the drums come back here I've got a diary log in the Landy of every trip and return trip with the diesel receipts", "nothing unusual?", "nope nothing unusual", "nothing moves without Devlin knowing, he checks everything, Blaggs said "and do you get on with him ok, Posh said "yeah ok he is a funny bugger but always the gent."

"Good make sure you keep the details we might need them, what's up Blaggs you look like shit! "Thanks for that I feel it, too much going on right now". "Listen" said Blaggs "keep your head down if anyone starts talking to you, you don't know, you haven't seen and you don't want to know, just fetch and carry, ok!" "yeh ok, ok said Posh raising one eyebrow and frowning, what's going on Blaggs? I can't tell you right now but just keep your nose clean up there. Someone is shit stirring".

"Blaggs we need to get you into this", Posh Henry held up a corset, dirty cream coloured with old rusty eyelets and laces of nylon" what the fuck is that?" "this got me through last season when I pulled my back out, you might be able to row with this on.

"Cox will fucking kill you if you don't turn up for this one tonight Posh Piled on the agony".

Posh and Blaggs worked on getting him strapped up. It was hard to breath, but the support was ok and Blaggs admitted to Posh he felt better wearing it.

"If anyone asks said Posh Henry you fell down my stairs pissed up", yeh ok said Blaggs "cheers Posh I owe you one, no Blaggs you owe me £300 quid so far, I need money to eat and drink! "yeh yeh ill sort you out tomorrow". Just do what I said and keep your head down ok ..ok"?

"Ok replied Posh Henry. He made Blaggs a sweet tea and put a shot of scotch in it, here drink this it'll sooth the soul and kill the pain.

Posh found a baseball cap for Blaggs to wear during the race, keep you face low and out of sight of the crew, Posh took Blaggs keys and went to collect his gear for the evening's races, he washed out Blaggs vest and took it to his Sue at the ferryman's inn who had a tumble dryer and got the vest clean and ironed she was grumbling but only too pleased to help and support the rowing team.

Here you go said Posh, now it's only 10.30, I suggest you kip here for a few hours, ill bring some food in a while, I need to do my runs up to the farm and to Devlin then back to the boat, yeh Blaggs said make it look like all is normal. You get going ill rest this lot here. Thanks, Posh. No worries said Posh as he closed the door.

Posh Henry went to the foreshore and locked up Blaggs Workshop, he drove with The Plastic cans to the farm and filled them up, the guy called Andrew came and asked "why are you late,?" "because today I am" said

Posh Henry. He loaded the oil up and went to the farm at Tuckenhay. There Devlin was waiting for him, "why are you late again?!" was the opening good morning question, "because today Devlin I am im sorry a friend of mine was hurt, and I helped him get some treatment." "my dear boy how terrible how might this have happened? "He was pissed and tripped over my cat", Posh looked at Devlin with a contemptable stare, "Devlin just smiled back from under his hat.

"Now here are your two Posh continued and handed over the tubs of oil", I'll take these three drums of finished, two coffees, and empty oil tubs for tomorrow". "Is that all for me"? said Posh Henry.

"Excellent" said Devlin looking at Posh from under the brim of his fedora. "excellent Posh Henry thanking you" Devlin smiled his gentleman smile and opened the gate to let Posh reverse out.

Posh made the 18-minute drive back to the foreshore and loaded the boat up. He pushed it afloat and rowed the 100 yards to the sailing boat moored off on the visitor's buoy.

He was greeted by the stocky man who never spoke to him, Posh Henry handed up the first drum, the second he placed on the little deck and lifted the third.

There were two coffee bags to come, Posh rowed back to shore in a few minutes and retrieved the coffee sacks from the rear of his car, he loaded the boat up, some of the coffee beans spilled into this boat, it was only a hand full, but he wasn't bothered, he wanted to get finished and get back home quickly. He rowed back in less time albeit loaded up with coffee. The stocky man on the back of the boat was getting impatient and was doing his mumbling in Russian pointing and grunting, "Oh fuck off" said Posh Henry.

Posh rowed his boat back to shore anchored his boat on the shore got in the car and drove the Landy home, Blaggs was out of it sleeping well, Posh checked on him his face was still a mess some of the swelling had gone down, he made some dinner of corned beef beans eggs and heaps of toast, lots of tea. He went over to Blaggs, "come on mate shit shave and shampoo time", he bundled a half awake Blaggs int to bathroom threw a clean towel at him and said, "Impress me, you ugly bastard", Blaggs closed the door.

15 minutes later Blaggs appeared in a towel, his body was black and blue, his ribs and side and back were badly bruised, fuck me said Posh you are a mess you took a right kicking. I feel it said Blaggs, I need pain killers, here Posh passed some soluble paracetamol, "you are a very well-prepared man" said Blaggs. "I need to be with wankers like you for friends", Blaggs laughed then stopped as the pain rushed over his ribcage.

Posh insisted that Blaggs stay with him until the meet up on the jetty. At 3.30 they stared to get ready, Blaggs put on his corset and Posh gently laced it up using the moans of pain as a gauge of how tight was tight. Blaggs announced he was ready as he could be, he put on a pair of sunglasses which did a good job of hiding most of the swollen eye and purple eye sockets in both eyes. He was dressed in Vest and track suit top and club shorts. Blaggs said "thanks Posh, I feel like shit look like shit and probably going to row like shit" "Normal then" Posh Laughed. Posh had dressed his eye again and fed him a double dose of pain killers, "Yes well it's all on you today isn't it? You're a fuckwit!"

The two men walked out into the street, there

were a lot of tourists about, the two made their way in the Landy to Blaggs Parking space outside his house, Tommo and Fish were already there Posh, said alright then, the two looked around at Blaggs, "alright you two?", Blaggs managed a "yeh ok , then tommo caught sight of Blaggs's eye, "fucking hell Blaggs who thumped you again? "

Blaggs went for Tommo "watch your mouth" said Blaggs, his head was pounding, and he was in no mood for Tommo and his sarcastic taunting, Posh intervened "ok! Ok! Ok! come on, come on, he's fallen down my stairs pissed up ok? this is our problem not yours Tommo so for today mate just for this evening lets drop it ok!" "no up-setting Coxy, mate please, so nothing to talk about let's just get and do this job. Drinks on me later boys ok?"

Posh had disarmed Tommo and nothing was said, Blaggs helped Fish hook up the gig to the trailer and off they set slowly through the very narrow streets to the jetty and the pier. The four men moved the Gig on its trailer down the hill towards the jetty without incident or scratching a tourist's car with the trailer.

Cox was waiting with Jake and Jools, the were chatting in the sunshine, the crew, three each side launched the boat, Jools holding the Gig on its bow rope, Cox was wearing his grubby track suit top proudly showing off the badges, he was on the jetty and organising the club lock up as each crew picked up their oars, Blaggs was holding back, Posh Henry picked up Blaggs oar and walked with it for him to the boat.

Cox called out as he took his seat "crew on star-board step aboard please", three of the big men stepped in and sat down their oars passed overhead, "Port side on board please" said Cox and they stepped aboard all sat

down together got comfortable, Cox had noticed Blaggs was last to seat, all six oars were vertical, one was wavering, Cox looked at Blaggs and he seemed to be struggling holding the blade up straight," OK Blaggs?" called Cox, "yes Cox no trouble no trouble ok here!"
"Ok then let us make our way to victory".

The crew slowly let the gig drift into the stream of the river, the first few strokes were disorganised, and Cox called "untidy gentlemen" it took a few strokes to settle in, Cox took them upriver almost to the visitors buoys then slowly in a big arc turned the gig around the back of the big sailing boat Makonde moored up 30 yards away, as they passed it on the back of the deck was Devlin and Vasyli.

Vasyli was leaning with his chin on the yacht's big wheel a short drink in his sun-tanned hand, both men were staring intently at the gig as it gently passed, Posh Henry spotted Devlin staring through gold rimmed sunglasses he leaned forward and whispered to Blaggs, keep your head down son don't look up. "I know" whispered Blaggs.

So, gents let us get warmed up please give me 20 long and smooth ones we are 20 or so minutes away and so let us gooooohhh! Cox was clearly on form and ready for a bloody battle downstream at the start line in 1 hours' time. the local onlookers clapped them through as they swept down the river towards Spanish Boathouse, "Keep it tidy boys come on accuracy, power, 30 strokes per minute please nice and easy follow each other listen to my instructions, and gooooohhh"!

Blaggs ok? Posh asked, "yeh ok thanks." They rowed smoothly, the 6 whirlpool spots behind each blade left on the deep green water showed Cox the blades were being used efficiently, the boat was moving well little resistance being felt as they cruised with easy against the rising tide. Blaggs was feeling the pain but able to row.

They arrived at Kingswear some 25 minutes later, Cox ordered them to pull up against the hard on the far side of the ferry run, the water was slack there and the boat remained stable. Cox handed out drinks of flavoured water and biscuits. He still had his eye on Blaggs who was keeping his head down and sunglasses on. OK Blaggs "yeh im ok thanks" was all Cox could get out of him.

Cox's radio burst into action it was Tim the cox from the Kingswear team, Team Ditsham calling Coxy Cox are you there over, Cox lifted the radio to his ear and responded with a "Kingswear "we are indeed here and awaiting further instructions".

The radio clicked and Tim answered back "the harbourmaster has given us the go at 6.00 pm sharp, we must be clear of traffic by 17.50 and on the mark at 18.00hrs, gun will sound at 18.04hrs roger that Tim" replied Cox. "Where is the start line,"? over, the radio crackled then the start line gents is from castle cove to mermaids point, its marked clearly, the referee boat is there already, we shall see you there in 15 minutes".

"Bloody hell!" said Cox that's not what I understood, sorry guys we are a quarter mile further out than I thought, and it's a bit choppy on the rising tide and approaching wind so we might be getting wet."

The marker was in the mouth of the river, this was familiar waters for crew of Kingswear, there were some important markers to look out for, Kingswear were better equipped on this water and the Cox Tim knew it, Cox and Quentin had discussed tactics and the race against

Kingswear always bought a challenge the open water in the mouth of the Dart there was and is always a swell as the current mix and swirl, Kingswear crew had done all their practice starting in this open often choppy and swelly race start.

The radio crackled into life again Tim said, "we are moving into position". The crew of Dittisham under orders from Cox moved out into the mainstream, it took 10 gentle strokes to meet up with the Kingswear boat, the starter had requested both boats stay behind the line, the line wasn't as clear as Tim had suggested, so moving back and forth in the swell was difficult for all the rowers to keep the boat steady the bow and stern reacting to the swell under the gig was making it hard to keep the boat stable in a straight line.

Cox called oars up the boys lifted the oars just clear of the water, Cox was wrestling with the rudder trying to keep on sight, Blaggs and Jools oars dropped, and both caught a wave passing under the gig from the stern, the pressure of the water pushed the oar into Blaggs chest, he gave out a roar in pain as the oar pinned him to the gunwale on his side of the boat.

Immediately Cox knew Blaggs was in trouble, he shouted to Blaggs "hey Blaggs sort it out we are ready to go in 1 minute!!" "Ok all good Cox sorry" Blaggs called back, the horn sounded to signal the 30 second mark the next 30 seconds felt like an hour the only sound was the wash of the waves on and against the gigs, each man felt their heart rates increase and they waited the go and to explode initialising that first pull on the oars .... the canon from the castle walls to the right of the two boats went off exactly 30 seconds later, ...Boom! and off they set,

All hell let loose, the crew from Dittisham dug in to 30 strokes straight away, "give me all you got lads" shouted Cox, the clatter of the gigs oars and creaking and grunting form the crew was deafening, "Ignore them they don't exist"!! shouted Cox as the Kingswear boat went ahead by a short length.

The Kingswear boat was riding the swell, they were almost surfing into the race, the Kingswear Cox Tim looked over his shoulder with a smirk in his face. The delay in placing the position was now clear, Tim had deliberately placed Coxy and the Dittisham boat off the line so as Kingswear could take the inner position they wouldn't feel the effects of the swell off the rocks, Cox spotted his over confidence.

The riverbank on the port side was bouncing the swell off the rocks, this had broadsided the Dittisham boat Cox felt the wave come from the side and slow the pace, then 10 yards later on another, now he understood Tim's tactics, "come on boys get it up 30 strokes please he roared at the crew, the pace of the Dittisham boat returned as the Kingswear boat was now almost a length ahead.

The race was running close side by side the oars on the starboard side running in on the Kingswear boats oar pattern. "Too close Dittisham move away" came the instructions from the race master's boat, Cox was looking for the right line away from the diminishing swell as they passed the ferry line. The car ferry was on hold until the race boats had passed through passengers clapping as the boats shot by. Cox bought the gig across only 5 feet or so that kept the race master happier.

This race was 10,000 yards in length not a long distance but enough to test both teams to their limits,

Cox watched closely as the rhythm of the crew got in to pace, "and again", he called with each completed stroke "and again" he called, out of the corner of his eye he could see Blaggs grimace as each pull on the oars was agony, Posh Henry was sweating he was pulling a slice extra for Blaggs, He could hear Blaggs crying in agony with every stroke behind him, come on mate keep it on, Posh called to Blaggs.

The noise from the Marina Hotel was deafening; locals cheering for Kingswear on home turf was heard even from the far side of the river where the steam train sounded their whistles, Cox shouted "ignore it look at me boys, now go, give me 20 good ones, come on puuuuull!"

Blaggs was in full swing, his strokes were long and accurate he was following Posh Henry sat adjacent to him, it felt good the rhythm was spot on they were gaining slowly, the pain in his chest was still red hot like a hot knife but his pain killers had kicked in and he knew it, his chest felt like it was on fire, the more he thought about the bastard who beat him up in his own home the more the pain began to fade away, Blaggs was getting angry and keeping angry the adrenaline was his friend.

Cox watched the Kingswear boat three quarters length ahead, Cox kept the speed on it, not to ramp it up too quickly it would only spurn Tim on harder.

The turn buoy was just in sight at the boathouse bend in the river off white point. The gig was spinning through the water fine, the pressure on the oars was efficient, the pace good, Cox called to the crew "steady rhythm now boys keep your eyes on me" as he looked forward 6 pairs of eyes were transfixed on him.

Cox could hear Tim in the other boat shouting

"row, row, row, go, go, row". He was happy his crew were working in silence, keeping pace with Kingswear, they were 3000 yards into the race, one length ahead "keep it right there boys".

Tallet Blood was pumping the water beneath was flowing well, red faces, sweat and a fast boat were coming together, "cruising now boys, good work, good work, when we turn, we will push on hard." Cox was concentrating on his engine room It was working as planned".

"1000-yards lads", he called, the crew settled into a drum beat of effort, the Kingswear boat was well over a length in front now, Jools looked over his shoulder and stared back at Cox, he mouthed "what the fuck" Cox called "500 yards boys come on steady now."

Grunts and huffs were the only measure of the power being transmitted through the 6 oars, Cox Bellowed above the din "Listen to me, Im the fucking captain" at 250 yards the race master's boat was alongside 20 yards away, Cox signalled to give him more room as he moved over to the port side by 10 feet, the race masters boat was giving off a wake, Cox didn't want his crew affected by the draw of this wake, so he pushed for more room. At 150 yards the Dittisham boat was in a cruise and moving well and closing slowly on Kingswear.

In the Kingswear boat Tim's red baseball cap was like a beacon, Kingswear was still 1 length ahead, Cox thought "Just where I want you Timothy matey boy! I can still smell you", Cox looked to the side the water was turning "oily smooth again" "perfect" he thought, the rasp of the water was clear to hear against the hull of the Dittisham boat. Thinking ahead boys we are at 70 yards, remember on my word we dig in and turn, now give me

10 at 40 strokes and go, rapidly the boat sped up gaining on Kingswear.

Tim could hear them gaining on him, he in turn ordered his boys to give more, at 30 yards Cox weighed up the number of strokes using Kingswear boat as a gauge counting the paddle marks on the water behind Kingswear, the buoy was getting closer and closer, He was pushing Kingswear hard.

20 yards Cox was nearly there, 10 yards and the Dittisham gig was upon the stern of Kingswear. Tim on Kingswear was looking for room, Dittisham was on him bearing down behind 6 feet away , Tim looked round and shouted at his team "more on the turn boys", the Kingswear boat shot past the turning buoy turning port-side across the front of the race directors launch to get it into its turn, his team working hard to row the boat around in a tight arc 20 feet beyond the Buoy.

Cox aimed the bow directly at the turning buoy, he shouted at the crew and turning in 3,2,1 now dig in the oars on starboard dropped deep into the water the nose of the boat was on the buoy the oars on the other side raised out and then straight back in as the stern of the boat swung fast and tight on the buoy the tightest turn without touching the buoy they ever have done, they shot away the portside oars dropped in and they were away.

"and give me 40 strokes a minute please for 80 strokes and goooooah ! my lovelies" Cox roared as he looked back, Kingswear were still paddling a turn they hadn't got past the buoy, and were in a chaotic scramble to get back on line, Cox watched as the race master was turning ahead of Kingswear.

Dittisham were already 50 yards ahead still giving a maximum effort 42 good strokes. Even the race master's boat was looking to see where Dittisham had ended up, "and long and power!" Cox called, with a smile on his face "come on give me one! give me one, give me another!", Cox glanced at Blaggs, Blaggs caught his eye, Cox nodded back, a whole conversation was exchanged in that second of communication. Blaggs was in pain a lot of pain, he was flagging, but he knew the rest of the crew were into this on full power and he wasn't going to back off.

The Dittisham crew pulled the boat through the water against the tide it felt effortless to the crew, they were flying, "come on boys we can have this, come on let's go! good work Dittisham boys good work" lets sick it right up them!

Cox's encouragement was fuel in the bellies of his crew he was a great sounding board, able to draw effort from a tired, wet, cold crew, 3000 yards boys and a lovely day for it!" he called again. Cox looked over his shoulder Kingswear were 50 yards behind his crew, now the more tired team after a fluff of a turn, the race master's boat was alongside Dittisham boat again, Cox signalling for it to move away.

Cox looked over his shoulder again, they were gaining, and there was still 1000 yards to go, "boys cox shouted at his crew, can you see these wankers behind? "Over to you boys this is your race, and goooooah!"

The sound of the oars digging in rattling in their gunwale pins and the rhythm increasing to 43 or 44 strokes was loud and clear, the crew aboard Dittisham knew the sound, it was a good victorious sound, just like the Viking attack he used to demonstrate the art of rowing to the victory.

The Dittisham boat just accelerated away increasing their lead in the next 500 yards by two and a half lengths, Kingswear were now lagging, they were passing the point of no return and for regaining a lead, there just wasn't enough distance left to pull ahead or even close.

Cox was really enjoying this, the finish line was now in sight, "we are flying boys!" shouted Cox, come on! my lovelies give it to me!" "come on let's show those cocky bastards what gig rowing is all about". They passed the hotel marina the clapping had subsided as they swept past, "now you don't like it do you?" shouted Cox, the boys kept the pressure on as they went ahead closer and closer to the finish line by almost 3 lengths.

Coxy pretended he was smoking an exceptionally large cigar as they got 200 yards from the finish line all the crew exhausted, they still were laughing at Cox.

The Kingswear boat was giving up as the Dittisham crew Crossed the line of the ferry and took the water that used to belong to Kingswear, Hey Boys do you see this water? Well, is our water now!

They gained on the finish line with gusto they could smell victory now and there was the line the siren horn sounded to mark the winner of the race, all of the crew in the Dittisham boat shouted hip, hip hooray, hip, hip hooray ! Oars up lads and rest now. Coxy applauded his team.

The Kingswear Boat crossed the line, they rowed toward the Dittisham boat, as they approached Jools and Tommo shouted to the Kingswear crew "where have you been guys? "what took you so long?".

Tim stood up in the boat he was holding his hands out "hey Coxy what the hell was that? ""what was what" Coxy said , "do you mean that win?", Tim shouted "no what the fuck was that illegal turn?" "That was no illegal turn Tim, that was how to win a race".

Cox was grinning at Tim, "no you touched the buoy that's illegal" Tim was gesticulating, "hey, hey Tim watch your mouth, "we didn't touch the buoy", "yes you did you got the race boat moved so you could go at the buoy." "No, No" Said Cox you were too focused on our boat being right up your arse that you forgot to turn, we didn't forget!! Timbo, we beat you good! beers are on you Tim".

Tim had a terse look on his red face he ordered his crew and his crew rowed away, Cox watched as he sided his boat against the race master's boat, he was in deep discussion pointing back at the Dittisham boat. "Oh it may seem we have a complaint on the way boys".

After a few minutes, the race director arrived, Hello Cox, they have raised a complaint they say you touched the buoy, what say you? Cox smiled "well you are the race director Raymond, so I am asking you, what say you? "we didn't see the turn Cox; you were at that point behind the race masters launch as such we were not watching you.

Cox thought for a second or two the race director and his timekeeper stood above them, Cox tipped his hat back "well there is your answer gentlemen, you didn't see us touch the buoy, did you?" "we, err" started the director," "did you?!" snapped Cox, "er well no" "under those circumstances Mr race director you are in default for not keeping your eye on both boats it is in the rules I think you will find, so against Tim's complaint you can't raise a fault because you have admitted you didn't witness it, So, do you want me to tell Tim?"

"No Cox, We concur with you, we will not be raising a fault in this case the race director Raymond held out his hand and Cox took the handshake, Cox said to the race director, Listen Raymond we have known each other for over 20 years, to draw a line under this Ray, we didn't touch the buoy, my word is my word", Yes I know that Cox thank you for clearing it up. Ok thank you very much. Hip hips boys for the race officials Cox requested, as the race directors launch moved away.

As the Dittisham gig passed by the Kingswear boat the crew of Kingswear were looking despondent slumped in the boat Tim looking on furious faced and pissed at Cox, the Dittisham crew held a finger and thumb on their foreheads in the looser sign, loo - sers,! – loooo - sers,! The called went across the water. The crew of Dittisham let the Kingswear crew who was the winner and who was the bad loser.

"Home boys, beers are on me, nothing worse than a bad boat full of bad losers", Cox announced, the crew set to a steady row back, Cox stood up in the boat and said "just a minute boys before we get going, Blaggs, me and you swap", Blaggs was reeling in pain, come sit here Son, the crew bundled Blaggs rearwards so he could stand and swap with Cox, Cox took his seat next to Posh and Jools, they sat Blaggs down, he took hold of the steering wires on the rudder and they continued and took a steady route back towards Dittisham and its Jetty.

The 25-minute row was mostly silent each man including Blaggs disappointed for the reaction from Kingswear a victory is a celebrated affair the race mostly good humoured and the preamble for a beer filled session with likeminded good sports Cox couldn't pretend he wasn't pissed off at Tim. As they arrived a gathering of onlookers were clapping as the Gig and tired crew arrived.

Calls of "great win" "good win" "best boat and jolly good fellows" soon were heard across the lake as the victorious and strangely quiet Ditsham Gig arrived and docked on the end of the Jetty followed by a long applause.

Cox bought the boat alongside the end of the jetty, He stepped off the boat and went to the back of the boat, Blaggs, "Posh come here, Posh take him to hospital this isn't right, Blaggs was bent over in real pain, Blaggs was holding his side and breathing heavily," Blaggs looked at Cox and said "im sorry I let you down, yes you did said Cox but I'll kick your ass for it another day". Posh said "can someone pick my kit up." He grabbed Blaggs by the arm, "Come on Blaggs lets get off."

Chapter 11

The rest of the crew beached the boat and accepted a pint each from Sue at the Ferryman's, she asked where Posh Henry was? Cox said, "he's off to A&E with Blaggs" "why?" Sue asked, "he's bumped his head" Cox said "he's ok just want him to get checked out he'll be back later".

The boat was locked up outside the pub, for the night Jools and Jake said they would put it at Blaggs house in the morning. Cox and Tommo were talking they agreed the complaint from Kingswear had been something to take the shine off a good win, good tactics and a clear stat plan had worked.

A car arrived in the car park of the pub, the race director and his record keeper get out and made their way to Cox, "Hello Cox and Dittisham Tallet crew, congratulations on an excellent win guys", "thanks said Cox, the race director said "you have enough team points now to be in the final of the south downs gig championships", Cox said "Yes Ray good news, I believe so".

It will take place in two weeks' time on Saturday 11th of next month, can we have a week before then a list of your crew and the name of your designated craft. "Yes, you can" said Cox, he looked at the race director and said "keep your eye on us next time Raymond, who is in the final with us,"? there was a pause, the director knew the rivalry was intense, erm..... it's Salcombe"!

A round of comments and ooh's and ah's filled the

air, "is that confirmed asked Cox, Cox's eyes were like saucers, yes Cox it is they won their qualifier this evening, I just had the call from Dave Jessops at Salcombe HQ, and by the way, we will be watching your every move Coxy.

It's a 2.00 pm race at Salcombe 10000 yards, first past the post, Cox stood up and shook the director's hand," great we accept and look forward to a fair race Raymond".

"See you on the 11th boys", "thanks Raymond", the director and his officers drove off up the hill. "Salcombe eh?" Cox mumbled, "this will need some clever boatmanship boys, meeting here Sunday 4.00 pm".

Posh Henry and Blaggs had arrived at The local Treatment room, at St Margaret's hospital the Nurse had seen Blaggs and asked what had occurred Posh Jumped in with a "He was pissed and fell down my stairs" the nurse took a look at Blaggs and said "yes of course you did,

Xray young man!" she handed him a card, she wheeled up a wheel chair and pointed down the long corridor its down there" Blaggs climbed into the chair, Posh pushed Blaggs to the Xray Department, the Xray nurse appeared, come on in John, "John said Posh, Yes John said Blaggs.

A few minute later she appeared, you need to see a doctor, she handed him a large brown envelope Posh pushed him back to the reception "John" Posh said "is back to see the doctor, the nurse went to another door and the doctor came out, come on in John he said, can you sit? Yeh Blaggs said, he sat on the edge of the chair.

"you sir are very lucky" the doctor said, "you have 3 fractured ribs a broken finger, and a cracked eye socket, what hit you?" Posh started to say "he" Blaggs stopped him, "I was beaten up, I don't know why or who so I can't answer those two questions, im finding it hard to breath", yes well it will be painful for a while to come, can I still row?" asked Blaggs with a desperation in his voice, "No definitely not said the doctor, rest, no work, no lifting, no rowing, I'll prescribe pain killers, and short dose of anti-biotics".

"Whoever did this John knew what they were doing, they knew how to hurt you, the Doctor was inspecting the bruises on Blaggs back "Christ man how are you walking?" "painfully"! scoffed Blaggs, "your eye will sort itself out but any problems with bleeding inside your eye socket come here immediately" "anything else Doc?" "Yeas young man keep away from naughty boys, I don't want to see you in here again", "OK thanks" said Blaggs, he put his shorts back on and zipped up his bruised torso in his track suit and walked out.

Posh didn't say a word as they arrived in Posh Henrys parking space. "Posh Cheers mate, I appreciate your help today, do you want me to keep deliveries going? Blaggs groaned as the pain in his chest smarted "For the time being yes, I don't want any trouble for you Posh".

"Im ok Posh said," I can look after myself". "Not with these animals you can't, they will go the extra to teach a lesson". "So be careful, keep doing it, but we need a way out of this with minimal aggro".

"We will talk but keep this between me and you, I don't want Cox knowing, ok understood? Yeh ok said Posh Henry, so you can bunk down at my place tonight if you want"? posh offered,

"Nah mate im ok I'll lock the doors and get some kip, I'll see you Sunday", "Sunday?" asked Posh Henry –"Salcombe meeting!!" "Oh yeah call for me well have a pint before?" "Will do" said Blaggs. Blaggs got out of the Land Rover and walked in a hobbled way into the lane to his house.

He let himself in the place was a mess, broken cups and mugs, a lamp was on its side and the sofa was in the fireplace.

Blaggs found the whisky bottle out and sat in the bedroom bay window watching the river in the distance, the few twinkling lights across the river was a focus. He drank a couple of big whiskeys, his eye was pulsing, and his sides really hurt, the scotch was taking the edge off. He relaxed a little bit still not able to get his head in order to try and sort this shit storm out.

There was a quiet knock at the door, he got up and groaned as his sides hurt again, who is it he called, "Silvia", "er no thanks love not again go away." She whispered "Blaggs I need to talk to you", "we will talk tomorrow," "no Blaggs today it is important" she was insistent. "No! Blaggs shouted "fuck off leave me alone". "Blaggs! Please just 2 minutes". "Blaggs unlocked the door and stood there, "So?, what is it?", "Oh fuck no"! she said, what has happened?" , "ha you are so funny, like you don't know Silvia whatever you name is ! I got fucked over because you were here."

"When was this?" Silva ran her red fingernailed hand across Blaggs chin and eye, he flinched and pushed her hand away, "Last night" he said, "just after you left." "Did you see who did this? "No?, for fucks sake Silvia I was lying on the floor having my head kicked in".

Blaggs took another gulp from his whiskey glass he poured another drink, and turned to the window, "So, Silvia, unless you know who this hit man bastard is, I suggest you get out of there before he comes to hit me again or worse hit you."

"This is serious and a warning Blaggs", "why a warning im doing nothing wrong" Blaggs snapped, "Vasyli will be working to unnerve or unsettle one of the team as soon as that one person shows a weakness, he will pounce".

She touched Blaggs "on the hand she looked into his eyes, "he will play dirty; he has no moral compass. So, beware Blaggs and tell your boy too. I leave you now".

"Silvia"! Blaggs called to her as she made for the door, "you too look after yourself". She nodded, Silvia turned up her collar on her long black coat and passed through the door. Blaggs locked it behind her and put the bolts on. He sat in the window again and slept for most of the night comfortable wedged into his favourite chair.

Chapter 12

The next morning was bright and according to the weatherman and the forecast starting off still and getting a little breezy a westerly 3-4 turning south westerly later as the day progressed, there would sunny periods and cloudy later, "Perfect", Fish thought as he rowed the tender to Bacardi from the jetty to the 34 foot sailing yacht moored off Spanish boathouse, he scrambled on board and opened the deck covers the smell from beneath was musty, not quiet unpleasant by needed to be aired, Seagull shit was all over the decks and the sun had faded the curtains on the narrow aluminium cladded windows, the boat hadn't been used this last season, the boat had only been out twice the year before, Fish's uncle and father own the boat and since his father passed away the start of the year it has hardly been off the mooring.

Fish tried to open the main doors, but the key was stiff and unwilling to move. In a toolbox Fish had bought with him was some oil spray, he got his out of the tender and sprayed a little in the lock and pushed the key in and out a few times, this seemed to do the trick as the lock still very stiff slowly yielded and the door was open.

The stench that hit him in the face was a real stench, it wasn't so much as a rotten smell but one of a citrus undertone something organic was quietly breaking down, there were dead flies all over the inside, on the cupboards tops and inside on the bunks there must have been a hatching this was going to take hours to clean up, something he hadn't calculated for, he could hear shouting, he opened the forward hatch trying desperately to hold his breath, it again was stiff but did with some pushing and shoving slide open.

The shouting was still going on, he put his head through the hatch and took a deep breath of fresh air. He could see Tommo on the shoreline waving, he had two boxes with him, Fish slid down into the boat, he opened the small door to the bunks in the forward cabin, again an unwelcome stench came from in there too, this was going to be a nightmare to clear up thought Fish.

Fish made his way through the cabins and onto the rear deck, he scrambled down into the tender and set off to collect Tommo from the shoreline 100 years away, "are you deaf"? said Tommo as Fish arrived, "maybe but my nose works fine," "oh yeh why is that? "It sinks in there, Fish was turning his nose up im not sure we should go", , "rubbish! Fish my boy, a few minutes with the hatches open" said Tommo "a bit of a scrub up and we will be fine", "err me thinks not Tommo said Fish, there are flies everywhere and it smells like someone has died in there" "eeeeyukkk! Said Tommo.

Fish and Tommo set to work on a clear up, Tommo swept the work surfaces to clear the flies, Fish stripped the bunks and laid out two fresh sleeping bags, the worktops were cleaned down and the boat started to smell a bit better on the inside, Fish found a bucket and dried-up mop, he set to work on the gunwales and decks Tommo had bought some bleach and washing up liquid this became the cleaning liquid of choice both inside and outside the boat.

Tommo looked at his watch it was fast approaching 7.00 am, time for a cup of tea then we are under way.

Fish set up the outboard motor and fuel tank and within a few pulls the little Evinrude was ticking over nicely, the sun was up and the day was looking good. As they moved away the tender was left on the buoy and they weekend had started.

As they passed the jetty Cox was there for an early morning visit to Busty Belle "aya aye boys where are you off", "just a weekend Jolly to Rozzo said Tommo see you tomorrow". "Stay safe boys replied Coxy as they passed Busty Belle Coxy shouted "you're both fuckin mad"! "yeh we are"! shouted Fish but it's all good, see ya Coxy" Tommo and Fish waved at Cox and pottered down the river towards Dartmouth.

25 minutes later they arrived in Dartmouth, Fish moored next to the town quay, he needed to drop into the harbour masters office to log their trip to Roscoff, "can I log a trip to Roscoff said Fish as he spoke through the hatch, when are you leaving? , asked the harbour-masters clerk, we are off now, ETA in Roscoff? Latest 22.00 hours, returning by 22.00 hours Sunday 4th moorings booked? "Yes, Port de Plaisance de Roscoff" Replied Fish, Radio frequency 228mhz said Fish "name of vessel?" "The Bacardi" replied Fish, "number of passengers?" just two of us." Ok all set enjoy your trip, please log in here on Sunday when you arrive back, please a radio check in is acceptable and advise us if you have a change of Sailing plans please.

"Yes of course" said Fish. Fish left the office with a new chart, a weather printout for the next 24 hours and a new tide table. As he approached the Quay, he could see Tommo talking to two young girls with back packs on, as he got closer Tommo caught his eye, Fish frowned at him and mothed who are they" "Hi Fish, Tommo said grinning look what I caught, er this is Charlotte and this is Olivia" "Hey girls you two look all set for a long march," each girl was tall blonde dressed in shorts and a tee shirt with Canadian spice on their tee shirts.

"Hi yeah we are looking for a lift across to France for a day trip and Tommo said you were on your way", "I know you are the owner of the boat, but could we come for the trip? We won't be any trouble", Fish looked them up and down, "how old are you asked Fish well Charlotte is 23 and im 22 said Olivia," "ok and where are you staying in the UK"? Charlotte said "we are hostelling it across to Plymouth and then Lands' End then back to London at the end of the month",

"I see" said Fish with a quizzical look "we just wanted a day in France so we could win" "win?" Asked Fish, Yeah, the prize for the best day out, sort of a wacky prize thing. " Ok, so, Me and Tommo are going to Roscoff for tonight, we need to be back tomorrow in the afternoon so this is a quick sea trip not a staying over and hotels and all that stuff "Fish explained. "Yeah, Tommo told us that that's cool with us."

"Do you have passports? Asked Fish, yeah sure" they both answered can I see them said Fish, "sure no problem" they said opened their backpacks and pulled out a clear plastic wallet inside were the passports they offered them to Fish, he took them and had a look, the names matched the pictures and the dates all tallied up, "ok Canadians eh?" said Fish "Yea Vancouver Island", real friendly bunch we are up there" said Olivia, Im sure you are girls, friendly that is and girls, both girls giggled.

Fish looked at Tommo he said "well if you are responsible, and no funny business and you buy us a beer in Roscoff." "Im called Fish and he is Tommo, we come from

Dittisham and we are the local axe murderers", Tommo smiled and shook his head at the innocence of these two. Okay said each girl excitedly, well come on then we must go like now" each girl slid off their back packs and handed them to Tommo, Fish followed them on board, he went down below and sat down at the table, Fish announced in a formal way "Ok girls So some basic house rules life jackets are there to be used, they are not as pretty as you are, but they will save you life if we get into trouble".

"Okay the girls said, "oooh its small in here, "and sleeping bags do you have one?" Tommo asked," yeah we have our own" said the girls, "Okay you both can sleep in the front cabin", there is a loo, er toilet, it is a sea toilet make sure you follow the instructions, "Ok said the young ladies.

"So, me and Tommo will get the boat ready now I suggest you two get comfy down here", Okay said Charlotte.

Fish cast off the back and Tommo cast off the front with a push he leaped on board and Fish motored the boat towards the open sea. Pretty soon they had hit the sea swell at the mouth of the River the boat bucked and rolled, and Fish could hear screams coming from below, "Christ Tommo said it sound like they found the axe murderer already Fish gave a semi laugh as he was concentrating on motoring through to calmer waters on the opposite side of the buoy at the entrance to the river.

Tommo was removing the shrouds on the foresail and packing them in the billy box sail locker on board, all the sheets looked in order and Tommo raised the foresail slowly he winched the triangular sail and immediately Fish could feel the boat reacting to the westerly breezy,

Tommo listened to the click click of the winch until he locked it out, Fish backed off the motor and cruised for a while whilst Tommo removed the main spar shroud to reveal a new looking mainsail packed in ,"this looks brand new"! he called across to Fish who was on the helm, "more like never been used much" said Fish.

Tommo worked with the sheets for a short time then managed to get the winch to work it was stiff and noisy through non-use but up the sail went, Fish was excited, hey Tommo that's great look at that, the boat tugged on the sheets as Fish got the boat to settle on the wind, there was a discernible increase in speed as the boat leaned and the wind took over from the out board, Fish turned it off and off they set under sail.

The morning Sun was coming midway in the sky, there were a few other boats heading off in the same direction. Tommo had set the heading on the sat nav and all seemed to be working well. Is it time for breakfast said Fish Are those galley slaves able to make tea?" I'd better go and see said Tommo, "I've bought two flasks and some cans so we should be Okay" said Fish. Tommo swung down below, both girls were chatting, they looked around, as Tommo arrived "alright then ladies, Okay Skipper Olivia said laughing, "We need tea" said tommo do you know how to use the flask, Tommo pointed to the box on the gally side, yeah ok skipper leave it to us". Tommo said "great thanks girls, come and join us when you are ready, bring biscuits too".

A few minutes later the girls appeared, Fish and Tommo couldn't keep their eyes of the two scantily clad beauties that emerged from below. Each girl had on a bikini and little else for the imagination, perfect hair and sunglasses finished off each of them, Tommo was spell bound, both girls looked stunning. "I told you we had God on our side said Tommo", Fish said "you'll go blind Tommo", "oh I think I'll risk one eye" laughed Tommo.

"Tea skipper" shouted Olivia, "aye aye" said Fish "just right, thanks." As Olivia passed him a lukewarm cup of flask tea. Olivia sat next to Fish and Charlotte sat with Tommo. Over the next four or five hours the four chatted about life, personal history, Tommo talked about his job in a haulage company and Fish explained at length that as schoolteacher how the children were either little darlings or horrific monsters and that their parent just didn't understand, social justice wasn't always on the side of the teachers and as such they should have more pay, and that he loved the sea, the river and rowing.

The Canadian girls talked about their expectations in life, family, traditions, travel, Canada and work, which for the part neither of the girls have had a career job, each had a plan of returning to studying and settling into a lawyer's office or accountancy or medical practice.

Despite the boat being a little neglected and Tommo's arms aching from pumping out the bilges she was in good fettle and a stable sailing boat easy to handle and sail from the helm and for that Fish was feeling quite nostalgic and thankful for his father's lifelong tuition on the water which had given Fish the relative experience to enjoy today.

The girls went down below to prepare something to eat, it was approaching 2.00 in the afternoon all four were feeling peckish there wasn't much and in terms of a meal it was snack food and crisps as Tommo wasn't expecting these beautiful Canadian visitors and fellow passengers he had shopped accordingly.

The weather was holding and the wind stable from the west, Fish and tommo had swapped steering a couple of times, all was going rather well. The girls asked if they could sunbathe on the front of the boat, there was room on the foredeck to put some towel's down and lay back, Fish said it was ok but if the water started to get any choppier then no, they must come back to the rear.

Both girls settled down at the front, Tommo was dealing with the outboard motor and tidying its hoses and cables up, Fish and tommo were chatting, "Tommo, Tommo"! said Fish have a look at this, Tommo got up off the small seat at the rear of the boat what he asked scanning the sea ahead, "look on the front of the boat, oh my god I've died and gone to heaven" said Tommo Jesus look at these two. Both girls had removed their tops and were sunbathing topless, Tommo and Fish looked at each other, Fish said, "they will never believe us!"

Back in Ditsham Cox had cleaned off the Seagull poop off Busty Belle, the old girl was looking bright and white and ready for her ladyship June. Mary had called from across the lake and suggested a lunch with Mary and Quent at their house in stoke at 4.00 ish, it was fast approaching 3.30 the sun was beating down the river was its normal Saturday busy with locals and tourists in hire boats buzzing about enjoying the beauty of this part of the Dart river.

June arrived, loaded with cakes and a trifle "Coxy rolled his eyes "what?" said June "why all this stuff im sure Mary will have a desert ready", "yes well its good manners to take something", June said "have you got the champers?", "no I have not said Cox what bloody Champers?, well pop in to the ferryman's and get a bottle off Sue", "ok, ok" said Cox, June was placing the boxes of dessert on the side seat, Cox started to walk up towards the Pub at the end of the jetty, " and make sure it's a cold one" shouted June, "Yes dear" responded Cox, he entered the Pub Sue was serving food ," Hello Coxy my love I'll be with you in a second," "Ok" said Cox as he leant against the bar, Sue came over came round to her side of the bar , "So Coxy what can I get you?", "Do you have a cold bottle of champagne please Sue"? "Ooh something special being celebrated is it?",

"Yes said Cox my graduation as a bloody mind reader"! he laughed, I forgot to get a bottle or I didn't know I had to get a bottle, or I forgot I didn't know I had to get a bottle!".

"Pint for the journey too Coxy? Broadways? Er ok a quick one will aid navigation I would say , cheers Sue". Coxy sipped the top off the beer, turned his back to the bar to keep his eye on June in Busty Belle at the end of the jetty, she could see she was on her mobile phone no doubt complaining that They were late because he hadn't done something, his eyes glanced to the steep wooden ramp leading up to the jetty, there in the sun on the corner sat Blaggs.

Alone just sat there with a coffee in his hand, Sue appeared, here you go Coxy love how much Sue, well to you coxy £22 all in "Bloody hell Sue im only going for a run out in the boat, it will be lovely" she replied,

"I see Blaggs sat there," "yeah" Sue said "he was in here a few hours ago looking a bit battered. He plays with the wrong people" said Sue, oh yeah are you referring to us rowers?

"No, no", Sue continued, "those Russian guys and her", Sue pointed and on Blaggs right shoulder he could see the outline of Silvia, big sunglasses immaculately dressed, her black hair blowing in the breeze, he immediately recognised her from the new development. "Ah so, Silvia the mysterious," Cox looked as it was clear Blaggs and Silvia were deep in a conversation which to all intense and purposes looked like an argument.

Cox turned to Sue and said "thanks for my pint Sue, perfect start to a little motor out. "Cheers Coxy enjoy the rest of your day" Sue replied as she cleared away his glass, Cox stepped out of the Pub and wandered a little closer to Blaggs stopping just behind his left shoulder, he could hear Blaggs talking, "ill fucking kill him when I find him, and if I don't kill him ill bring more attention down on Vasyli than Aleksander can cope with", "no!" Silvia said, "you must not, we are only here for another 6 weeks then we return to Monaco". She continued "We need zero attention the contract is almost complete".

Cox took a step back then marched forward as if he hadn't seen Blaggs, "Hey Blaggs are you ok lad getting some sunshine?", He looked at Silvia who was drawing on a cigarette, hello there he said, Silvia said Hello Mr Cox are you celebrating yes?" "oh the shampoo yes, my friend is waiting for us across the pond", "Pond?" Silvia didn't understand, "The other side at Stoke", "oh yes I see" she said, "How you are feeling Blaggs" Cox asked, "Im ok Coxy, yes thanks, can I come and see you after the meeting on Sunday?" "Yes, mate anytime", we can have a pint here if you want, yeah please just the two of us ok? Yeah, fine" said Cox. "ok you two, I'll be seeing you",

"Come on Cox we will be late June was calling as he approached the Belle, "ok im coming replied Cox. The Busty Bell started up its muffled rumbling engine sound echoed across the water, Cox let go front and rear ropes, he reversed a little then motored off towards Stoke Gabriel.

The boat left hardly any wake, As Cox cleared the overnight moorings, he made a little diversion of 150 yards or so and rounded the rear of the imposing Makonde moored still out in the temporary moorings, it was closed up, no sign of any one on board, there were two side windows open, and he could see the top of two people heads, one was wearing a hat and the other jet black hair, they were using a large telephoto lens camera.

Cox had seen enough he veered off so not to attract any attention to him or the Busty Belle, he aimed for the quay at Stoke Gabriel and pottered in and out of moorings and around the outside of yachts and motorboats, on approaching the Quay he could see Quentin and Ugly waiting for them on the quay side.

"That's nice, a welcome committee" called June, "Of course replied Quentin and only for the best visitors to our humble back water". Quentin and Ugly took the ropes and held Busty in as Cox bought her alongside. Pass me the Shampoo said June I'll get off to see Mary, She's waiting for you June love just go in. "So, how is the lovely Busty Belle?" asked Ugly she is a peach said Coxy, sure is I must say Coxy im jealous, "well we should go out for a boys cruise of the river pub cruise eh?" "Goodness me" said Cox in a posh voice "the long arm of the law is proposing a drunken sailors event "! Quentin said "its not a bad idea after the year I've had I could do with letting off a bit of steam", Cox spotted that ugly was wearing a set of binoculars round his neck , "are you bird watching again Tony? No Cox far from it , me and Quentin were comparing notes on the Makonde boat over there," "There seems to be comings and goings there, yeah strange bunch if you ask me Cox said, I do some plastering work for them, they are Russian or Ukrainian.

"Ok Oh really?" said Tony "Quentin said you had an issue with the skipper who didn't know how to sail it", "yes a few weeks ago they crashed the jetty at Dittisham blocked the ferry lane off Quent had to intervene and moor her up there", Coxy have a look at this, Tony handed the binoculars, look at the plimsole line on the rudder", Cox looked and focused the binoculars in yeah well look at these photo snaps Quentin took on the day of the crash". "Oh yes Cox said sitting a lot higher than then eh?" "yeah, exactly and look at the mast at the rear, yes well look at the photo, that is not the same boat!" or they have swapped a mast out over night!"

"So, Cox what do you know about the Makonde crew, I mean is there one?". Cox tipped his hat back and scratched his head "Well, I do know this, Blaggs had a good kicking on Thursday, I sent him to the emergency room, I saw him just a while ago he seems ok but im concerned he is getting in too deep with the Russkies, they are a shady bunch, so much so I can't stand them".

Tony said, "I think I'll have a chat with Harbour control and see if they have anything to report". Ok Tony let me know if I can help, Cox said as he finished tying Belle up. "and by the way Cox "said Tony "Congratulations on your appearance in the finals at Salcombe", "eh yes great news thanks Tony, hence why im here today, im going to pick Quentin's brains".

"He has done Salcombe a couple of times whereas me has only done it once and it was oooh 10 years or more ago".

"Well good luck and we hope to be there to cheer you boys on" said Tony, "oh great said Cox I'll look forward to it" The two men walked along the quay following Quentin, at the car park Tony made for home and Cox and Quentin walked the 300 yards to Quentin house.

Mary and June were already into a glass or two of the champagne, Hello Coxy love said Mary she gave him a hug and kissed him on the forehead, June thought this was funny. "What are you trying to say?" said Cox, "you're short said June, "very funny" said Cox.

Food was on the table drink was in hand and the four friends ate and chatted and talked, and then Mary said "I have some news", June started to well up, "oh yes Mary love what is it?" I have had clear scan, the cancer is in retreat, and all is looking good, "oh Mary" shouted June, Cox turned to Quentin "that's great news Quent", "It is good news, but we have some way to go yet, this is the first result showing some progress, it's very positive and we are holding on to that, but Mary has some more challenges to get over and we are going at it together".

More champagne appeared from Mary's fridge and the four friends drank and ate until 7 ish when Cox said, "June love we need to be thinking of getting back it'll be dark in an hour". Quentin and Cox spoke about boats and Quentin wanting to have one. they didn't really get on to the race plans for Salcombe. Then Cox remembered who he was there.

"Quent I need your help on the Salcombe race, Coxy asked, "anytime said Quent you know that. "Well, I need a Strat plan and some inside on their crew, who, experience, crew layout. Ok Quent lets meet up. I have my 2017 race notes somewhere, all I now is they are a big crew, good boat layout and a woman Cox.

"A woman"? Cox said, "who is that? "there are some cracking women Cox's in south Hams district, but

I didn't know Sally had one", Yeah im sure its Dave Gibbs daughter Quent said, "So, that fat bugger does the training, and she bawls at them to make sure daddy gets his way, she is a third of the weight of Dave, so training is a heavy boat then race day, Dave feels poorly and she steps in".

"Ah I see said Coxy. Ok can I have a read of your notes please Quentin? I need a plan of the course too. Let me find it all and we can take a trip over there and take it all in? sounds like a plan. Cox agreed, the four walked down to the Quay, Mary and June hugging like limpets saying goodbye, "we have had a lovey afternoon Mary thanks again", "the best news helps and we both hope this is the start of the end, well yes said Mary that's exactly what it is, it is the start of the end."

"We will obviously be going to the finals so are you up for coming?" June asked, "Want to bet we will be there no worries at all" said Quent.

Cox started Busty Belle up the rumble from the copper exhaust pipe on the water line burbled away as June climbed aboard, see you soon Coxy said Quentin Mary blowing kisses as they left the Quay and burbled off into the distance.

The mist was starting to descend from the steep valley sides as Busty Belle "pop popped" across the lake, a reddish orange hue filtered the late sunlight into almost a Turneresque scene the water was absolutely still, mirror like.

Cox had his eye on the Makonde as he passed in front, he could see someone closing the doors on the back of the huge boat and then climbing into the tender which in itself was a bigger than usual yacht tender, it powered up and set off towards the lower jetty a little way from the main jetty and quay at the ferryman's Inn, by the time Cox had gotten half way across the lake the launch and occupants from Makonde had arrived and were getting off at the jetty, the wake the boat had created was working its way across the unblemished water scape towards Cox and June In Busty Belle. Cox was thinking to himself "yeah not the only water you lot are sullying round these parts."

"It was good news today Coxy, said June, she sat in the front of the belle with her feet stretch out and resting on the seat opposite, "it was June", "im so pleased for Mary, she has hope now, last time we saw her I sensed neither Mary nor Quent were in a place where they could believe there might be a way out." "they both looked happier, didn't you think?" "yes" Said Cox.

Belle motored for a few moments and neither Cox or June said anymore, Cox looked at June sitting there taking in the familiar view of the river they loved, thinking she was still as good looking as the day she married him, "are you ok June?" June looked at Coxy, she was tired and contented, "I am Coxy" she said blowing him a kiss as he made for the jetty.

"Come on Coxy" she said, "let's get home", "Yes it's been a good day but a long day" Coxy said as he pulled alongside the quay, he jumped off and held the boat with one hand and put his other hand out for June to hold as she stepped up and off the boat. I'll see you at home June said, No Love just wait for me here, I'll get the kettle on, "No June, please, just wait for me here. He looked at her and she knew he meant it. June didn't say anything but stood as Cox put the covers on the boat and the seagull wires. He took June by the hand and they made their way up the ramp and up Steep Hill.

As they passed the new house, the tall grey gates were opening, there from behind the newly planted clematis plants Vasyli appeared, he looked as if he was tending the plants, cox suspected differently "good evening Mr Cox and Mrs Cox, have you had a pleasant day?", yes thanks said Cox, Cox and June continued to walk on by, Vasyli stood towering over Cox and June "when are you coming to finish the wall Please?", "Tuesday" said Cox, "not tomorrow? asked Vasyli frowning at Cox, " No Tuesday!" repeated Cox ,"

Only Aleksander will be returning on Tuesday evening and we agreed...", Cox cut across him, "It was agreed that my work would be best served if I made the decision to paint it when I say it will be ready for painting, and I made that agreement with the house owner not you, so I will see you Tuesday" said Cox "good evening" Vasyli bowed a little and said, "good evening".

Cox and June continued up the hill, Vasyli closed the grey gates again saying nothing more. When Cox and June got to the top of the hill June said, "he is creepy isn't he? they all are creepy said Cox, im sure my parents are thinking the same up there somewhere".

Chapter 13

Tommo Fish and the two girls were on course for an early arrival at the Roscoff moorings, Fish had radioed into the port authority, channel 9 to report their arrival, it was 5.00pm and the port was ahead and insight, the approach was messy as there were ferries running until late so Fish asked the girls to get life jackets on wrap up warm as the wind was getting stronger and it was good if they arrived clothed instead of the half-naked crossing, which to both boys had been a treat.

Tommo too was told to close all the hatches and set anything lose in the cabin and galley down, Olivia and Charlotte were undaunted by these orders from the helm and were happy to stay down below for the remaining half an hour or so of bouncing about in the boat as it rode the choppy waves near to the coast of France.

After a short time, and some bumpy water they arrived at Port of Bloscon they dropped the sails and motored with a half furled foresail, which was much more manageable albeit the small Evinrude was under powered but just capable of getting behind the breakwater, a small boat appeared alongside, a man on board called across to follow him, he took Bacardi into the berths and slowed right down pointing to a berth number 568 wow said Fish "that's the one I booked, how did they know?"

Tommo amazed at this thought Fish was some sort of genius, thank you called Fish as the boat slid effortlessly into its berth, Tommo jumped of the front roped off the boat in the mooring, Fish turned off the Evinrude engine and they were there, the pontoon manager appeared and offered leaflets and information, Fish thanked her in French "Merci madam", she answered in perfect English.

The girls had appeared from below, the pontoon manager came back and said "I didn't realise there are four in your party. Yes, sorry said Fish a last-minute change of plans", ok she said no problem she marked on her sheet two more, "but can I see passports please, just a formality yes of course" said Fish, the girls found their passports and handed them over and Tommo handed over his ok all good said the pontoon manager here is the code for the gate, please lock it when you enter and exit. have a nice evening",

"Right!" Fish said "quick change then we can lock up and get into town for food and a drink", Tommo was ready in a matter of seconds Fish made secure the doors on the boat and off they set for the walk into Roscoff.

They walked through to the old port, still frequented by local Fishermen, is a 10-minute walk away, in the heart of the historic centre of Roscoff, a small town full of character with imposing 16th and 17th century granite houses. "Looks like Dartmouth and Weymouth" said Tommo.

They made for a bar and restaurant, 5 minutes further away up a steep hill, the girls were enthralled with the French feeling and ate and drank to prove it.

Local onion soup and garlic infused risotto and moules for Tommo, Fish reminding him of his poor constitution, Tommo denying it and putting it down to rich complicated food which this meal he considered was not anything like that.

The foursome engaged and enjoying the company and the banter was good clean fun. The girls soaking up the attention and relatively good manners of the Dittisham boys, each girl taking a turn in telling stories about Canada, bears the northern lights and bigfoot.

Time was getting on and the mood became a bit more relaxed, calmer. Fish and Olivia had hit it off, Tommo and Charlotte had started playing drinking games, Fish said Tommo please take it easy it's not a rowing night, "I know" said Tommo "chill out."

The night wore on and Fish was tired, the sailing was fun but at the helm for 8 or 9 hours had worn him down, He yawned a few times Olivia asked "are you tired of me already?" laughing, "no im sorry" Fish said " im wacked out", so why don't we make our way back and take a walk and leave these two to enjoy the Riccard", Olivia said, "they know the way back", Fish called , "guys do you know your way back", "Yes, yes, ok mother", said Tommo, we will see you there in a while, don't be late, said Fish, it's another early start".

Olivia and Fish took a slow walk back towards the marina, Fish showed Olivia some of the sights ana architecture of the old town, she was taking lots of pictures with her mobile phone, the continued walking on leading to the marina and the pontoon. As they walked Olivia said Fish, yes, he said can I ask you a question, yeh whatever, "So, why do they call you Fish?" "Ahh well if you believe the truth my na".… before he could finish Olivia planted a big kiss on Fish, he was taken aback a little, but revisited without hesitation passionately into the kiss, "well that's nice" said Fish "that's a thank you for a wonderful day here in France, we wouldn't have got here had

it not been for you... so?" ...."So what" ? Said Fish......"
why do they call you Fish?" "give us another kiss and I'll
tell you", she laughed, they kissed again.

They stopped and took in the view of the twinkling lights of the ferry terminal half a mile away, "real
pretty eh?" said Olivia, "yeah looks like a Spanish city to
me" said Fish, "Like it always did" she sang, hey Olivia
said "we know the song", "Like a Spanish city to me when
we were kids,!"

They're began wolf whistles from the roadway
above the marina it was Tommo and Charlotte who were
very merry and noisy, guess who said Olivia "I've had
a great day too" said Fish "naah thanks Fish said Olivia
that's so cool!"

The four of them sat on the rear of the boat with
hot chocolates and wrapped up together in sleeping bags
and talked about nothing in particular, until late, Fish almost nodding off, "come on let's bunk down it's a 7.00 am
start."

The boat was basic inside and the night was cold,
Tommo had crashed out in the front cabin Charlotte the
same, Olivia came to Fish and slid into his sleeping bag, it
was warm and secure she and Fish found a warm position
and snuggled down for a comfortable night.

Chapter 14

Vasyli had returned to his office on the ground floor of the enormous house, he scanned the cameras on the bank of flatscreen monitors on the back wall of the office, he could see one of the security men in the gardens, he was overlooking the bottom of the 2-acre plot looking towards the riverside.

The gardens were placed on a slope leading down to a pathway which was public access, Aleksander had complained about people walking through the little green lane down there but unable to stop the foot path being used.

Privacy was a problem for Aleksander he was overbearingly paranoic about it, hence the security men and the surveillance cameras places at 8 points around the perimeter of the plot. This on its own had caused many of the locals to regard that there was something going on in the new house and village mentality was fuelling gossip which was fuelling discontent with the occupants and the village alike.

Silvia was in her apartment at the back of the new house development, she was working on a catalogue of African art pieces for Aleksander, Silvia had graduated from the university of Belgrade holding a first-class master's degree in antiquities and fine art. Her speciality was Madagascar and its art, she sourced sculptures and artwork from Madagascar and other Indian and African countries for Aleksander for his ever-increasing collections dotted around the world.

His empire was far reaching, from Singapore to London to Brazil and Honduras Mexico and the Crimea. He held a small collection in all these locations and from time to time would offer his most valued pieces up for auction. He spent his time travelling and arranging deals both in fine art and other commodities. Silvia was his trusted expert for his art collections, she lived part time in Devon at the new house and part time in Amsterdam where she had her own gallery and Canalside house.

Her phone rang in her apartment, she picked it up she said "yes?" "Ah Silvia can you spare me a few moments please?" "Vasyli is it important? I must complete work for Aleksander this evening. "It will only take a few moments" said Vasyli. "Ok I will be down in 5 minutes", "Thank you" the phone clicked, she continued reading for a few minutes, she put her black coat on and her heels. Silvia made her way downstairs, there in his office was Vasyli, "Silvia, we have security issue, well as you are head of the security im sure you will be dealing with it, what is the issue?"

"We suspect it is an internal issue", "really" said Sylvia as if she was really bored now of this man's deliberate theatrical playing on words, half of which he can't translate from Ukrainian to English, "how?"Silvia asked.

Vasyli continued slowly. "The receipts for all departments are correct they tally up, they are in balance, Vasyli sat behind his desk hands clasped together his forefingers pointed out tapping as he spoke, "but we are running 1 to 2 kilos of lost materials grade A each month, the current value is 150,000 per kilo so this is a lot of money to be missing, Silvia lit a cigarette so how much are you processing each month Vasyli?,"

He looked at her directly with open staring eyes, " it is difficult to say" , but you just said all the numbers add up? Yes? Vasyli so you must know, yes but it's not how much it right now Silvia it is just how?"

"Aleksander returns tomorrow evening we must have this closed off and an explanation by then, what do you suggest? Vasyli continued to stare his cold 1000-yard stare, an empty stare his brown almost black eyes engaged in almost hateful exchange.

"I would suggest Aleksander employs a security expert who knows what he is doing and takes control of security. Other than that, it is your job, I am employed to do other things Vasyli!"

"Yes, I know you are Silvia, we are all charged with solving this dilemma, and Aleksander's confidence must not be damaged in any way, this operation is of value to all of us am I right?" "Yes Vasyli, but why are you so concerned about Aleksander's confidence?"

He didn't answer, "enough of this bullshit" said Silvia, "this isn't my concern", So, how do you explain your night-time visits to Blaggs?" "it is not any concern of yours Vasyli," Silvia stood up and pointed at Vasyli, "I was concerned for his wellbeing, that is all, he looked very worried after the last meeting with Aleksander, he has done nothing wrong".

"And your little tate a'tete chats on the harbour-side this morning? How do you explain this?", Vasyli lit a cigarette he drew on it deeply and readjusted himself in his chair, he reached forward, he turned on his swivel chair and took hold of the remote control for the Surveillance monitors and one by one they clicked off as he pressed the buttons in a deliberated way.

"I don't have to explain anything to you Vasyli

you are not my keeper or my employer"! She flicked her black hair over her head, Silvia raised her voice," if you or your gorillas had anything to do with his beating then it is you alone who is bringing attention here, something you will know Aleksander hates and will not tolerate".

"You are the fool Vasyli, and you are the one who should be under suspicion!"

Silvia turned on her heels and left the office. She rushed up the stairs towards her apartment as she turned on to the long gallery leading to her door.

Standing in her way was Devlin, his immaculate 3-piece Harris tweed suit and tilted hat greeted her in the shadows as she tried to walk past him, he removed his hat to reveal his terribly scarred head and oddly shaped hair.

"Good evening Silvia my dear what seems to be the rush?" Get off me" ,"Let GO!" she shouted as he grabbed her by the arm and pulled her back towards the landing on the top of the stairs, "come here, let us talk like sensible adults", he said, "I said get off me she shouted again leave me alone", "calm down clam down" he repeated, Devlin pushed her backwards into the waiting hands of Vasyli, who had come silently almost to the top of the stairs, he in turn pushed her forwards back to Devlin.

" Now I see, You really are the real problem with this operation", she shouted "leave me alone", Vasyli grabbed her again and held her shoulders as Devlin got close to her mouth and quietly said "Now listen here you interfering pathetic Crimean bitch, we are in control here and if any your friends for example Blaggs is under any misguided misapprehension that something under-hand is going on in this operation then it can only have come from you my dear, So?, are you going to keep your mouth shut? You will disassociate yourself from Blaggs or do we hurt Blaggs or our loyal Mr Posh some more?"

Devlin had her chin in his hands, he held her harder, staring into her eyes as she struggled to get away from him, "im waiting for an answer you bitch!" Vasyli had her arms locked, Silvia spat in Delvin's face, he turned away, Vasyli said in Ukrainian *"gryaznaya zlaya suka"*. Devlin slowly lifted the silk handkerchief from his top pocket of his Harris tweed jacket not looking at Silvia but at Vasyli.

He wiped his face and lips like he was trying to remove thick paint, "that wasn't very friendly he whispered", the back of his hand swiped at Silvia catching her mouth and lips, Vasyli held her firm as Devlin rolled in another punch to her sides, Silvia fell to the floor blood dripping from the corner of her mouth. "oh dear you seemed to have slipped" sneered Devlin.

Devlin picked her up by the wrists, Vasyli put one hand behind her arm and neck, Devlin stood in front of her again , "feisty little bitch aren't you" Devlin said "Silvia raised her legs and licked Devlin in the stomach her stiletto heel embedded into Delvin's groin, he bent over as she used the force of the kick to launch herself back a Vasyli, he in turn moved sideways and Silvia slipped by and fell down the top flight of stairs, she screamed, out of control, sliding part way on the chrome bannister, she tumbled over the rails and fell 20 feet down from the galleried atrium to the marble floor below.

Devlin stood up; he dusted himself down and put his silk handkerchief back in his top pocket, Vasyli was on his way rushing down to the ground floor.

Silvia's lifeless body was sprawled out on the marble floor, her arms were stretch awkwardly behind her body, her head was bleeding, a large pool of red blood encircled her head, her white house coat collar was soaking it up, her deep blue eyes were lifeless, Vasyli desperately checked for her pulse, first on her wrist then on her neck.

Devlin calmly walked down the stairs one step at a time, lighting a cigarette on the last step, he offered no urgency, no emotion, and no compassion.

Vasyli turned "Devlin she is dead", Devlin looked at Silvia's body in a crumpled bloody mess. "dear - dear, fucking hell Vasyli old boy" said Devlin "that is a nuisance." "Is that all you can say? Vasyli screamed.

"well, well how touching, what the fuck do you want me to say?" shouted Devlin, He drew on his cigarette "the bitch is dead! one less thing to worry about old boy", Devlin said to Vasyli "get a grip, get it cleared up and get her out of here", "where shall I take her" "use your fucking imagination Vasyli!".

Devlin kicked a sail bag from Vasyli's office "use this, I'll get some towels." The two men put Sylvia's body in the large sail bag they wrapped her head in towels and her black coat, the bag was only just big enough.

"Now what?" said Vasyli, "take her to the boat we will go out to sea tomorrow morning," said Devlin, "I can't manage this on my own" Vasyli complained, "yes you can", Devlin snapped, and you will, Im going back to the farm."

"I will call Aleksander" to update him Vasyli shook his head "fuck fuck" Devlin "what shall we say, "I will say nothing, for now we will say that she is her own minder, remember? she told us that, we don't know where she is", understood Vasyli Ok?

Vasyli and Devlin dragged the body in the bag

through the door together they put the sail bag in the boot of the Black BMW, make sure you disinfect this tomorrow Vasyli, "dogs smell things ok!

Vasyli looked grey and exhausted his shirt sleeve was blood stained, he fetched a dark jacket from the rack in the office, "yes I know" he replied, Vasyli drove slowly out of the grey gates the 150 yards down to the quay, he stopped and turned the ignition off, his headlights died, he held his breath as his senses looked for anything suggesting he was in sight or being watched by anyone there were no sounds, all he could hear was his heartbeat drumming in his head.

He got out of the car and had a good look around, the air was cool damp and fresh the smell of seaweed filled his nostrils, there was a single orange streetlight on adjacent to the quay but no one in sight. A dog barked in the distance, the water was rippling past and there was a mist hanging low across the river, he was sure that if he couldn't see anyone then no one could see him, the mist was his unexpected cover. he opened the boot there was the cream-coloured bag with G82 embroidered in red on the side, he lifted the bag out of the car and dragged the bag onto the bow of the launch.

It was pitch blackness, and he had trouble finding the key slot for the starter, his eyes slowly got accustomed to the darkness, he got the engine going and very slowly moved out onto the main current which was flowing fast as the tide was on its way out.

The launch had small but powerful spotlights to light his way, even so the darkness and the water seemed to meld together, giving a difficult perspective on where the water ended, and the blackness of the night began.

It only took a few minutes to reach the Makonde,

he bought the launch to the rear of the boat bumping into the big boat as the current worked against him, he searched for the right place to stop. He looked around again, pulled the bag to the side of the launch and stepped aboard the yacht, tying the launch up to the rear stanchions.

The bag was heavy and ungainly, he took another look all around the bag was conspicuous in its colours even in the darkness, but for now it was convenient.

He managed to fumble around and getting his footing he pulled the bag on board over the rear of the boat, he got it onto the rear deck. He dragged it across the deck a smear of blood left under his feet, Vasyli found another rope, he tied the rope around the handle of the bag securing it to a deck ring, over that he put a tarpaulin to cover the bag and on top of that a selection of sail bags, a deck matt and another deck cover.

Vasyli climbed back into the launch, he looked at the hump on the back of the boat and satisfied it was secure he made off back to the quay.

After securing it at the quayside he climbed into the Black BMW and reversed back up the hill as he slowly turned the corner, he caught a stone wall and scratched the car bumper, "fuck! fuck! fuck!" he said to himself, he continued as the whine of the gear box took him back up the hill and into the courtyard of the new house.

He pressed the button to close the grey gates, the gates slowly closed behind him, he looked at the long scratch on the cars bumper it was noticeable a reflector was missing, but other than that it was intact.

Devlin appeared, "well?" "well, what "? Vasyli said, he felt like Devlin was going to demand something else, "is it on the boat", "yes" "what have you been doing?"

Vasyli asked, "packing her bags", Devlin loaded a suitcase into the back seat of the car, "Im going to the Farm, I will pick you up at 5 am, get the place spotless", "ok I will" replied Vasyli.

Devlin drove off in the car he powered up the hill, Vasyli went up to Sylvia's room, it was locked, he went back to the office and got the spare key, when he opened the door the room was tidy, nothing seemed to be out of place, her post was opened, teddy bears were on the bed and the bathroom was clean and fresh smelling.

"Devlin had done a good clean up in here" thought Vasyli. It looked as if she had left it as she would have liked to have found it. Vasyli slowly closed the door and locked the room up, he went down to the office, he cleaned the office desk up pouring himself a large whiskey. He cleaned and mopped the floors banisters the glass work on the stairwell and the door handles.

Vasyli retired to his room in the basement, he looked in the mirror, he was grey in the face, his hands and shirt were bloodstained, he started the shower and removed his shirt trousers and shoes, he showered in the hot water thoroughly, hair, fingernails and hands scrubbed hard, feet he rinsed off and put the dirty bloodstained clothes and shoes into a plastic bag and stuffed it into the dumpster.

He dressed again in cream chino's and a pale pink shirt from his wardrobe, it was 3 am already time was moving on, He was tired and emotional these were big undertakings, Devlin would be back in an hour, the sky outside the roof window was getting lighter, it was a sunrise of reds and oranges with dark blue sky, after pouring a coffee, he went to the garden room and lit another cigarette, he thought about the events of the last few hours, his military training told him this was progress towards a goal, a goal of money and return on greed.

Vasyli had been a long-standing part of the team who had successfully worked in the south, working under cover, so far, the operations had been satisfactory and lucrative to Devlin and Aleksander, but now this was a step change, he considered that operations would have to be moved and quickly.

He held his head in his hands, what seemed like only a few minutes he heard Devlin arrive back in the car, the door opened, Devlin shouted "Vasyli! Come let us go now," Vasyli was startled but alert. They walked briskly down to the quay, the launch was soon powered up and on its way to the Makonde. They arrived and jumped aboard, the hump on the rear deck was clearly visible, Devlin opened the boat and started the engines.

Vasyli unhitched the bow of the boat from the buoy, it started to drift, Devlin engaged the drive and off they set. "slowly" said Vasyli "slowly". Devlin said, "here you steer", Vasyli took the helm, Devlin went below, there was banging and dragging of a chain, he reappeared, to the chain was an anchor Devlin placed it at the back of the rear deck. Vasyli smoked another cigarette, they slowly maneuvered the Makonde down the river past peaceful marinas and moorings.

The engines droning an echo off the sides of the valley as they passed the upper ferry and then in a few minutes the moving bridge ferry. Then onto the open water of the river mouth. As they passed the buoy on the wrong side Vasyli opened the boats twin engines and she powered off into the misty open water,

They motored for 3 or 4 miles directly off into the English Channel, passing the occasional early morning or late-night Fishing boat, but it was quiet. Devlin attached the chain to the sail bag, he dragged the bag to the rear of the boat, Vasyli watched him as Devlin without any emotion. Threw the anchor of the back of the deck at the rear of the boat, Vasyli stop here, Devlin demanded.

The engines were cut it was quiet, the boats engines ticking over was the only sound. Devlin then pushed off the anchor, the chain unravelled out Devlin with both hands picked up the bag by the handles and threw the bag into the sea, the water was still and calm, the bag bubbled as the air was forced out of it, it sank beneath the water.

Eventually the colour of the cream and red disappeared out of sight, beneath the green water both men looked on as the evidence vanished. "Job done!" "now that wasn't too hard was it" said Devlin "we have work to do Vasyli old boy" let's get back to the mooring".

Vasyli didn't say anything, he lit another smoke and drew hard on it, thinking to himself that Devlin was nothing more than an animal, He turned the boat around and headed back towards the coastline, clearing the mist as they entered the mouth of the River Dart.

The sun was up it was 6.00 am and the light was bright, the town quay starting to get busy. The floating ferry taking its first 7 am passengers and the white vans of the local trade's, bakers and decorators. It was time to motor up the river not attracting any attention "slowly" said Devlin "let's talk about the weather, after all old boy that's what the Brits do for a pastime", "How would you know" said Vasyli "you're a hell of a long way from home." "watch your mouth Devlin replied and why Devlin or should I say Danslav?" Vasyli sneered at Devlin.

"you are well informed Vasyli, but you should

not throw your caution to this breeze" replied Devlin," you may think you know some minor details about me Vasyli, but I assure you the whole picture isn't always as they say on the face of it."

Devlin went below, Vasyli continued to motor the 52 ft yacht slowly along the river, this time he was cautious and turned the boat in a big arc under power on the lake, as he approached the visitors buoy the boat slowed, Devlin shouted from below, "we have water in here Vasyli, this is a big problem!"

As the boat turned it leant to one side, Vasyli could feel the boat was becoming sluggish in the turn, not something he had noticed before, as he straightened the boat up and approached the buoy, he called to Devlin to get to the front and tie the boat onto the buoy.

There was no reply, He called again and still no reply, Vasyli took a boat hook from the main cabin roof and made his way to the front of the boat, he managed to hook the chain attached to the buoy and slowly bring the buoy closer to the boat, Devlin appeared from the forward hatch and between them managed to attach the bow rope to the chain.

The boat settled into the flow of the river, Vasyli and Devlin exchanged glances, "the boat is full of water" said Devlin, "Let me see" said Vasyli.

The two men went to the back of the boat which had leant over more, "is it sinking?" said Vasyli, "no but look", Devlin pointed to the galley and front cabin the carpets were wet and the water had lifted the floorboards there was a danger that the water might contaminate the product on board, so he needed the water out quickly.

Vasyli ran to the front of the boat again and looked

over the bow, there below was the damaged bow, "shit, shit" he said, "Devlin the bow is holed, we have been to sea and the water has got in we need to have this fixed".

"I will call Blaggs, and get it done today Vasyli, I will stay and run the engines and pump this out", ok" said Vasyli, he took the launch back to the quay and then walked up to the house.

Devlin had the engines running and was pumping out the bilges, it took nearly an hour for it to be pumped out, Devlin checked the hole on the front of the yacht, it was above the water line but only just.

Devlin raised his mobile phone to his ear, in his strong developed British gentleman's voice.
"Ah hello there Blaggs its Devlin here, really sorry it's so early old chap, we seem to have a problem with our yacht," "Oh yea?" said Blaggs "what's it to do with me at this time of the night? "I was ringing to see if you can seal up a hole in the bow of the Makonde, it will take some patching up old boy, I say you're the man I would see to do this work can you help me please" "Ok said Blaggs I'll have a look tomorrow morning"!.

"Can you make it today Blaggs old boy, as she is leaking in water and only, we are off for a sailing day?" Blaggs thought for a short while, "Hello Blaggs are you there?" said Devlin.

Blaggs thought some more then after a pause he answered "I'll come down at 8.30" excellent Blaggs thanks old chap" Vasyli or myself will be on board!", Blaggs slammed the phone down with a "fuck you!", Devlin continued to run the pumps to empty the boat of its bilge water the boat slowly came up right again and settled looking normal .

Vasyli called him on the mobile, "are you done?"

No Devlin said, "but I'm close", Vasyli said "ok all the paperwork at the house is done, I have it in a case". Ok said Devlin, "we need to work at the farm to remove the stock and work in progress, where are we going to put It?", Devlin said "in this fucking boat and leave and quickly!"

Half an hour later Blaggs turned up, Devlin heard him scramble aboard, "show me where it is" said Blaggs "no good mornings Blaggs? said Devlin, "Not a good Morning, what is the problem," Blaggs was clearly not in the mood to talk to Devlin, " See" Devlin pointed down to the hole and crack in the front bow of the boat, Blaggs said "ill patch it up with some epoxy and matting will that do?", "yes please just to stop the water leaking in".

" You need a pro job on this" Said Blaggs "Yes we know old boy but for now just patch it!". Devlin wasn't going to give an inch to Blaggs, the tension between the men was obvious, Blaggs thought it best to not get into a conversation, less for fall out about in one sense and as he was still bruised and feeling not fully fit, he had a clue Devlin had attacked him, but he had no real evidence to hang it on him.

Blaggs went back to the shore in his rowboat, he picked up some epoxy and matting and rowed back, he worked on the hole on Makonde from the rowboat. It took him 30 minutes or so, the job was completed. Devlin! Blaggs called, Devlin appeared, "the hole is fixed, it will need a pro job on this at a good boat yard", Devlin said "Yes I know Blaggs put a bill in will you." Blaggs said "It will take 2 hours to set. Keep it dry until then", Blaggs rowed his boat back to shore, Devlin called Vasyli to come and collect him.

Later they took the BMW to the farm in Gallows

lane, there they filled the BMW with packages of white powder from the machines.

Chapter 15

Back in French waters the Bacardi was underway, Fish and Olivia had managed to motor the boat out of the Port of Bloscon moorings at an earlier time and had sailed well in to the 9- or 10-hours journey, the timings and the tide were right for a 4pm arrival back in Dartmouth.

Tommo and Charlotte arrived on Deck looking tired and a little bedraggled, "oh dear look at you too", said Olivia "too much or too much", "a little too much" said Tommo. Smiling, wrapped in a sleeping bag, I don't know what you mean" said Olivia! "Better that way" joked Fish.

There was an easterly wind the sky was clear with some clouds far off, it was good the boat was hitting 7-8 knots and the sea was lively, with a minimal swell, the boat sailed well, and all was good on the Bacardi, she was cutting through the water well almost rushing, Fish was enjoying the sailing, they were making particularly good time.

Tommo yawned, "where are we"? "about a quarter of the way back" replied Fish. Olivia and Charlotte said, "we will prepare a brunch boy's". They went below leaving Tommo and Fish to compare notes, "well"? said Tommo, "well what"? said Fish," You know what"? Fish replied, "I do not know what!!"

The two lads laughed Tommo punching Fish on the arm in a playful way, certainly this was a subject to be revisited later.

The girls reappeared half an hour later with a tray of crisps two bananas and yesterday's chicken salad sandwich, "oh that looks delicious" said Tommo where is the caviar? turning his nose up, "well Gentlemen" Charlotte said, "that's all there is, so it's a sharing platter boy's! but we have hot tea and coffee so who wants which? "the two boys looked at each other, "Tea all around yeah!" the four continued to chat and share stories the lads telling the girls about pilot gig racing and the rest of the team.

The hours passed and the boat got closer to the coast, a celebration of spotting the coast was toasted by more tea, "this tea is a very British thing boys im getting used to it" said Charlotte.

As the Bacardi got closer and landmarks could be seen, they were buzzed twice by the coastguard search and rescue airplane and the coastal search and rescue helicopter, Hey Fish, Tommo said "they are looking for something", "or someone" said Fish.

They continued on and passed the bar into the River Dart, the water became calmer, Tommo dropped the main sail and reefed the foresail, Fish started the outboard it burbled into life, He said to Tommo "take the helm Tommo I'll check us in", the quayside was buzzing, police and coast guard personnel in their white vans all over the town, Fish said "it's too busy here to drop you off girls so come back to Dittisham with us and we will drive you to where ever" "great!!" said both girls. "we will go down and pack our things" said Olivia.

Fish called the Harbourmasters office, "Harbourmasters office" said the voice on the phone, "Hi it's the Crew of Bacardi here just checking back in as advised", "reference number please? Said the man on the phone

"8854" said Fish "ah yes Bacardi from Roscoff, yes that's us said Fish "two crew"? said the harbourmaster's clerk as he ticked off the boat on his computer, "yes that's right" said Fish, "nothing to declare Sir?, "no, Fish responded, a quick trip all good thank you, err before I go, it seems busy has something happened?", the clerk disinterested answered, "it's a missing persons investigation it has been going on all night and today it's not just for the Dartmouth office its right down the coast to Plymouth a big operation today".

"Thank you for checking in Sir, "Yeah cheers" said Fish he ended the call, "I'd better call Cox", he said to Tommo, "we will be late", Tommo said, "oh shit, I forgot about that meeting".

The phone rang out as they motored on up the river, Cox answered the phone, "ok where are you"? "we are just motoring up the river, we are late but record crossings meant we are not going to be later, ok we will get the beers in see you in a short while".

Bacardi passed the Vipers Quay the two girls came topside looking a million dollars each, the two days of sailing had given them a glow, the girls were wearing shorts and vest tops, their blonde hair blowing in the wind, Charlotte stood next to Tommo and Olivia put her arm around Fishes waist, it was a photo opportunity not to be missed, Tommo and Charlotte took pictures of Fish and Olivia and the favour was returned.

The jetty came into sight as the Bacardi rounded the bend in the river on the opposite side passing to the Greenway's quay. Fish and Tommo could hear the cheers coming from the Ferryman's inn as the rest of the Dittisham Gig crew and Cox celebrated their return.

Cox got up and went to get the beers on order, Bacardi berthed at Spanish boathouse and the four passengers got into the little tender and it motored back to the jetty at the Dittisham quay.

As they approached the tables outside the pub Jools shouted, "Ay aye, hey up lads are those women with you?", "Hi Guys how is it going"? "yes, this is Charlotte and this is Olivia", "this, girls is Cox", Olivia said "hi Cox I've heard so much about you," this is Jake and Jools and Posh Henry and Blaggs, both girls said Hi guys, really nice to meet you at last, Tommo came out to f the pub with two glasses of beer for the girls. Oh no Tommo its beer, yes said Tommo it tastes like blood, Tommo and Fish laughed.

Posh Henry asked are you American? "No," said Olivia, "we are from Canada", "Canada?" said Cox, yeah said Charlotte, "well we have been hearing an awful lot about you two", "really" said Charlotte, "how is that said Olivia, "are you by any chance part of a visiting party of exchange students from Canada, Vancouver Island, are you? "sure yes, we are", said Charlotte.

Fish and Tommo said, "how did you know that Coxy? because most of the south coast coastguard and search and rescue police and forensic teams are deployed across the south Hams area is out looking for you two!", "What?" said Tommo "no way" said Fish, "yes, "Cox said "it's all over the local news and all over the telly, you two girls are in a bit of trouble.

"You are officially missing!" "Oh no said Fish this is bad", Tommo said "girls! where are you supposed to be if they are missing you?" "Plymouth" said Charlotte, "we were supposed to call in yesterday but with all the excitement of us getting to France we forgot".

Olivia said, "I think we need to call our lead team

member and report we are safe"; Cox said "it's better you do it that way, then call the police or Coastguard".

"Coxy said, "Boys you are idiots, this could bring the crew and name of the boat into disrepute!" "Er we will handle this said Tommo, Sorry crew Sorry Cox, we will be back, Practise night tomorrow 6 o'clock here! Tommo and Fish no excuses we are in need a race plan."

Tommo and Fish went to get Tommo's car, they loaded the girls in and set off to Plymouth some 30 miles away. On the way Charlotte rang her group leader, "Hello Marot, its Charlotte here "Charlotte are you ok? - oh my god, we have been so worried about you - oh my god where have you been? – "is Olivia with you?" "yes, yes, Margot we are fine and safe and everything has been wonderful", "so why didn't you answer your phones?", "well, we were out of range of a signal, I guess" "and where were you when you were out of range Charlotte?" "France!" whispered Charlotte "FRANCE!!!

"I hope you will find your way here this evening?" Margot dictated "yes, we are on our way now, Charlotte, you must ring your mother and father immediately they are besides themselves with worry and tell Olivia to do the same then call me back! I will call the police and then you can explain yourselves to them." "Ok thanks Margot"! she hanged up the phone, "Shit! shit! shit! shit! said Charlotte holding her head in her hands, "we are in deep do do's"! she said to Olivia. "Yeah, but the best of do do's we have had eh Charlotte". "It has been so cool "Tommo laughed.

"Girls, girls!" said Fish "seriously now, let us park up and you can call home, it is the most important thing right now. Fish Pulled over into a layby, he turned to the girls offering his mobile phone, he said, "please girls call home and put your parents mind at rest, then we will get you to Plymouth", "Do we have to?" said Olivia. No, said Tommo "but it is important you are recorded back as safe"

After a few attempts the phone connected in Canada. "Hi Mom, its Olivia, yes Mom im ok safe, well, nothing wrong, we just got carried away and have had the best of time, its all-good Mom honest, just bad communications, im sorry for you being worried, yeah Margot is with us now, ok Mom I'll call you tomorrow, Charlotte is fine yes please let her Mom know yes fine ok im ok please don't worry".

Charlotte had a similar conversation with her Father, he was less sympathetic to the report of good times had, he sent his love and assurance that her Mom would be settled knowing they were safe.

So, let's get our stories right, the four new made friends spoke for a while to work out the next 12 hours. They found their way to Plymouth University where the indomitable Margot was waiting.

What they didn't expect, was that the local press and television crew were waiting for their return. On the TV local news that night was a full report as to the return of the wayward missing Canadian girls, and how two local lads rescued them from a camping fiasco from a local island called Mew Stone, where they stranded themselves in a leaky inflatable boat, they managed to survive for two days on sea bird eggs and mackerel and sheltered under a torn sail from the biting wind and rain until the local lads spotted them and rescued them.

Coxy had watched the late news he saw the news cast and laughed "those bloody crew are unbelievable.! "June I am off to bed I have a room to paint in the morning", "ok love I'll be up there in a few minutes June was sewing with her spectacles on the end of her nose.

Cox was early to rise and text a message to Silvia saying, 'he would be there in an hour to finish off the blue room as agreed'.

After an hour he set off to the new house and tried to get in, he rang the doorbell several times but there was no reply. He rang again, eventually a voice said in broken English," no man here what do you want,"? "Morning its Coxy I've come to paint the blue room, there was a long pause "ah ok, h'ok I know you Cosx" after another short pause the gates clicked and the imposing tall grey gates opened, Coxy drove his little grubby white van in to unload dust sheets and paint brushes.

"I Mikhail I open door - you paint then go, ok"? came the voice from the intercom, "ok" said Coxy! is Silvia there? "No! I know not where she is today, thank you please come in" said Mikhail. The door clicked and buzzed for a short time, Coxy pushed the tall front doors open and went inside.

As Cox went in it felt something was not as it should be, there were no lights on as previous visits the place looked like an empty cold night club, it was cool and dark, he was let in by a stocky man he had seen sometimes there Coxy said to him are you Mikhail? it was clear he was a security type employee but Coxy didn't know him. Yes, the man replied I am Mikhail, "Where is everyone"? asked Cox, "I not know today, all gone business trip I think", he held out his hands and shook his head like he had been left holding the fort.

"Ok" said Cox, he climbed the stairs up the two flights in the glass atrium to the top floor and the room he was to paint. Nothing had been moved the tables and sofas were still in place, Coxy threw his dust sheets and covered the floor, tables and chairs, he masked off some of the window frame and poured himself a cup of tea from his flask.

He stood back and estimated to himself this would be a 2-hour job. He turned his little transistor radio on and listened to the local station, planning in his head the training for Tallet in the upcoming Salcombe race, as he painted the repairs on the walls.

After an hour or so, he heard the main front door in the atrium buzz then open, and a voice shouted "Mikhail, Mikhail"! Silvia!, Cox looked over the balcony there below was Aleksander standing there with his hands on his hips spinning on his heels, He looked up and raised a hand to Coxy, Ah Mr Cox how are you?", "Im fine thank you Cox replied and smiled, Aleksander said "why are all the lights off? is there anybody here?, where are the staff is Vasyli here? do you know?", er no replied Cox "Im sorry Mikhail said they are all away", Aleksander stood there and said "Is Silvia away too?" "well she isn't here and I haven't seen her today, Cox said, "so I guess so", Aleksander said Oh so she didn't tell me she would not be here, Cox shrugged his shoulders and said "I wish I could help", I will be out of here in 15 minutes oh no rush for you Mr Cox. "I Think Mikhail is in the gardens Cox pointed in the direction of the garden". Aleksander went to the inside door to the gardens and bellowed out "Mikhail! Come here please".

Aleksander looked up to Coxy "I have come a long journey Mr Cox and wanted to speak to my staff that's all I want eh? they never here when I want them eh?" "That's life im afraid" said Cox.

Mikhail arrived; looking flustered, the two men

spoke in Ukrainian *"gde id kazhdyy Mikhail?"* Aleksander was holding his hands out as Mikhail replied *"ponyatiya ne imeyu, boss zdes' nikogo net"* shaking his head obviously hadn't got any idea where everyone was.

Aleksander came up to the top floor where Coxy was just finishing off, Aleksander had a mobile phone which was ringing next to his ear and a pair of binoculars and was looking across the water to the large boat. He looked down over his double chin and said quietly "Silvia never has her phone switched off said Aleksander under his breath. He turned sharply on his heels and shouted down "Mikhail are they at the farm?" "I not know Boss; I not see anyone today".

Cox said he was finishing off and would be out of the way shortly, "no, no please, Mr cox said Aleksander "please take your time, the doors are on security locking so when you go out you can't come back in so please don't worry I trust you, help yourself and leave when you are ready".

Aleksander looked over the portion of the wall that Cox had finished, thank you very much Mr Cox you have done an excellent job", "oh my pleasure" said Coxy, "Im pleased you are happy with it, it will be dry in a couple of hours, then it is finished". "Very Good Mr Cox I thank you and when I find my secretary Silvia, I will make sure you are paid right away". Thanks, said Coxy, I'll clear up and leave you to your day".

The two men walked down the stairway. Aleksander said, "what is that?" he rushed down the last flight of stairs ahead of Cox and went over to a red leather sofa, on the sofa half hidden under a cushion was a patent black and white stiletto heeled shoe, "This is Silvia's, this is her shoe", he held it up in Mikhail's direction *"Mikhail pochemu obuv' Sil'vii zdes"?'"* I not know Boss" Mikhail looking embarrassed for not having and explanation. Aleksander carefully replaced the cushion.

Aleksander walked back up the stairs with her shoe in his hand he called the mobile number again, as he climbed the oak and glass stairs, we walked across the landing into Silvia's room.

Everything was in place and tidy, he felt her bed, slipping his hands under her pillow, it hadn't been slept in the sheets were freshly ironed and cool to the touch, he moved across to the wardrobe and slid the mirrored door open, there was a rack of shoes, Jimmy Choo, Christian Louboutin, Casadei, he whispered to himself "why this woman likes all of these overpriced shoes eh? tut tut!".

All the shoes were immaculately lined up, they all were in pairs, he noticed her long black coat that she always wore was hanging on its hanger, but back to front.

On her desk was the work she was preparing for their meeting tomorrow; her handbag was on the back of her chairs, he felt this wasn't a good situation, He placed the odd shoe on the rack and closed the door. He looked at his reflection as the mirrored door closed, he stopped for a second, it was a concerned look on his face and he was now very concerned, He slowly left the room backing out as he closed the door behind him, "Mikhail bring the car!" he shouted from the top of the stair way. This wasn't a request it was an order.

Cox had just finished loading up the van with the dust sheets he got in his van and Mikhail opened the gates. Cox waved a cheerio as Mikhail started the black Range Rover.

Mikhail wasn't looking back and had a seriously

terse look in his eyes,

"Oops Cox thought to himself "somethings not right there". Cox turned left at the top of the road towards his house. The black 4x4 sped past him as he was opening the door.

"Hi June, im back", "hi Coxy how did it go?" June asked, Coxy said "well job done all completed im pleased to say that's the back of it", "well I think you have done alright there Coxy considering it was your Mum's place!". Yeah, well that's all gone now" said Coxy.

June sat down and passed a cup of tea to Cox. So, what's your plan now? she asked , "what today? asked Coxy I want to go over to Quentin and have another chat. Oh, ok can I come?" June asked "Yeah, give Mary a call and see if she is free, I just want to get on with the race plan". "Ok love," she reached for the phone and called Mary's number, it rang for a few rings "Hey Mary love, are you doing anything this afternoon?" "no June nothing special why? Mary replied "great, Coxy wants to bore the pants off Quent, So, if you're up for chocolate or a walk ill come over too"? Mary said "sod the chocolate June bring the prosecco!" "Im so pleased you said that!!" said June, we'll see you in the next hour".

Coxy went up for a shower and June got changed. June picked up a large bar of chocolate from the fridge and a couple of bottles of Prosecco, "good god June both bottles?" Coxy exclaimed. "well, it is Mary love" said June "it's for "just in case!!", Coxy said well I suppose so, your pair of live wires". "but I need to be back for 5 or so I have a meeting at 6". "Ok" replied June. The two of them made their way to the jetty hand in hand, the sun was shining, and it was warm, they called out to Sue who was clearing tables outside the ferryman's Inn.

Posh Henry was inside the pub so Coxy doubled back and had a quick word with him, "Hey Posh, "tell Blaggs to bring the Tallet down tonight I need to go through a few things". "Yeah, ok Coxy, are you off somewhere? Posh replied, "over to see Quent" "Nice well have a good trip mate", "see you later" said Coxy, "err by the way, how is Blaggs?" enquired Cox, "He's ok Coxy, a bit quiet but on the mend, he will be ready no worries." Coxy left saying "see you later".

Cox uncovered the Busty Belle, folding the covers carefully and stowing them under the rear bench. In a few minutes they were waterborne June sat in the cuddy and chugging across the lake toward Stoke Gabriel. The water was calm and still, reflecting the blue of the sky, and the green treeline across the riverbanks, the wake off the bow of Busty Belle was gentle as was the rumble from her engine. June looked back at Coxy with a smile and mouthed "elephant poo" he mouthed back "I love you too," she burst out laughing and blew him a kiss, he frowned, it was always her little joke.

As they arrived Cox called out "blimey Tony it's like ground hog day on this pontoon, you're always here with your binoculars". Tony Laughed "you are right It is a bit like ground hog day as whenever I'm here you two turn up, Hi June" said Tony.

June was helped off the boat by Tony, she made her way into the village, leaving Cox to tie up Busty Belle. "So, Tony what's new here in the centre of the world?", well Coxy not a lot but this boat is causing some attention" Which one the Makonde? Cox pointed "Yeah, yesterday it was listing right over", really? said Cox it looks ok ish now, I didn't pay much attention to it on the way across? Are you still working for the owner?" asked Tony, "well actually today was the last day, and they are disappearing fast he said, yeah it was like the Mary Celeste in there today", "Why? asked Tony, Cox said "don't know just no one about the place was all closed up the owner turned up and was pissed off about it.

The owner? asked Tony who is that it's a guy called Aleksander, Aleksander who asked Tony, I don't know its Kaprarov or Karpov something like that" "and who is the other guy? Tony was pumping for information now, Vasyli is the house manager Cox Continued, he looks after business at the house, I think. Anyone else there? Tony asked, "Yes a grunt called Mikhail and Silvia a secretary but she's more than that, she does the art stuff.

Art? asked Tony, yeah, I told you before, they import African art. Really? said Tony, that's interesting. "Why? said Cox, Tony put his hand on Cox's shoulder "Im sorry I can't say Coxy, but they are being watched so good thing you're not working there anymore".

"Anyway, are you over here for long?" Tony asked, "Im discussing Salcombe with Quent said Coxy as he finished securing the boat", Tony said "well don't be too long there is a storm coming in", "yeah I heard that the radio earlier and we have a practise tonight". "We'll see how it develops but it will be on us by 8.00 pm tonight".

"Cox said cheerio to Tony and made his way to Quentin and Mary's cottage, Mary and June were already getting loud, shall we sit in the garden Coxy? I think we might be able to hear ourselves think, these two are already half a bottle in," "yeh good" said Cox.

Cox and Quentin rolled out a large map of Salcombe water, they put stones on each corner, the two friends became deep into conversation over several cups of tea, the subject was intense and detailed, wind direction and tide flows, tide timetables reference books were crowded on the table on the table, Quentin had footage of the race he Coxed 4 years previously, they played it over and over looking at landmarks, wind and water references were all important to Cox , he wasn't going for a row , this was his final Viking charge of the year.

This was a big year for Cox, the Salcombe regatta was a big event in the rowing calendar. The name "regatta" is for a series of boat races, either rowing or sailing, and this regatta was this year in its 167th year! The Cornish gig races are always popular and extremely competitive, Cox had no doubts he and the crew needed to pull all the stops out to beat the other crew, Tallet needed to be in the best trim, as light as the rules would allow and still let the hefty crew show off the sleek lines of their beloved 133-year-old Pilot gig built in Dartmouth.

Chapter 16

Mikhail drove the Range Rover through the country lanes at speed, Aleksander was silent as they turned into Gallows Lane, the trees were already blowing hard shedding branches onto the road, as the car turned into the disused dairy farm there was no one to be seen, the yard was empty, Aleksander told Mikhail to stop and wait in the car engine running.

He climbed out and walked to the side door, it was locked, he walked across the yard and spotted the BMW parked in the next courtyard under a carport. He tried two other doors, but all were locked. Then he banged on the main shutter doors, they rattled in their keepers as the noise echoed inside. Footsteps could be heard, He stepped back as the side door was unlocked, slowly the door opened and there stood Vasyli. Looking sombre Vasyli beckoned Aleksander in "Come In said Vasyli.

Aleksander walked in he could see Devlin in the next bay behind his desk, "Vasyli there had better be a good excuse as to why my house is unattended, what is going on, why are you here? why has no one called me? Is there a problem?". "There is a problem Vasyli said come through to the office we can discuss things there, as they walked through the complex of small workshops Aleksander said where is everyone? Why is production stopped.

Devlin rose to his feet as Aleksander entered the office, without a greeting to either man he asked "Devlin, please explain what is going on here, why is all stopped? Where are the workers".

Devlin looked over to Aleksander, "I have sent all the workers home for a day, to give s time to prepare", "prepare for what?" asked Aleksander, prepare to move out close! of course", "you had better explain to me why Devlin, this operation has been the best we have run, ever! Aleksander was angry, "where is Silvia? ".

"Aleksander", Devlin got to his feet, in a quiet voice he said" listen to me please, Silvia was behind all the losses; "how could she have been behind it explain Devlin and what do you mean was, where is she?" Aleksander was getting impatient with Delvin's pandering and lack of an explanation.

"Aleksander Silvia is dead", what!? shouted Aleksander, "how?" there was a fight, she was violent angry, she lost her balance, she was angry that we had discovered her, she fell from the balcony in the house," So, where is she now? Vasyli stepped forward, "Boss we had to" ......he stopped, he looked at Devlin "had to what?" shouted Aleksander".

Devlin stood up a drew on a cigarette he said, "we had to bury her at sea, there is no body, there is no evidence there is no reason for the police or authorities to come here looking for her, we cleaned up we washed down we cleared the house of all evidence", "why did you? Aleksander asked "In case you hadn't noticed Aleksander we are refining class A Cocaine here we don't need any fucking attention, He continued Aleksander said "Do you know why im here Devlin? Vasyli do you know why I am here?" ...there was silence in the room... "let me tell you why, I am here because you left her shoe in the house, one shoe, not a pair, you hanged her clothes up wrong , her handbag is still on the chair, her bed isn't slept in her glasses are still on the table this minor fucking mistakes are things that will bring the house down on us all in a missing person investigation.

"You are good Devlin, but you are sloppy in the finer details and that goes to you Vasyli", Devlin said "but who will report her missing? we had to decide, and I took the decision that we close and move, and quickly move Aleksander, the last thing we all need is any attention, we need to move and move today. And no, we did not call you; the phones do record all the movements."

"Oh my god! this is a fucking mess" said Aleksander "I go away for a few days to make us better people do good business, and you two animals fuck it up"!

We have the house, I have the London Gallery we have this place, there is progress, good progress, the distribution is set up it is perfect, the Brazil guys will not be happy about this Devlin this is a fuck up!", "no!" said Devlin "it is time to go Aleksander, understand this, I have looked at all of the options there is no plan B Aleksander! this is it, we must pack up take the powder with us to Spain on the boat and keep our heads down."

Devlin banged his fist on the wall, "We can continue business with Brazil from there, a new location in Laredo, a new identity", what about the people here, Aleksander said, "Devlin continued, "we will be long gone before they start to shout", remember Maritsa? "we made good money there", Aleksander didn't agree "ah no, no it was too far from an airport".

Vasyli carried on, "Laredo in northern Spain is where we can safely do business. It is close to Santander Airport and directly in contact with Brazil". "This is all too much to handle right now," said Aleksander.

Vasyli stepped forward "I respectfully suggest we lay here low until this storm passes, you go back to London Aleksander, I can coordinate any transportation for artwork, you take Mikhail with you, and don't discuss anything with anyone."

Aleksander looked at Vasyli and said in a low voice" "what the hell do you know about respect".

Undaunted Vasyli continued spelling out their plans "look Aleksander stick to African art and football. It is Monday today we must be loaded up and gone by Tuesday night latest. I have 4 shipments, 8 kilos to Bristol and Aberdeen, they have sent the money, then we are clear and ok to run, that shipment will keep the system full until we are in Spain and then all will be quiet. Aleksander sell the house it is the winter season, so, the place will be quiet no tourists or locals poking their noses in".

"Tomorrow we use the Zurich bank to transfer to Tbilisi in 100,000-euro blocks, then wire transfer to Malta. Aleksander, we have taken care of all the important pieces of the problem I assure you, if it was not for Silvia being greedy, we wouldn't need to take this action" Aleksander paced back and forth.

"I can't believe she has done this to me, I treated her like a daughter, why would she double cross me like this, how much did she take me for?" Aleksander asked for an answer. Devlin said "150,000 per kilo and we estimated 10 kilos in the last 9 months, a little here a little there. Vasyli said, "she was caught Aleksander it was simple, in a corner, it was clear, she came out fighting like a Turkish ship rat".

Devlin continued, "her death was an accident Aleksander, she fell off the top balcony, she fell onto the floor below, we didn't touch her, you have our word".

"And what is your word worth Devlin? eh? what is your word worth Vasyli answer me this? is this how you repay me? I gave you this escape, it was me that respected you", He stared at them both giving them each a harsh look, he felt between them was a betrayal.

"I financed you developed you, before you met me you were pathetic war criminals fighting for a kilo here and kilo there, 2 common Balkan bastards of war, criminals, liars' thieves, chancers. and look at you now Devlin you are almost a fake Englishman."

Devlin got up from his chair, he lit another cigarette, "that's right" Devlin barked, "Aleksander remember the millions we have made, we made for you too, so we all have won, we all have made our fortunes, Silvia has gone, and we must in order to preserve all that we have achieved move on too".

"It is time to go, turn off your mobile phone, go and clear out the house and then London, we will be in Santander, we will contact Brazil with new banking details and you Aleksander will live a long and happy life. But we must do this now!". "How much product is there to be moved Vasyli? 55 kilos there are 2.5 kilos per box I have taken 13 boxes so far, I am trying not to bring attention to the trips back and forwards to the boat, the people are too inquisitive. I have 5 more to go this afternoon".

Aleksander tapped his glasses on his lips and looked to the ground in a long contemplation, "Well this is a sad state of affairs Devlin, this is a deep shock to our otherwise well-balanced business in England, I am bitterly disappointed in both of you, Devlin, I hold you responsible for its failure and charge you with a new responsibility to get us out of this mess, if not, the consequences Devlin are considerable I am sure you understand me?".

Devlin turned around slipping his green tweed jacket over his arms and putting it on, he straightened his tie and pulled his waistcoat down and pulled on the cuffs of his shirt. Devlin looked up at Aleksander, his piercing dark brown eyes looking fearlessly straight at Aleksander, "I am sure we will all recognise the risks here Aleksander, I do not have any doubt, at all and im sure Vasyli agrees with us whole heartedly we always had, we always will, go onto mitigate those risks at whatever the cost, either casualty wise or financially wise."

Devlin picked up his silver cigarette case and lighter from the table, he slipped it inside his jacket and continued," Nevertheless, Aleksander, in this situation we have no choice but to break it down and move on. That is my recommendation and I suggest you accept it Aleksander, and we live another day.

So, what now? asked Aleksander, Devlin put on his long brown overcoat he dusted off his immaculately shine brogues again he looked up at Aleksander "for now we carry on filling the storage boxes on the boat, we take as much as possible with us, we sail tomorrow evening, everything must look and feel normal, Silvia is out of the country, she went to see her relatives it was urgent. No more details. You will leave for London with Mikhail, as normal no drama, no fuss, no attention".

Vasyli will continue to load up, we have a storm on us now, it will be clear by dawn, we load up with food and water at Dartmouth then sail off as if we are taking a trip to France to fill up with cheap wine, we will be back in a few days' chaps, if we are asked. Aleksander turned for the door and said this had better work. He closed the door behind him. He and Mikhail left the farm the stormy weather now starting to blow hard.

"Vasyli, we continue with our own plan, said Devlin, we sail to the Azores, then on to Brazil, we take the refined cocaine with us the rest of the rubbish we leave here. Agreed" said Vasyli, both men closed the building and drove off in the BMW.

Chapter 17

"Come on June it's time to go the weather is turning", Mary said "this woman is not for turning!" "Not you it's the weather, it's raining now so can we get a move on …please! Im going down to the boat see you there", Cox was insistent. Cox marched off, June and Mary who were still giggling followed Quentin who was helping Coxy untie the busty belle,

Tony was still there on the pontoon, "bloody hell tony you are fixated on that bloody Makonde, yes I am said Tony there are two guys on it now, I wonder what they are doing this is the 4th trip there today, Coxy could I grab a lift from you across there now, ?" "yeah of course June won't mind, it is going to be wet you know, Tony looked at Coxy and said "really? can we cruise close to the Makonde so I can take a look?" "yeah, no worries we can swing round the back of the boat if you like."

June stepped aboard after her hug from Mary, "see you later" said Quentin" give me a call Coxy later tonight" "ok pal thanks for today a great help".

The rain was starting to come down hard, the surface of the water now rippling with raindrops and the visibility dropped, the wind was blowing in from the sea up the river, which gave rise to a real gust or two as the wind was funnelled up the valley onto the lake, it could become a bit choppy, Cox was aware of this and opened up the taps to get a move on. Busty Belle roared off from the pontoon into the murkiness of the Dittisham lake, the banks for the river were at a low tide and the muddy banks were less than scenic.

Cox offered Tony a yellow waterproof jacket June sat there in her waterproof over coat and an umbrella hoisted above her head whist ducking under the cuddy. Busty Belle moved north to come across the stern of Makonde, as they approached two figures emerged from the rear of the boat, Vasyli saw the white Busty Belle with Cox at the helm, "Hello Mr Cox he shouted, not a nice day for a cruise, "No indeed", "How are you Mr Cox?" called Vasyli, "Wet"! replied Coxy Tony was all eyes over the huge broad beamed sailing yacht.

He took out his mobile phone a took some shots of the boat just as Devlin appeared again from below, Tony silently clicked away, as the rain increased the noise of the rain on the water, Tony got up and crossed over to the other side of the boat as coxy steered the busty bell down the side of the yacht.

"Hey, you no photos please!" came the English sounding Devlin "oh sorry mate" said Tony "lovely boat you have, how long is she?", each man looked at each other and Devlin said 50 feet Vasyli said 55 feet "oh nice" said Tony, as he was talking as his mobile phone was videoing the pair on the back of the boat. Tony sat down and they roared off toward the jetty. Tony waving as they left trying to instil that his photos was a harmless intrusion. "Enough Tony?" Cox asked " oh yes said Tony just right".

When they got to the jetty Tony helped June out of the boat, looking at the Makonde Tony saw the two men were getting into the launch, Tony said "Cox can come with you to home PC Graham will come and pick me up" "ok mate no worries" Cox replied, the three covered up

Busty Belle as the launch passed them making the jetty and pontoon bounce up and down as its wake washed into the floating boat park, the two men in the launch moored up some way off near the old cottage.

Tony June and Cox made their way up the jetty to the street, the water from the rainstorm washing litter and rubbish into the Ferryman's Inn car park.

June made it home and immediately put the kettle on. "Let's have a cup of tea" said June, Cox said "Tony please help yourself and use the house phone to give PC Grahams a call", "Ok thanks" said Tony using a towel June had passed him to dry off.

Tony arranged the lift, but from his wife, and said she would be there in 40 minutes, "I can give you a lift back if Grahams can't make it", "its ok Coxy my wife doesn't drive a police car, she is less likely to attract suspicion.

The three sat at the kitchen table June poured the tea, Cox said "is there something going on there with those two on the boat? Hard to tell really" said Tony, we had a tip off something wasn't right, they are not sailing folk, he sipped his tea, ... are they? "clearly not" said Cox. "so, how is Blaggs asked Tony, "Im not too sure said Coxy I should see him in an hour or so, we of course hoping he is fit and well for next Saturday's Salcombe race. I have a gig meeting at 6. looks like it will be inside the pub we are not going out on the water in this weather.

Excuses - excuses! said June, Tony laughed, "come on June you know how this works" , yes its so exciting", are you and Fiona coming?" yes we are, I hope we can get in, Don't worry Coxy said I've set aside two tickets for you and Fiona, it will be great to have your support on the day. You will have that for sure Coxy, said Tony, Tony heard a car pull up outside, "here she is said Tony bang on time!" Ill be off both thanks Coxy, and can I ask that this is under your hats please, there in an investigation but I don't know all the details, of course Coxy said nothing will go any further.

Coxy waved to Fiona in the car Tony got in and off they went back to Stoke Gabriel. The time was approaching 6 cox said June I have got to fly he put his coat back on and set off in the wind and rain.

Coxy arrived some minutes later at the ferryman's Inn the crew was gathered in the bar, Posh Henry was serving, What are you doing behind there asked Coxy, Im performing miracles said Posh, a pint then said Cox, ok give me a minute, Jools Jake Fish and Posh were there where is Tommo Cox called out, he'll be here in 15 said Fish, where is Blaggs, Cox repeated the question , don't know said Posh he will be here, the weather is bad so hell be closing up and coming from work.

OK let's find a corner and we can have a discussion, Posh said above the noise of the bar, "Coxy here's your pint, and by the way Tallet is at Blaggs place I guessed we may not have been out tonight", "good lad" said Coxy.

Ok hear up hear up team Tallet, I want to talk ultimate tactics tonight, so if you are here from Salcombe bugger off! The crew shouted Yeaaaah! Cox started to talk about the Salcombe crew, so they are a big team, nice boat, nice guys, but we are faster fitter, and our boat is prettier, the door opened and Into the bar walked Blaggs and Tommo, look who I found said Tommo, yeahh! the crew called out. Blaggs was looking ok still some black eye but he was smiling. Two Pints Posh Blaggs said.

The evening rolled on, Cox issued each member with a large map print of the Salcombe bay and river estuary on it he had marked the course and the position of the buoys some landmarks and the depths of the water, he had included the tide times and heights.

Coxy got really technical with his crew, strokes per minute, the turn which they would practise only 3 times Tuesday night Wednesday night and Thursday night, Friday they would be travelling to Salcombe a hotel was booked for the 6 lads Tommo and Fish would share a room Blaggs and Posh Henry would share a room and Jools and Jake would share a room, Coxy and June would share a room too. So lads we have a storm here right now , but we will be on the water tomorrow night at 6.pm low tide, understood, all we are doing tomorrow is speed trials, I want a straight line course from the Lake to white rock we will be stepping it up , getting accuracy and timing spot on, Wednesday we will be on turns, tight accurate and quiet, Thursday will be a 4 mile row to Dartmouth and back again so that's 8 miles under pressure some straight line 44 beats 46 beats then long strokes. "Quiet?" Said Posh Henry "you said Quiet?" " What do you mean Cox?" "I mean quiet, no noise, you expend energy when you lot grunt and puff, that will be kept quiet until we are in sight of the finishing line…………… then I want to hear your inner Viking lads.

"All the crew took to their feet and chanted together *"In the Halls of Valhalla, where our brave sons live forever - Tallet crew has come to ruin your day!!"* The war cry went up, all the crew raised their glasses!! *"Huhggahhh Skol!! "*

"Coxy punched the air and knew he had his dream team and knew they were his committed crew.

Ok lad's tomorrow night 5.30 Tallet on the water ready to go, straight lines ok? ok Coxy left the pub and made his way up the hill the rain was driving and heavy the wind was blowing strong, as he passed the new house, he saw the lights on, standing in the blue room overlooking the river was Aleksander, he waved and Aleksander waved and beckoned Cox in, Cox hesitated and the gates opened, he ran to the doorway and the doors buzzed, Coxy pushed the door open and there stood Aleksander Mr Cox good evening, the weather is awful come in please, Hello Aleksander did you find your people? Ah yes, they were away on conflicting business, just bad timings, would you join me in a scotch whisky, er well ok yes please that would be nice.

I have been think about you today Mr Cox, Just call me Cox Aleksander, everyone knows me as Cox, Ah ok thank you we can be less formal with a whiskey in our hands, well Cox I had been thinking about you today and thinking how uncomplicated your life is compared to mine, and that I would swap with you in an instant, "oh really said Coxy, well im not sure I would like to swap really", "oh why do you say that Cox,? he passed Coxy a large glass of single malt, "well several things, the most important is that I live in this perfect part of the country and always have done, im a river man, I hope I always will be, my work is not too stressful, "ah yes stress! Cox it is a killer", yes and my wife is a local girl, and my racing boat is part of my life and I love my crew nearly as much as I love my wife".

Aleksander stood in front of Coxy legs apart his gold and diamond Rolex glistening under the roof lighting "There you go Cox it sounds perfect I'll take it". They both laughed.

"It is a lot of responsibility I have for many people who all rely on me and my businesses, it makes me be awake in many hours of the night, and the stress is big I feel it here!", Aleksander beat his chest, "Yes, I imagine it is Aleksander, but there are compensations I guess, a nice home like this and a big boat, in the harbour", said Cox, "it is not my boat, it belongs to my manager Devlin" "ah yes said Cox I've seen him a few times and Vasyli is he your guy too?", " yes, Aleksander continued he has been with me for over 20 years, good men, but ruthless men too, "yes" said Coxy not really wanting to know more details.

"We are from Ukraine, I have been a businessman all my life Cox, big deals expensive risks which have for the main part paid off and allowed me to have some luxury, but this is no compensation for not having a simpler or easier way of enjoying life, I would swap it all for less risk more calmness and so less stress, do you understand me Cox, do I make myself clear Cox?"

Aleksander was looking directly at Coxy, "yes you do Coxy replied "and I hope one day you find it." "Thank you, Cox", there was a pause "you are clearly a good man; I have enjoyed meeting you", Aleksander held out his hand and Cox engaged him in a strong handshake. Cox thought it was like someone giving a goodbye.

"I am going to be away for several months, but I will be returning". Cox necked back the last drop of his whisky and placed the glass down, "are you going far?", "Africa Cox to collect art" said Aleksander, "I wish you luck" said Cox and So, on that philosophical note, I thank you for the malt, but I must make my way back to home" Cox turned towards the door, "Thank you Cox", Cox replied with "thank you! Aleksander, take care, and by the way did you manage to have a word with Silvia about my bill, I have not sen her said Aleksander", he bowed his head averting his eyes from Cox's gaze, he pressed the button to buzz open the front doors, Cox ventured out into the wet and windy courtyard as the grey doors closed behind him.

He let himself out of the side gate and up the street to the top road where he stepped into the kitchen, he was cold wet and windswept, June shouted through "take you jacket and shoes off Coxy its wet out there". "unbelievable!" Coxy thought to himself.

Coxy put the kettle on and made some tea." How did it go love?" June called through from the lounge, "all good said Coxy the boys are all charged up, if I can keep them sober for the rest of the week, we have a chance".

"Im really looking forward to this weekend Coxy", "me too love" Coxy said sipping his tea, "60 minutes of chaos will be a fitting end to a long year, eh love?". June sat next to Cox she snuggled into his shoulder, Coxy said "I've just spoke to that Aleksander guy from the new house", "Oh yes" June said, "did that woman pay you?", "er no he hadn't seen her she is away on business, but im sure she will when she gets back. Coxy continued "he was telling me he would swap his opulent life for our poor poverty-stricken existence what?" said June "really?" "yeah really!" "He sounded really down and disenchanted with his lot," "I wouldn't be Coxy, I hope you said yes, when do we move in?" "Nah June love, there is a lot to be said for keeping life simple and enjoyable and we are good at it ", "oh Coxy we are what we are, and as you say we are good at it."

The following morning the weather had improved a little, Coxy turned on the radio to hear the weather forecast, the local radio was in the middle of the news   (.........."*previously reporting a rise in burglary, mar-*

ine crime and local crime for Plymouth stated were now on the decrease, the chief constable said it was encouraging news, as the end of the summer holiday influx of visitors was at an end, Chief Constable Sarah Francis considered the successes had been bought about by more vigilance of home and boat owners in the larger Plymouth rock area. "West Pier news!" back to the main news this morning, a body has been washed up south of Port Minster beach in Bigbury, Police are searching the area and have appealed for the public to stay away, Sheila Prescott reports, it has been a stormy windswept night here......)

"*June* love do you want your tea up there? Cox shouted up the stairs as he picked up the post off the mat from the hallway, "no love im coming down". Ok Cox wandered back to the kitchen as the weather forecast came on, *(the weather will continue to be blustery this morning later things will return to a quieter temperature and clearer skies as the high pressure returns.)*

"That's sounds better Cox, what does? Said Coxy", "the weather you and the boys will be able to get some good practice in this evening".

"bloody hell"! Cox burst out "What love?" June looked over concerned" "look at this, it's a cheque for £5000!" who from Coxy, it's from Aleksander" said Cox, "this is too much im sure the bill is for £2200", Cox put on his reading glasses and pulled his copy invoices out of his file, yeah these are the last three invoices, and they total £2208. "Have a word with him love to see if he's made a mistake?" "Yeah, I'll call him later". Right im off to see Blaggs and to mess with Tallet for a few hours. "Ok, love, have a good day", Cox put the cheque in his pocket and walked down to Blaggs place.

June picked up the envelope left on the table, inside was a compliment slip 'Aleksander Makonde African art Dealers Chancery Street London', obviously Cox had missed it, In a handwritten note it said "Enjoy the life Mr Cox, I owe you respect and the best of good wishes, please accept this cheques as the conclusion to our business. Regards Aleksander Makonde",

Immediately June reached for the phone and called Cox," Hi Love" he said, "Cox come home now!" "what? what's up now love" "I'll explain when you get here come now", "ok" Cox said he turned around and walked back home, June was waiting on the doorstep "read this Coxy", "what is it?" Coxy opened the letter and read the compliment slip, "Bloody Hell" Cox said quietly, "OK love here, he passed the cheque to June, go pay it in love," "Are you Ok Coxy , oh yes love im more than ok, just pay it in," Cox turned and walked away, as he passed the new house it was darkened the gates were locked, the place looked empty. Something told Coxy and he sort of knew Aleksander had gone for the time being.

Cox pulled the Tallet trailer out and removed the cover, there was his weapon, long sleek and full of rubbish, he oars were laid in the bottom of the boat and rudder was marked and dirty, Cox in a flash decided to smarten them up, He went back home and drove the van down to the carpark at the back of Blaggs house, in the van he had varnishes and paints and some masking tape, in an hour he was ready to paint.

Blaggs opened his door and was greeted with a sight of a man possessed, "hi Blaggs Cox" said "we need to smarten this beauty up mate, have you seen her?" "Yeah, she needs a clean alright", the two men spent the next couple of hours scrubbing and rubbing the hull, the inside, the foot boards and the gunwales, some new thole pins really bought it all together, she was given a re varnish on the top side and inside all the foot boards and seats were re painted a dark grey.

Cox had rubbed each of the 8 oars down 6 racing oars and two mid boat spares, each oar had a red tip painted and two white lines, over the top of that he Fished them off with a smart coat of varnish, each oar was checked for damage and to see if the leathers were in good order, some minor repairs were done.

Blaggs had re painted the name on the stern of the boat, and the rudder was refitted with new brackets, paint job and new wires. Cox and Blaggs stood back and the re vitalised Tallet was finished.

She looked longer sleeker and brighter than she had done for many years, on the stern her name in Italics *"TALLET"* was proud and loud, "what do you think Blaggs? "asked Cox, "she looks a beauty *"in the halls of Valhalla* eh? Coxy", "exactly"! replied Cox, June appeared and quietly stood next to Cox, "my god she looks lovely boys, what a change!". "Yeah, she deserves it" said Coxy.

Come on love its teatime, what!? Coxy said Blaggs said "look at the time Coxy we've lost track its 5 already", "we need to get her down to the jetty"!, just then the rumble of Posh Henry's land rover turned into the car park, "bloomin eck!" shouted Posh, "look at the boat, who's been a busy boy then?" "wow! Coxy she looks swell mate".

Coxy said he was going to get washed up and would see them in 20 minutes, June and Cox made their way back to the house, June said, "I've paid that cheque in the bank Coxy", they wanted to know what we wanted to do with the money invest it or pay it into a savings account".

Coxy said I hope you just paid it in?", "Oh I did Coxy why? We might be going on a little holiday. "oh Coxy love that sounds nice, where? "Don't know that's for you and Mary to sort out!" Coxy gave her a long kiss June said, "I love you foxy Coxy" he replied, "not as much as I love you moony June!", He said "gotta go", he put his old track suit top on picked up his notepad and maps and walked out down to the quay.

Waiting was the Tallet crew, they cheered him as he arrived *"great job"*, *"wonderful job"* *"good job Coxy"* they all joined in and the congratulations were all around Cox, Coxy said not all me lads, Blaggs did the finer work, but I agree it's a better-looking boat, Tallet was looking fine on the water and the oars stood up against the Jetty wall looked picture postcard fresh and ready for business.

"Right, you crew of the Tallet, let's get aboard and do some lengths", the crew lined up, Oars held high, each man stepped onto the freshly painted deck and sat down on their freshly cleaned and painted seat, the foot boards were clean bright and varnished. "It felt good" said Jools, Jake agreed and Posh was already wiping the water off the floor.

Blaggs was the last man in the boat, he sat down and pulled his oar across and dropped it through the thole pins, he looked aft and saw Coxy looking at him, Cox mouthed to him "are you ok" Blaggs gave a smile a nod and a thumbs up.

Cox raised his voice "Tallet, nice and steady start tonight", a crowd had gathered, and cameras were clicking, and mobile phones were taking video as the long boat and colourful crew paddled off the pontoon and into the golden sun, it was a good early evening, the weather was calmer, and the sea state settled, some parts of the lake were being whipped a little by the breeze coming off the white point head land.

Cox called for 50 at 20, this was for 50 strokes at 20 strokes per minute, off the Tallet went cutting a fine profile through the cool water, Cox steered the boat past the end of the ferry pier and out into the larger part of the lake, on Cox's knee was his stopwatch, looking down on it he called for 50 at 30, "lads concentrate on the beat, you set the beat now listen to Tallet".

The boat began to creak as the strokes got longer and the oars went deeper, this was cox's secret, the crew knew his methods worked, they were mostly faster than any boat in the south Hams area, but they didn't row faster, the crew rowed just a little deeper, Cox and Quentin always had their theory that more power from the rowers backs and legs being transferred into the net speed of the boat came with a deeper oar.

The Tallet had covered a good piece of the lake, Cox coasted the boat around several buoys and in a large arc turned the boat back down river toward Dittisham , soon Cox had Makonde's broad beam in sight, Cox noticed it was not on the buoy, It was moving, on the back of the broad beamed yacht was Vasyli, "oh fuck he said out loud", the crew looked over their shoulders, Blaggs looked too, he glanced back at Cox and shook his head in as much to say go the other side.

Coxy looked for a clear run as they could pass Makonde on the far side, the yacht was starting to slew across the narrow pass near the ferry crossing Cox decided it was too risky, Cox called for a "slow stop lads for fucks sake!", the boys dipped their oars and bought Tallet to a slow halt, "what's up?" asked Jools Fish turned around to see the Makonde drifting to one side, "he's got weed on his prop look" Fish pointed to a huge ball of green weed and old rope and plastic bags wedged under the rear transom of the Yacht.

Vasyli was wrestling again with the big helm wheel, side to side he was drifting the prop was loaded with weed and old mooring lines probably caught up from the mooring.

Cox called out to Vasyli get your craft under control, stop! stop! The Makonde continued to zig zag through the narrowest parts of the river, passing the old house and into the big bend off Old Owle's, Cox and the crew followed behind frustrated at the pace, they were all ready to burn some calories and make the Tallet fly.

As they turned on the bend Cox saw an opening, get ready lads lets pass here, give me max power now !, the six rowers dug in the boat took off like a speed boat, the bow surging back and forth as the oars delivered, Cox steered the 32 foot long wooden boat past the port side of the stumbling yacht, as they got alongside the Yacht it moved across, getting closer as the Tallet was just feet from the far mud banks, hey, hey, hey, hey! - stop, stop! called Cox.

Vasyli was looking down on the Boat below, "hey-hey" called Cox again "stop" move out Starboard! Vasyli shouted something Blaggs shouted back "move over for fuck sake man!

Devlin appeared on the back of the deck, the oars were just about to contact the yachts hull, the boys were looking to Coxy for the next orders.

Up Oars! Cox shouted the 3 rowers on the starboard side lifted their oars, the rowers on the port side felt the mud just below their oars as they dragged their blades on the bottom the Tallet slammed into the yacht towering above, Devlin looked over the side he shouted "ho – ho! you below get off my boat," Blaggs stood up in the gig "fuck off Devlin he waved his hand back at Devlin", "move your boat over we have called starboard now fucking move!.

Delvin's eyes widened and his piercing black eyes stared right back at Blaggs.

He stepped forward looking over the side rail "Blaggs he growled through gritted teeth, he stood up straight and reached for his belt he produced a gun and took aim at the crew below, he made a shot Crack ! the shot echoed down the steep valley of the river, he aimed again it looked deliberate and the gun cracked off again the Tallet was still wedged between the Makonde and the mud bank, Cox and the crew ducked for cover.

The yacht carried on grazing the pontoon of the lower town marina, Cox reached for his mobile which had fallen into bottom of the boat, he called Quentin, Mary answered almost immediately Cox just shouted down the phone.

"Quent get Tony there has been a shooting from the big Yacht, urgent! Mary passed the phone to Quentin "Get Tony"! as he spoke, he looked along the line of his crew, all were now sitting up apart from one, Blaggs was writhing in his seat, "Posh Blaggs!!" Posh Henry turned away from the scene on the river Blaggs was bleeding, from his right shoulder, "no no no" Posh shouted.

Makonde was still making way down the river the engines now in full roar blue smoke coming from one of them the boat was still turning uncontrollably from left to right

Cox clambered along the boat climbing over Jools and Tommo to Blaggs, and Posh Henry "no no no" Blaggs cried out, "my arm my arm!", Posh took a look under Blaggs sweatshirt it was soaked in blood Cox took off this tracksuit top and rolled it up he put it on the bleeding area and said to Posh Press hard, push his arm down. Blaggs let out a cry as the pressure came on, Jools called to Cox, "anyone else hurt are you all ok!" Cox registered four "yes's It's tony on the phone, He passed the phone to Jake to Cox.

"Ok listen!" said Cox "shooting Blags hurt Makonde, Town Marina just coming onto hotel Devlin shot him guns on board all yours Tony", "Ok" Tony said.

Cox turned to his crew "right the four front oars men row like the wind back to Ditsham Go"! the crew turned the Tallet around and rowed back to Dittisham, Cox called to Posh to make a call to The Ferryman's "tell Sue we need medical help call and ambulance," Jake made the call

"Sue we need ambulance, no Posh Henry fine, it's for Blaggs urgent! urgent! at the quay 999 yes now!"

Jake handed the phone back to Cox "she is on it" Cox, Cox nodded Jools and Tommo and Fish were rowing hard the boat was on its way up the river against the tide, it was producing spray Blaggs was crying out "Arrgh!"

As the boat moved n Posh Henry was rowing, Cox was holding the pressure on hard for Blaggs, there was Blood everywhere, "So much for a clean-up Cox eh?" "shut up Blaggs you're on clean down duty tomorrow you bloody PITA!!"

10 minutes they were at the quay, the crew pulled the Tallet up alongside the floating pontoon, Blaggs was in agony, Cox looked out for the Ambulance he could

see the blue lights flashing in the car park of the Ferryman's, Sue appeared and pushed her way forward through the crowd of onlookers "here, here, she shouted "Cox use these".

Posh Henry looked up Sue gave him a glance, she had a blanket and towels, Cox covered Blaggs up in the blanket and removed the blood-soaked track suit top and Posh Pushed a rolled-up towel into the wound, blood was still pouring out.

A paramedic arrived with a medical bag, he looked at Blaggs and said "I need him in the back of the ambulance can we get him off the boat", the 5 rowers without saying a word lifted Blaggs off the boat in one lift, Blaggs managed with support from Posh Henry, he stood up but quickly passed out and collapsed at the feet of his crew members.

The paramedic said as quick as we can please gentlemen, Posh Henry picked Blaggs up and threw him over his shoulder, he marched up the floating pontoon with Jake and Fish clearing the way through the onlookers.

Blaggs was delivered by Posh Henry to the back of the ambulance, another paramedic was waiting and immediately took over, the doors of the ambulance were closed.

Cox called the crew together, "Is everyone ok, no holes in anyone else? "all good", "ok" im ok", me too" said the five rowers, "ok im going to ask you to zip it! ok for the time being don't say anything to anyone and if you think it's the press just walk away, understood? Im sure Ugly will be here shortly and he is the only person we should speak to ok "ok" "understood" replied the crew.

"I suggest we get Tallet off the water quickly and

put it away", "Can you deal with that Posh ,Tommo, Fish and Jake?, Jools here Cox handed him some money, "here, get some drink in I'll be there in a while", Yes Cox ! good lads be in the pub in 20 minutes.

Cox reached for his mobile, he rang June, June it's me, Hi Coxy "I can see blue lights", yes love listen Cox said, im ok, but I might be some time, what's gone on Coxy? June asked with anxious concern in her voice , "I'll tell you later love, im down at the pub if you need me."

Chapter 18

On Makonde Vasyli was still powering on one engine he had shut down the other, steering was harder as was progress as the boat on one engine wanted to steer to port. They had made almost 2 hours progress on to the open water away from the river dart, the boat wasn't making as good progress and only just holding 6 knots, they were using diesel fast and if it wasn't for the good fortune, they were running on one engine would have run out of fuel over an hour ago.

"We are going to need sails soon" said Vasyli, "So, we are the consummate sailor now are we Vasyli?"

Devlin went below and was moving things around some crashing and banging could be heard up top by Vasyli, he reappeared with books and charts, he without saying a word, threw them overboard. "We might need those" said Vasyli. Devlin went below again without saying a word.

Devlin reappeared from below minutes later, he had a bottle of whisky and two glasses, "what is that for?" said Vasyli "a celebration", "if you like old chap" said Devlin in his usual calm charming and moderated tone, "these things are sent to try us aren't they, here drink this and stay calm, by the time those mongrels have sorted themselves out we will be another boat with another name heading off for another destination."

"Vasyli said "why the fucking hell did you shoot? have you forgotten all the training? no attention is the rules Devlin", Devlin stood up straight an rolled his shoulders, he smiled , took a deep breath and continued to pour the drink "No Vasyli, I wanted to kill Blaggs, as he is the only one with any link to me or you Vasyli or Aleksander for that matter, even if I have wounded the crass peasant bastard idiot, at least he won't want to talk for fear I will return and finish our business together, he also has information on Silvia, which he will think twice before he reminisces with any member of the English Police or investigators, and that Vasyli can only and will buy us more time".

Devlin chinked the glass in Vasyli's hand "chin up old chap, Now, I need to change the name of this floating hulk."

Devlin disappeared below and reappeared with a tube inside the tube was roll of signage for the name change on the transom, Vasyli said "you are well prepared", "So, this is part of the training too Vasyli? said Devlin, he laughed and said sarcastically "you are in good hands old boy".

He rolled up his sleeves took off his fedora hat and exposed his badly scared head, he replaced his fedora with a baseball cap and stepped down onto the rear transom deck, he peeled and scraped for half an hour removing the old "Makonde out of Monaco" name leaving a trail on the water as they motored on.

He stuck another graphic reading *"Ruvuma of Lisbon"*, he smoothed it out and threw the backing paper of the back of the boat. "there you go Vasyli" Devlin climbed aboard again "we are now "Portuguese", Vasyli looked at Devlin still with and look of disgust and said change all the key fobs, change and dispose of the paperwork, I already have old chap stop panicking we will be successful, we have Luck on our side my friend.

A coast guard aeroplane made a pass over the yacht, wave Vasyli be friendly now. Both men waved at the low flying aeroplane as it dropped it's wings on one side and made a firm observation and identification of the yacht. "we have only half a tank of fuel Devlin we need more fuel, do you understand? I have only 4 hours of cruising left. We need more fuel, Ok", "ok let me have a look. we have 100 litres below; this will get us under motor how far?

"It can get us to Roscoff " said Vasyli "or down the coast to Plymouth", "head for Plymouth" said Devlin we can get to Roscoff later tomorrow", "So much for more time" said Vasyli, Devlin reared up, "Vasyli if we are going to get through this and to Azores and Brazil we need to work together!", there was a silence, after a few seconds Vasyli said "I hear you". Vasyli tapped in a route to Plymouth it was getting dark and Plymouth was only 4 hours away, they could make repairs to the engines and propellers clogged up with weed and rope and load with food and fuel for the

Chapter 19

At the Ferryman's Inn Sue had made up some food for the crew, she had put a notice on the snug door "Private Function", Inside Cox and the remaining crew were almost silent waiting for News on Blaggs,

The Paramedic came into the pub asking for Coxy, he came outside quickly, the paramedic said "luckily he has sustained a wound from a bullet, he has lost some blood but not life threatening, however they were concerned that his reaction in terms of shock made them consider that he needed to be in hospital over night for observations and an intensive course of antibiotics and a drip, and that because it was a gunshot the police would be informed and Blaggs may be questioned".

Cox said that PC Tony Handsome was already aware, the paramedic asked does he have any relatives who need to be informed, Cox said he would deal with that and someone would visit him in the morning. "Ok we will look after him for you", the door of the ambulance opened and there was Blaggs looking grey but eyes wide open oxygen mask on with a thumbs up for Coxy.

"See you later" shouted Coxy, behind him gathered the rest of the Tallet Crew all raised their glasses and "broke into the war cry *within the walls of Valhalla where our brothers live there forever, the Tallet Crew has come to ruin your day*" Blaggs laughed and gave another victory salute.

The doors of the Ambulance closed, Cox looked at his mobile phone he had 3 missed calls from Tony, He called Tony back moving over the stone wall where there was less noise.

Tony asked "Hi coxy how is Blaggs? Cox explained, "he is just off to hospital for treatment he will be in overnight but should be ok, he looks grey Tony, he is in shock right now", "yes im sure" said Tony "and how are you Cox? and I trust no one else was injured?" "Im ok and we all are ok , the shot looked a deliberate Tony, fucking hell, the guy called Devlin shot at Blaggs and straight at him, and twice, missed then aimed again, he seemed to single him out, not at anyone else but who can tell, im ok but I am worried my lads will feel this more later on when it sinks in,! "

Tony said, "Yes maybe, try not to worry, I was calling to say the big boys are now on this, special operations and the coast guard with support from the royal navy are on the tail of our Russian friends, it is hoped we make some stoppages later".

"In the meantime, I have requested an armed officer is posted to sit with Blaggs at the hospital, two things Coxy and I would appreciate you help on all of this, 1 this will protect Blaggs if this is a life threat and 2 unfortunately it might attract the press who will wriggle through rumour and supposition back to you and the crew Cox", "Yeah well we don't need that Tony because of this weekend but I understand these things develop like this".

So, the words I would like you to use are "*we know little right now but are continuing to help the police with their investigations*" Just keep it simple" "yeah ok, Tony no problem" "and drill it into the crew to say the same."

"Yeah ok Tony understood, will do I'll do it now before they set off home". "Ok Cox one last thing, in the new house you said there was another guy Alexzander?" "yeah" said Cox, "he's a nice enough chap Aleksander" its pronounced with a K."

Tony enquired again "ok no second name?", "er well no actually Tony I never knew he was introduced to me as Karpov or Kaprarov but he signs things as Makonde that all I know" ok mate but he I think has an art gallery in London, and there was the girl , "yes" Tony said "what about her, well she disappeared a couple of days ago, she still hasn't answered my text message" "and when did you send that?" Tony asked, just a minute, Cox opened his messages on the phone.

He scrolled down a couple of texts then said "8.10 yesterday morning". "ok thanks Cox the less said about here right now the better" Tony continued, "but do not delete that text", "ok mate, take care of yourself I will come and see you tomorrow all being well, Im based at Dart HQ but will be moving down the Plymouth later tonight to help with coordinating some aspects of this tonight, good luck over there" "OK thanks" Tony Cox said "speak later ".

Coxy called the crew back into the snug in the Ferryman's Inn, "now lads quiet please, this is important, this evenings event have obviously buggered up our rowing, but this is unravelling to be a major incident for all our sakes listen up, please pay attention to what im going to say to you".

"I've just got off the phone to the police, who are coordinating operations to bring this mad man to account, but they are well aware the press might jump in for a story, so the words you must use until these idiots are arrested are *we know very little right now but are continuing to help the police with their investigations*" Keep your heads down and keep quiet, we don't want any undue attention or newspaper expose this side of Salcombe", "what about Salcombe Cox? asked Posh Henry "are we still going ahead? "

Cox stood at the bar before the crew, "my thoughts are this boys, Right now I am thankful we are all safe, I really am it could have been so much different and so to all of you, we should carry on as planned, albeit we don't have Mr Blaggs right now, but we should practise as best we can and focus in the mind we are going to take that Salcombe silver salve trophy, and if we can do it for our mate and crew member Blaggs we should, he's had a lucky escape tonight and im sure that is only just sinking in right now." "Huaggh! Skol" went the chant from the crew.

"So," Cox suggested, "we meet here again tomorrow evening half five sharp and we can then show the world our stuff. Ok now all of you get off home. No texts no mobile calls please; if you need me call my home number."

A collective of "Ok's and nods" broke out from the 5 rowers, the last of the drinks were downed and a quiet subdued Tallet crew left the pub for home. Cox went to the bar, Sue came over oh Cox love you look shattered, she turned to the optics and poured a Brandy here love have this one on the house "yeah it's been an unusual night Sue that's for sure", Cox whispered across the bar "er Sue, can I ask a favour, and offer a word to the wise, er should any reporter come round can you try and I know it's hard but can you try and put them off the scent," "of course Cox no need to ask , we don't need this sort of this shit in the village, bloody outsiders causing a riot". "Yeah, Ok Sue thanks.

Coxy turned and there in front of him was June, he looked at her and just broke down, "Oh June love, I've been so scared" "come on Coxy lets go home, Sue looked on "take him home June it's been hell for him."

Chapter 20

Out at sea, the Ukrainian yacht was still moving towards Plymouth, Devlin was on the helm, he was following the sat nav and could see the lights of Plymouth sound before him, Vasyli was making coffee below, the night air off the water had turned cold, they needed to be alert , the Navigation was precise and the screen was well Illuminated there was a swell and an 4knot running tide, they each knew the boat was limping into Plymouth at best they were making 3 knots, they needed 5 to 6 knots to keep moving forwards.

In a combined operation Tony Handsome and his team from Dartmouth with Devon and Cornwall police at Plymouth in close cooperation with the "The Ministry of Defence Police Marine Unit at Devonport had been following the Ukrainian yacht, they had made a positive identification of the boat and had been following its course and progress for the last two hours, they were in position with drones and a coastguard helicopter.

Tony was convinced the taking and arrest of the two suspects on the yacht would be better if it could develop into a fake rescue situation, but that outcome would remain a slim chance and would be in the lap of the gods, however a window of opportunity was possible as they approached the Plymouth Sound the sea state was getting worse.

On the yacht the radio clicked *"good evening this is QHMS Longroom Plymouth Channel 14 calling vessel*

Makonde, Makonde please respond", Devlin Shouted below to Vasyli, "Hey come quickly, they are calling us on Makonde, why how? Vasyli thought for a moment and looked to the top of the main mast, there is a transponder, it will be set to the Makonde registration not so easy to change the name of the baby now is it Devlin the transponder is set Makonde for all three of the boats.

The radio Clicked again *"good evening this is QHMS Longroom Plymouth Channel 14 calling vessel Makonde, Makonde please respond,* Vasyli shouted over to Devlin, "should we go not go in?", "I will say whether we should go in stay calm! "I will reply."

"Hello Longroom QHMS this is yacht Ruvuma calling, over how can we help, " the radio buzzed " *hello Makonde please give your intentions please?"*.

Devlin put on his best English accent and replied, "we are making slow headway to Plymouth", *"thank you Makonde, please confirm your destination in Plymouth sound port area and your heading please, we have no registration details is your visit business or pleasure.,*

The radio clicked again Devlin Shouted again Vasyli where in Plymouth are we heading, Vasyli was quickly looking through the maps and charts, he found a chart and looked for Plymouth, tell them we are going into.... Into where Vasyli? Plymouth Western Channel tell them that! Hell fire! said Devlin, QMS we are going into Plymouth Western Channel Marina".

The radio clicked again, *"this is QHMS Longroom Plymouth please repeat?* Devlin said, "ignore it Vasyli, we just go in and find a berth".

The radio clicked again *"This is QHMS Longroom Plymouth to Vessel Makonde Please set up an approach via the Eastern Channel in the white sector of Plymouth Breakwater*

East Head Light Beacon, a pilot vessel will meet to assist you.

The Yacht carried and limped on for another 20 minutes, it was being tossed about by the converging tide and flow of the receding tides, this was a notorious part of the Plymouth Sound estuary and the big lumbering boat was starting to feel the weakness in it's one engine approach.

Vasyli looked behind the boat there were other boats moving in the same direction, he said "Devlin there are other boats going our way we just follow them as they pass us", Devlin said "I can't see how far off they are, Just keep going" Devlin shouted above the din of other boats horns going off, the radio clicked again *"This is QHMS Longroom Plymouth a pilot vessel has been dispatched to assist you, please slow and allow alongside" ,there is an emergency operation on the sound Makonde please assist. Confirm please".*

Vasyli was watching from the rear and Devlin was at the bow looking ahead, above them was a circling helicopter which didn't seem to be moving on but was using a search light off in the distance, "Vasyli I can't see where we are heading point" the noise from above drowned out Devlin's voice, he looked rearwards, he could see Vasyli, but Vasyli couldn't hear him.

The Lynx helicopter shone a spotlight on the water, it followed across the water and lit up the yacht a circular beam of light surrounded the whole yacht, the light was blinding Devlin could not see further than the edge of the boat the dark brown water below making his footing a challenge.

At a sudden point a naval security boat came in to the beam of light and pulled up alongside the boat, Vasyli was startled and surprised at the speed of the approach, high powered spot light blinded Vasyli, a loud explosion from a Thunder flash and smoke grenade was detonated on the rear deck and the flat sunroof, another boat slammed into the yacht from the port side, Six masked men came aboard, six automatic machine guns were pointing at Vasyli and Devlin, "get down get down get down" they were shouted down onto the deck.

Two men jumped on Vasyli's back pinning him down whilst wrist restraints were put on him, Devlin was told to stand still hands above his head 4 machine guns pointing directly at him. Move slowly hands up come this way Vasyli was bound up wrist and feet and slid along the side of the deck.

Devlin came down from the side gunwale, three of the men pulled him down to the deck face down, his hands and feet bound with plastic tie straps, the other three held machine guns at him, his head pushed hard down onto the deck, "get off me" he shouted, the more the shouted the more the men held him down crossing his legs into a stress position and strapping him up.

He resisted but was overcome by the three special forces officers. They silently patted him down, the men stopped the engine, each of the two patrol boats were lashed to the 50 ft boat each side. Vasyli and Devlin were covered with a blanket and a ubiquitous canvas bag over the head.

Devlin could feel the ensemble of boats motor off, after 15 minutes or so Devlin became aware that lights were on him, it was bright he could see little through the canvas sack on his head other than it was bright lights.

The two special services motorboats each side of the yacht fell silent. Vasyli could smell heat and hot diesel fumes; after what seemed like minutes, he could hear footsteps and many of them military boots on hard concrete and the clatter of belts machine guns.

He was lifted by his arms he was dragged across the deck of the yacht and onto the adjoining motorboat, he was then lifted high off the boat and across a concrete floor, he could feel the rough surface as he dragged his feet into a room and across to a chair.

Devlin was dragged complaining from the other side and other service boat. He too was dragged kicking and making a noise, he was taken silently to a room, it echoed as if it was an empty room, he was forced to sit down on a hard chair two firm hands pressed down on his shoulders. It was cold but smelt of military. A musty smell Devlin knew well.

Devlin could hear footsteps and someone entering the room, the canvas bag was removed from his head in one swift move, the lights were intense, and it took a few seconds for his eyes to adjust, sat in front of him were two uniformed service personnel, two Policemen and behind them were two armed officers, at the door were two more.

He could make out the masts of the yacht outside, it looked like they had been taken to an under covered wet dock, the two grey and green camouflaged special service motorboats were moored each side of the yacht gently bobbing in the covered wet dock.

"Well congratulations gentlemen, what a welcome!" Devlin sneered in his best Englishman's deep tobacco'd voice. The two policemen and Special Services agents stared at him, they waited for him to say something else, "So gentlemen how can we help you"? again, Delvin's sneering English voice raised no reaction from the six officers sat opposite.

One of the officers turned over a sheet of paper, "are you Devlin James Constantine also known as Danslav Nikiforovskii?" "Do I have to answer that?" Devlin questioned the officer, "May I have a cigarette gentleman?" after a few second the officer said, "no sir this is a non-smoking establishment, are you Devlin James Constantine also known as Danslav Nikiforovskii.?"

One of the officers leant forward and said "*kh-vatit pritvoryat'sya starikashkoy Danslav, vy potratite zrya vremya I nashe tozhe. sotrudnichat', I eto budet men'she prob-lem dlya vas i vashego druga.*" (stop with the old boy pretence Danslav, you will waste your time and ours too. Co-operate and it will be less of a problem for you and your friend over there.)

Devlin slowly looked to his left, there sat in an office directly opposite on the other side of the wet dock was Vasyli he was still sitting bolt upright with his canvas bag on his head, Devlin slowly turned his head back and looked directly at the officer asking the question.

"So, I will ask you again, the uniformed officer continued "are you Devlin James Constantine also known as Danslav Nikiforovskii?" Devlin took a few seconds to answer in his deep tobacco'd voice .... "I may be", "I am arresting you on suspicion of involvement the murder of Silvia Alina, the trafficking of slave labour to the UK and in dealing with the handling and distribution of class A drugs" and the use of a firearm in the attempted murder of a Mr John Blagden yesterday 16th September. "You do not have to say anything, but it may harm your defence if you do not mention when questioned something which you later rely on in court. Anything you do say may be given in evidence. Do you understand?" "perfectly!" "my lips are sealed old chap "sneered Devlin with a wink, almost breaking into a laugh, "can I speak to my lawyer's now please? which is I think one of my rights to justice .....gentlemen?."

Tony looked at him in disbelief then continued "You will be detained here under special HMPS home office section 23 Terrorism Act 2006 emergency measures and a warrant to hold you here, is incepted".

"Danslav, there is one more thing, a second officer rose to his feet "and what in holy god's name might that be?" sneered Devlin,

A Dutch official stood up "I am Gertz Van der Bruggen, I am from the International Residual Mechanism for Criminal Tribunals, in the Hague, you have affirmed you are Danslav Nikiforovskii," "not true, I said I might be, interjected Devlin, his eyes wild and dark.

"We have good reason and evidence to believe you are and identified you as Danslav Nikiforovskii, you are wanted for war crimes in the former state of Yugoslavia, you were identified and named as being responsible for the deaths of 60 people in a war crime atrocity in the town Srebrenica of December of 1996.

"You are responsible for the grave breaches of the Geneva conventions, violations of the laws or customs of war, genocide, and crimes against humanity."

Devlin said nothing and rolled his eyes and slumped back into the chair, whilst the gathered six officials organised their papers and enveloped documents.

Devlin then sat bolt upright alert and had a determined look on his face and hissed in his deep voice, his lips quivering and hands clasped tight *"I will rage against the dying of the light. Wild men who were caught and sang to the sun in flight, have learnt, too late, they grieved it on their way to the gallows, and so, I do not go gentle into that dark night."* Devlin's eyes were wild dark and staring his arms were shaking and hands clasped tight in a fist.

Tony Hansome put his glasses on, he huffed, looking down at his notes and documents on his crossedleggs where he was resting his note pad. he looked up, and said directly to Devlin "very entertaining I didn't consider you were a sensitive man, any reference in this instance from or to Dylan Thomas, however incorrect you so recall its content, it is a highly inappropriate trope of a desperate and guilty man, it makes no sense Devlin...or Danslav, You are a wild, cruel desperado of the very worst kind, you and your kind are not welcome in my country you are not an Englishman, an Englishman has a morale code worthy of the true and accurate kind words of Dylan Thomas"....... Devlin protested calling Tony Hansom and imposter and demanded again a cigarette, Tony raised his voice "please be quiet! whilst my colleague asks you some questions".

The Dutch officer continued "when our British counterparts have completed their investigations and relevant custodial sentencing, you will be transferred to Scheveningen, Belgic Park, in the Hague to face these charges made against you".

"We will see gentlemen!" Devlin sat back in his chair, he was trying to appear almost relaxed, he sat there with a sneering smile on his face, the six officers stared back and said nothing.

Devlin said raising one eyebrow and looked around the assembly of secret service agents and International Police he smiled and hissed "Gentlemen are you happy now?"

"Take him away", said one of the international military policemen, he was handcuffed hooded and lead away. His feet shuffling as he was marched away, he was flanked by two officers and backed up by two-armed service personnel.

The six officers after a short, huddle and a conversation, looked on and watched Devlin as he was bundled into the back of a waiting prisoners van and cuffed to the bars inside the claustrophobic single seat cubical in the back of the Police van.

They then one by one made their way across a wooden bridge across the wet dock and the dark green water 10 feet below, they stopped to view the yacht flanked by the two military naval motorboats, a pair of sniffer dogs were on board with their handlers, one team on explosives to ensure the boat was safe for the following team of dogs looking for drugs, work was being done to start to search the vessel. Shortly it would be hoisted onto the dry dock side and the hull and its modifications inspected.

The Police and Special operations team moved on, they marched through an outer office and entered the room where Vasyli was sitting quietly under guard waiting, the two officers guarding him were dismissed and remained outside the room, Vasyli straightened his back as he heard them enter the room, he made a fist in each hand as he heard the approaching six officers, two armed officers stood with weapons across their chest inside a guard stood across the door.

Vasyli's head covering was removed, he squinted his jet-black hair across his eyes in the bright lights, Vasyli took a few moments to adjust to his surroundings, in front of him were the six uniforms.

One of them pulled his chair forward a little, "can you please confirm your name Sir?" Vasyli's head was now down looking at the floor, he raised his head slowly his jet-black greased hair dropped down across his right eye, looking at Tony Handsome with his head canted to one side, he then scanned the other officers in the room and had a look of total distain on his face and shrugged his shoulders.

"Sir I asked you to confirm your name for me please?" Vasyli slowly said " My name is "Vasyli Gilovich " Tony Handsome continued "thank you Vasyli", my name is Detective Constable Anthony Hansome, I work for the South Hams Police force, I work with a team from Devon and Cornwall Police, I would like to ask you a couple of questions", "Do you know why you are here?" Vasyli said nothing, "I want to ask if you know this woman?"

From a brown envelope Tony produced a photo of Silvia an enlarged colour passport photo, her hair straight, her dark eyes and red lips and smile looking straight back at the camera, Vasyli looked at the photo with no emotion in his face or voice and without taking his stare from Tony, he said "I do not know her" Tony leant back and said "are you sure Vasyli?", Vasyli repeated himself "I do not know this woman" "a pretty girl im sure you will agree " Tony said, Vasyli just stared back at Tony, a cold look, empty of empathy.

Tony took back the photo and replaced it in the brown envelope, "Ok so, how about this more recent photo of the same woman?

Tony was passed a second envelope by one of the officers sitting to his right, he produced 2 colour A4 photos which he held up for Vasyli to see, it was again of Silvia, this time her blood-stained hair was plastered across her swollen, bloated and disfigured features, sand was on her face, her eyes half open, lips blue grey and her skin a pallet of purple and grey, a blood-stained eye, a white bag partially covering her lower face and neck.

Vasyli looked and immediately turned his head away looking towards the floor again, Tony held the photo up in front of Vasyli's face, Tony continued, "not looking her best, wouldn't you say Vasyli? She seems to have suffered some distress I would say!".

Vasyli, In his broad eastern European voice Vasyli said "I don't know that woman" he started to fidget moving about in the chair, looking at the floor again, "are you uncomfortable with that image Vasyli" asked Tony?

"Why should I be?" replied Vasyli. "because you do know this woman Vasyli, you and Silvia Alina shared the same house for almost two years," Tony held another photocopy up, do you recognise this house Vasyli? Tony held up a photo of the new house in Dittisham, Vasyli said "I don't know this house you say" Vasyli continued in Russian, "nechego dokazyvat' glupomu angliyskomu politseyskomu". (*nothing to prove to the stupid English cop*). In a moment, a second officer from the left said in a low quiet voice to Vasyli "vam budet legche otvetit' na vopros po-angliyski, chtoby my mogli dvigat'sya dal'she. (*it will be easier for you to reply in English, answer the question so we can move on.*)

Vasyli continued to fidget, Mr Gilovich, who do you work for? Vasyli said nothing, "do you know this person," Tony held up a photo of Aleksander getting into a black car, Vasyli raised his head, raising his voice he shouted, "no I do not know this person!" "And you don't know this building?" Tony held up a Photo of Gallows Farm, "I do not know this place" "I do not know this place" Vasyli repeated.

Tony then took another envelope from the officer

over his left shoulder, from it he produced a photo of Vasyli and Silvia on the back of the Makonde, this was one of the photos taken by Quentin on the day he piloted the yacht to its Dittisham lake mooring, this time 'Tony' said nothing, another photo was held up of Devlin walking with Aleksander across the car park at Gallows Farm together both wearing sunglasses open neck shirts enjoying the sunshine.

Tony remained silent maintaining a fixed stare at Vasyli, A third photo was of Devlin and Vasyli on the launch on its way to the Makonde. The last photo was of Vasyli and Devlin and Silvia together in the garden of the new house.

Tony picked up the envelope containing the gruesome photos of Sylvia's body again, "So, Vasyli, can you tell me please, do you know this woman?" Vasyli looked up his eyes squinted, and teeth gritted he growled under his breath "fuck you, stupid English cop".

Tony turned, he said to his colleague "I think you also have some questions for Vasyli", "Yes thank you Constable".

A tall officer stood up, Tony got up and sat down, the tall officer moved in front of where Vasyli was sitting. He was in green combats and was wearing a beret on his greying hair, he took off his reading glasses, "You know who I am Vasyli, you will remember me, we have crossed paths before", there was a pause he looked at Vasyli looking for a reply, Vasyli looked back at him, he broke into a laugh.

"I am Nicolai Voss, I work for Interpol, Geneva representing the National Central Bureau. You may remember Vasyli, me and my team arrested you in Crimea 6 years ago." There was another long pause, "You are Vasyli

Gilovich, aka Vasyli Nikonchin, aka Vasyli La'Moyer, these are names you have used in various countries, where your criminal dealings have come to the attention of the authorities, yes?" .... The military policeman waited for a confirmation from Vasyli.

Vasyli remained motionless and silent, "Where shall we start Vasyli?" there was a continued silence from Vasyli an empty pause, Voss looked directly to try and get him to make eye contact with him.

Vasyli was showing no emotion or surprise at what Voss was saying, "So, is it class A drugs distribution, firearms smuggling, murder, extorsion, people smuggling, slave labour or prostitution?, Voss sat back crossed his legs, Vasyli moved on the chair trying to make himself more comfortable his hands handcuffed to one side of the chair, making his movements look awkward.

Voss continued "Vasyli, we in a few minutes will be searching your vessel out there on the dock, we expect to find class A cocaine, a high-quality version of the rough cocaine product you import from Georgiou Golva in Bolivia via a false keel, on several of these boats sailing out of Belem in Brazil" Vasyli looked up, almost with a look of disbelief on his face. Voss said, "Yes we know about this Vasyli".

Voss Continued "we, expect, as we have found this afternoon at Gallows Farm this to be a refined cocaine sold through your distribution network of lowly farm equipment outlets in the UK and south east of the UK including the Makonde Gallery run by Mr Aleksandar Valarie" or Karpov or Kaprarov, or Makonde."

"You need to understand Vasyli, every person involved with this crime is being arrested right now as we speak and will be faced with serious allegations and no doubt further prosecutions".

He continued "You Vasyli Gilovich are wanted in Georgia for gun running and arms dealing. You are wanted in France for the Murder of two women, and now the UK authorities want to question you in relation to 22 men and women kept in slave labour conditions at a plot at the rear of Gallows farm where you have been refining a class A drug".

"Do you have anything to say Mr Gilovich? "Vasyli stared at the floor, hunched up motionless, Silent, Voss continued, we have a collection of international warrants for your arrest,
of course, when the UK authorities have completed their investigations, prosecution's and your custodial sentencing you will then be repatriated back to Simferopol detention centre number 1 to continue your 20-year sentence"-.

"As you know Vasyli the law in Crimea is unique in as that if you break your detention, you will have to restart it again from day number 1". Vasyli looked up his teeth gritted, he was red in the face boiling with frustration, anger and shaking with pure hate. He spat on the floor and growled at Voss and looking round the room at the assembled in front of him "pizdy!"

Another officer approached, he stood over the bundled and curled-up and shaking Vasyli, Vasyli stared down at the officer's shiny boots, the officer said,

"Vasyli Gilovich "I am arresting you on suspicion of the Murder of Silvia Alina, the trafficking of slave labour to the UK and in dealing with the handling manufacture and distribution of class A drugs and substances".
"You do not have to say anything, but it may harm your defence if you do not mention when questioned some-

thing which you later rely on in court. Anything you do say may be given in evidence." You will be detained here under special HMPS home office section 23 Terrorism Act 2006 measures and a high court warrant to hold you here, is incepted".

Vasyli started to sob, Tony Stood up and stepped forward, "I trust this are tears of regret and sorrow Vasyli" Tony said, - "take him away".

The two special service guards with faces covered pulled Vasyli up, a third handcuffed him and led him away in the same direction as Devlin.

They both were taken to be locked up at Plymouth Naval lock up," the Glasshouse" then transferred to a secure solitary detention facility at Dartmoor Prison. Both men would be armed guarded 24 hours a day.

Tony went to a debrief meeting immediately, following the detainment of the two Russian drug dealers, in the meeting, the two men were passed over to the Military Prison Service, S Branch for seriously dangerous detainees, this was a greatly enforced detention protocol, set aside for those prisoners who the Home Office considered were dangerous and posed an immediate danger to the general public.

Tony closed the meeting an hour later, the 7 stakeholders and representatives of the countries where warrants were out for their arrest and had been for many years thanked Tony and his team of undercover detectives and service agents and their collaborations in bringing these dangerous criminals to justice.

News had come in that Aleksander and Mikhail had been detained at the Gallery in London and were under arrest and being detained in Southwark police station jail.

Nicolai Voss said to Tony that he and two of his men from Interpol were going to make their way to London, to make further arrangements for their detention and with the Met's Specialist Firearms Unit, SCO18 to bring Involvement in murder of Silvia Alina, drug dealing and distribution, people trafficking and firearms charges against them.

Tony thanked officer Voss for his help and that reports would be exchanged as they were compiled in relation to what was found on board the boat and back at the farm and the new house.

Tony sat in his car he called Cox, "hello coxy mate I know its late but just to let you know we caught them and they are staying at a local hotel owned by her majesty the queen - Dartmoor" oh my God thank you Tony, we can rest now, yes indeed, "Coxy, Im going to see Blaggs tomorrow morning, I know you're probably wondering how he got himself into tall this trouble, but I need to speak to him before the press get hold of the story, would you meet me at St Margaret's Hospital tomorrow morning?" "Er well yes of course Tony, I'll see you there at 9? "er yes Tony said, "that will be good". "ok see you in the morning, "Thanks Tony" "thanks Cox."

Coxy put the phone down, June said "who was that you're seeing in the morning then?", "It was Tony" ...." yes said June what does he want?" "I don't know but we are meeting in the morning at the Hospital to see Blaggs. June said "the sooner that man get his thinking head on the sooner hell stay out of trouble" yeah ok said Cox.

Coxy pulled into the small hospital car park in his dirty little van, he went in and asked the receptionist "could you tell me where John Baddaford was please?" she snapped at him in her high-pitched voice "it's far too early for visitors", Coxy was taken aback "well im meeting...., Coxy felt a tap on his shoulder, there stood Posh Henry and with a coffee in his hand behind him was Tony Hansom.

Morning Posh what you doing here", well I could ask you the same Coxy, "morning Cox" said Tony, so Tony what is all this about, "well I know it's the regatta on Saturday, and you are a man down right now, but im sure your man will be fit for the race," Coxy said "bloody hell Tony the poor bugger was shot last night", "yeah" said Posh "he was in a right bad state", "oh yes im sure he wouldn't want to go through it again" said Tony. "let's go and have a chat with him" Tony said as he led the way.

The three men walked down two corridors away from the main wards, they could see a uniformed armed policeman outside a room, without knocking Tony marched in, Cox and posh followed could believe their eyes there on a bed in the private room was Blaggs eating a full English breakfast, "Bloody hell lads can't a man eat his granola and a full English in peace Blaggs said, slurping a big mug of tea".

"wha? what? what the hell is going on Blaggs" said Posh Henry, "shush up im eating", Tony stood at the opposite side of the bed, "I think I have some explaining to do Cox and especially to you Posh."

Tony sat down on the edge of a table, he took a deep breath, "we arrested two notorious Russian criminals last night bad bad people, it was a big operation and has taken a lot of planning, Coxy, you know one of them you knew him as Vasyli the house manager at the new development and Posh you had met him a couple of times I think and, you met the leader of the pack Devlin. John here has been working with me for over 18 months, to work with us to infiltrate their operations on the river Dart and previously in Brixham. John has been instrumental in helping us understand how the system was worked and what they were into and up to".

A week ago, we discovered the 22 refugees living in terrible conditions at the farm, we also discovered mixing and purification equipment for refining cocaine, this was a sizable operation they were responsible for the distribution of coke in the UK and Europe worth over 30 million. So, on behalf of the Devon and Cornwall police the Home office and the Special Combined Forces units, we would like to say a big thank you."

Cox your call couldn't have been better timing, and Posh you made the difference and in a way kept our operation valid and balanced. The two Russian guys don't know what hit them last night as a result they are in the clink and will face some serious charges.

"Blaggs here will make a full recovery, I have spoken to his doctors and he will be fine, in fact Cox he wants to ask you a question Cox." Oh yeah what's that Blaggs, "Er well said Blaggs with a mouth full of sausages and egg, "Cox I know this has all been a bit surreal and strange and I've been a bit of a twat at times," "at times? Blaggs you're always a twat "said Posh Henry, "but to cut to the chase Cox er really er am I on the team for Saturdays race?

Cox looked at Henry and Said well how is your arm? And your broken ribs? "It is alright Cox honest, I've had stitched to close it up apparently the bullet went in and out the fatty bit said Blaggs "there's plenty of that" said Posh, "Oiy" Blaggs continued, "no long term damage

Cox, it is bloody sore I admit, but I should be ok for Saturday, and if a swap sides with Posh I will be pulling on the other arm, So ?? can I Cox…..Please?.

Coxy looked at Tony, then at Posh Henry, listen to me Blaggs you know the training is key, we have a session tonight and it's the last one till Saturday, "when will you be released from here? This afternoon Cox, ok great, but I don't want you training today, why? said Blaggs, "because I'll have no fall back if you fuck your arm up tonight in training, I will arrange something, you will be on the water tonight but not rowing ""Eh? what? said Blaggs and Posh they looked at each other.

"How will that work? Cox looked at them both, who is the Tallet Cox?" "you are" Henry and Blaggs said , "well done, so stop asking questions and do as I say, report to the quay 5.30 tonight

Tony said and if these nurses give you a bright white sling cover it up please "ok said Blaggs will do. and for the next few days you will be in the company of a plain clothed armed officer.

So, Tony said as he stood up, Im sorry to have asked you two gents to show up early but as you can imagine I have a long, long day ahead of me, but that leads me on to my last point and I know I've asked for you to comply with this before, I need to make formal police request this time gents, please abide.

Tony slid on his rain coat, as he fastened his buttons up and secured his belt, he said "guys, please, please, please do not talk to the press, they will be sniffing around today, the answer is

"we are not able to comment as the police are continuing with their investigations, please refer your questions to PC Fenton at River Dart HQ ", "ok yeah, no problem".

The three men Posh Henry Blaggs and Cox nodded and said they would. "so, who is PC Fenton I've never heard of him, is he new? said Coxy "It's she and very new" said Tony."

"Oh, and one more thing, me and the wife will see you Saturday at Salcombe, Blaggs, listen up, my wife drinks white wine and I drink pints ok? cheers all", Tony left the room.

"Ok so what do we tell the rest of the crew?" asked Posh Henry picking up a slice of Blaggs toast, Cox said "we must stick to Tony's request and that is tight lips for now", "Blaggs you will not discuss this with anyone in the crew other than me", "How will you get back from here later? said Cox "I'll pick him up later, we will see you outside the pub later."

Just them the door opened an in stepped a woman, short cropped blonde hair red top black jeans and boots and a blue jacket, attractive even though she had no makeup on, "hey up Blaggs the Doctor is here to give you that enema you keep raving about!"

"Sadly, not Sir" said the woman, "but, if you do misbehave, I will resort to other methods of concentrating your mind", wagging her finger, she laughed, and went to the bedside, she held out her hand to Blaggs to give a handshake", "hello you must be John", "yeah, I am said Blaggs" looking at her up and down, " I am PC Fenton, im going to be your armed guard for the next few days".

Blaggs took her by the hand and gave it a gentle shake. "A woman?" Said Blaggs in disbelief, "they sent me a girlie?" "yes, John, a full-blown girl" said the woman, Cox and Posh Henry were laughing, "Sometimes" said posh Henry you have a habit of rolling round in the shit and debris of this life Blaggs and then come up smelling of sweet roses."

PC Fenton continued, "Gentlemen, for the sake of this deployment I must ask you to work with me, please do not ignore me, but beware I am here to do a job, So, John, we will be together, first name terms, friendly but not too friendly and that is my first ground rule," and you will not be out of my sight ok!?" "aaah Blaggs its sounding just like married life already" said Coxy "they sent me a girlie"! repeated Blaggs.

PC Fenton turned to Cox and Posh Henry, I will be driving John for a few days, we have an unmarked car, so where will he need to be? At the Quayside Dittisham 5.30, Cox spelt it out, "Does he know where it is?" she said pointing with her thumb at Blaggs, "oh yes, no worries, where there is a quay there is a pub where there is a pub you will find him" Posh Henry pointed out, "not for a few days though" she said I've just checked his meds and he is on antibiotics for a week". Today's news is getting worse said Blaggs, first they send me a wife then no beers!

Blaggs said "So, PC Fenton do you have a first name, yes I do she said, staring at Blaggs, and what might that be then? said Blaggs, "Jenny she replied "Jenny? that's a nice name, can I call you Jen? Yes, you can John, "er it's not John," Blaggs said, "its Blaggs, and always Blaggs", "Ok Blaggs she said nice to know you".

Now then Cox, can I have 5 minutes with you to go over the preparations for Salcombe this weekend, er yes of course said Cox, I suppose you will need a room? No, I already have one thank you, Tony has been a busy fellow, Blaggs said "you can always share with me Jen love", Yes I could said Jenny, looking over her shoulder, but you know the ground rules, she laughed "Blaggs just relax. She turned and winked at Cox and Posh Henry, Posh gave out a "tut tut "! "Blaggs you got more jam than Robinsons mate!!"

Later that afternoon the crew of the tallet met at the Ferryman's inn. Blaggs arrived flanked by Jenny, she was introduced to Sue at the pub, Jenny told Sue that under no circumstances should she serve this man an alcoholic drink, Sue called over Posh Henry and said "Who is she and where the hell did, he get her from? Well, it's a long story said Posh Henry, but I think they make a lovely couple! Don't you?

Cox arrived, ok, ok," listen up Tallet Crew, tonight we are going to practise our turns, this is a crucial part of our winning formula, tonight Blaggs will be replaced by a guest rower of much experience and repute, Blaggs will of course be taking a rest but if all goes well will be on number 2 seat on Saturday. So Blaggs and Jenny you will take Busty Belle, Blaggs you will film our turns, at we will use this footage tomorrow night in the hotel and watch where we can make any improvements".

"Ok Coxy" said Blaggs, Cox continued, "sitting in for Blaggs on number 2 will be Quentin", "Quentin! asked Tommo and Jake, "why Quentin?" "two things" Cox said, "he was available at short notice and he will teach you buggers more about pace, cadence, oar balance and rhythm than "Bob Marley" ever could. He will be with us in a few minutes". "while I get ready, get the boat on the water and let us crack on".

The Crew gathered their oars and were aboard, the five oars upright at attention. When Cox and Quentin arrived, Quentin greeted the crew with "good afternoon boys", "Hi Quentin, how is it hanging" said Posh Henry, Quentin climbed aboard and took up seat 2 in front of Posh Henry and behind Jake. He joined them in hoisting his oar upright. "Ok" called Cox if everyone is ready let's just slowly get out there and head toward Pighole please, "Pighole?" said Tommo "we never go there. Cox said "Pighole! Tommo come on, stop talking start rowing."

Behind Tallet was the busty belle following 30 yards back off the stern of Tallet. Coxy radioed to Blaggs, "Follow us to Gurrow Point, we will make a turn at your Dads old buoy, then pick up the far bank to Pighole, you motor ahead I will raise my hand when we are ready to turn, you know the drill, then you back off and start filming then" "Roger" crackled Blaggs the radio popped and whistled.

PC Jenny Fenton was enjoying the trip and the sight of Tallet coursing through the water was both picturesque in the gold of the sun setting lower in the sky, she said to Blaggs "I didn't know it was this aggressive", "yeah the boys are putting on a good pace" Blaggs was concentrating on the boat. He started filming, then stopped, placed the camera down.

Cox called to the six rowers "come on give me some puuuuull! give it to me we are 500 yards in boys I want some speed please", the spray off the bow of Tallet was blowing Icey cold water on the vested backs of the rowers.

Cox called for more "come on dig in boys I want 40 x 150 at 10 knots come on pull" "sit on your seat Tommo! did I say stand up", "Quentin get in time lad", "Fish sit the fuck down! Cox's eye was looking at all the rowers his eye was critical and photographic "Jake sit closer to the middle, Jake shuffled across in-between strokes, that's better called Cox.

"We are flying now boys! keep it on!", Cox was aiming for a buoy it was 70 yards away straight ahead ,Ok

Tallet Crew get your selves ready, as they surged toward the buoy the water rasping on the hull, Cox raised his hands, Blaggs grabbed the camera and started to film as he held the tiller under his other arm, Jenny sensing he was trying to juggle the tiller and the camera, she moved across and took the tiller off Blaggs, he looked surprised , she smiled at him her perfect white teeth and warm smile, let me do this she said.

Blaggs started to film as Cox counted down and turn! The port side crew lifted their oars clear of the water, the other side dug their oars in deep, the Tallet turned in a perfect arc around the buoy, Quentin smiling as it happened, the lads on the port side gave a stroke as the other three joined in, like a Fred and Ginger dance perfectly timed and so graceful.

Jenny shouted out "look at that!", Blaggs said "shush im filming", "I have never seen anything like that" Jenny enthused, Tallet had cleared the turn and ws on the way back towards them, Jenny was so mesmerised she drifted the Busty Bell right into the path of Tallet, Blaggs took the tiller off her in a snatch and veered away, she yelled "Sorryeee"!!

Blaggs laughed and said, "Bloody land lubber!" Blaggs turned Busty's taps on, her bow raised itself as she stormed after the rowers, the Belle's pace picked up her engines roaring, Jenny looked over at Blaggs who was more than able to control Busty Bell at full speed, he winked at her and shook his head, soon they had caught up with the Tallet now streaming down the far channel heading for Gurrow Point buoy number 2.

Six big rowers heaving their way into the water making the tallet fly, Now, Now, Now called Cox, they were approaching 40 strokes, a hard test for any Gig crew keep it on, come on give me speed on and on and on and on Cox was growling at them, and go and go pull it lads pull it hard come on, we are turning in 20 strokes don't count it, just look at me!

Cox eyed up the Gurrow buoy, he aimed the bow of Tallet directly at the buoy, as they got almost there, he called the turn within feet of the point of no return "and turn about now", the well-practiced turn was swung into action it was perfect, the port side oars were up starboard side down deep almost under the buoy.

Tallets stern turned like it was on ice, the boat rose onto its own wake and rode off again the six oars reaching the water in perfect unison.

The boat creaked and the banging from the pins leathers and oars on the gunwale planking bringing Tallet alive, three oars came down and the other three oars come up, the beat of the rhythm was precise and without a word the well balanced rowers pulled hard, thighs pushing down and backs pulling the oars up, core muscles working hard to pull the long wooden oars through the oil like water.

Ok said Cox let's do a sprint, I want to see you lot sweat and sweat hard ! come on Puuuull boys give me rapid strokes at 45 for 100, go - wa! Cox was leaning forward shouting at the top of his voice, stroke, stroke, stroke, go boys, we want the silver tomorrow so go, go! the crew were sweating hard, red-faced arms and shoulders bulging, core strength full power hard on the neck, the boat was flying down the course towards Spanish boathouse.

Coxy looked to the side, the speed of the water passing the boat was breath-taking, it was now Cox was ready for Saturdays fight at Salcombe. "Ok lads one last turn".

The crew looked at him the Tallet was at full cruising speed, Cox eyed up a point in the middle channel, he called 3, 2, 1 and turn, this was the fastest turn he had called, the oars went in post side pulled their oars p the boat tipped up it rode up and down the following wake, the oarsmen pulled away from the turn again it was perfection in Cox's eyes. Tallet shot back up along the channels and along the frontage at Spanish Boathouse, "Ok crew stop rowing", Cox looked around and waved in Blaggs.

The crew stopped rowing holding their oars over the water, each man and especially Quentin were breathing blowing and trying hard to catch their breath bent over forwards laying back into the laps of the rowers to the side and behind, Sweat was pouring off each man's brow, back and the palms of their hands.

Blaggs bought the busty bell alongside Tallet, Blaggs Posh Henry and Jake held Busty on to Tallet. The tide was on the way in, the water was relatively calm, the boat slowed, the gentle flow of the river pushing them slowly almost relaxingly drifting back up the river. Cox handed out water bottles Jools passed them back and Tommo passed them back again. "Lads, crew of the Tallet, we are ready.

Coxy stood before them and said "right tomorrow we travel to Salcombe, we are staying at the Portside hotel, there is a bar, but....i don't want you getting boozed up, I can't make you not order a six pack and shorts but im asking you, we will have a nice meal at 7 pm, we will talk tactics and have an early night, I've sorted some place secure for the Tallet to be parked up overnight."

Tony Hansome is going tow Tallet for us tomorrow morning, Posh Henry will be taking the oars and all of your bags, there are four seats with Posh and 3 with Tony, Blaggs I take it you will be with Jenny? Er Yeah, Jenny said We have a couple of seats in the back, and so do we" said Quentin so plenty of room everywhere.

"So, Blaggs where are you at? Are you going to be fit I suppose is the question?", yes Cox I will be fit". Blaggs gave the suggestion of a slight air of desperation in his tone, Quentin said, "Just to underline lads im available if Blaggs can't make it," everyone in the boat obviously wanted Blaggs in seat 2, but not at any cost and certainly not at the cost of losing the race.

"So, lads, Tallet put away safely tonight, it that ok Blaggs?", "yeah, all good Cox", ok, Lads I want that silver salva, I want it so bad!" he made a fist. The crew laughed, Posh Henry said well lets go get it Crew Tallet! The crew shouted at the tops of their voices, ""*In the Halls of Valhalla, where our brave sons live forever - Tallet crew has come to ruin your day!!*" The war cry went up echoing down the steep sided valley of the river, all the crew raised their oars!! "Huhggahhh Skol!! "

Chapter 21

The Friday Morning was wet, it had rained over-night, the cool air coming off the river was chilling, Posh Henry arrived at the Ferryman's Inn early, Sue had made him a breakfast, he sat with her telling her of the exciting day in Salcombe tomorrow, she was listening carefully, he had tucked into his second round of toast.

Sue said, "Posh", "Yes Sue" replied Posh Henry with a mouth full of Sausage and tea, Sue continued, "can I come to the regatta?" Posh answered still munching on his fried bread, "course you can Sue weather looks good tomorrow, it'll be a nice day", Posh munched on his bacon and egg, she looked at him through her long lashes, Posh did a double take, "What?" Posh said, "well I was wondering if I could come with you today Posh?" "what? with crew Tallet?" Well, if it's too much trouble Posh I won't"! snapped Sue, "er Sue love, er well, er".

"I didn't tell Coxy you might want to come, so there's the small detail of where are you going to stay, you know?" she took a drink from her coffee cup, "I could stay with you Posh", she looked away staring out of the window hoping deep down her suggestion might find a soft landing. "What? said Posh Henry, how? Im sharing with Blaggs", "oh ok don't worry then Posh you boy get all loved up on your own!".

Sue got up and cleared her things from the table and went through the swing door into the kitchen. Posh Henry stopped eating and sat back, he held his head in his hands and whispered to himself "for fucks sake".

Coxy appeared "Hey, Posh what's up mate?" "Oh, nothing" said Posh "Same shit different day you know". "So, young man, have you got your Landy ready?" "Yeah, just got to fill her up then im ready Cox", "great......everything alright Posh you look troubled", "er well er yeah im ok, look Cox, can I not share with Blaggs", "oh Posh lad you're not", said Coxy, "oh right, ...what!" said Posh, "Er Blaggs is under guard remember? he will be in a room on his own, PC Fenton is or has been sorting his room out it's all a bit hush hush", "really?" said Posh, "yeah you're on your own Posh", "why? " Coxy if I pay can I bring a guest? Bit late notice said Coxy, who are you wanting to invite, Sue appeared and stood behind Posh clearing the breakfast table, Morning Coxy Sue said, Hi Sue love, all ok?

Posh turned to Cox and said "Sue Coxy" "Its Sue! - I want Sue to come with me", Cox looked at Posh, then looked at Sue, he was stumped for words, after an awkward pause Cox said, "ok Posh I'll leave it all up to you, my June has all the room details, she is here look".

June was outside holding six shopping bags, "Ah Posh here are some bags I need taking can you put them in your car, yes June of course, er June", "If I pay can I bring Sue with me to the regatta, June looked at Posh and looked over his shoulder at Sue working in the pub cleaning up.

Is she closing the pub then, it would seem she wants to support us in Salcombe, Posh's eyes were fixed on Junes face, She could see his dilemma in his face, a mixture of pain embarrassment not wanting to disappoint, June put her hand on his shoulder, "no need to pay Posh ill sort it out of funds", "Of course it will be great to have Sue along, but, she will have to share with you."

"What!" ? Posh said, June winked, with a knowing

smile, "yeah come on". "Thanks June".

Cox reappeared with another bag, here we need this one too, I'll be back in a minute Coxy hold on, Posh Henry went back into the pub.

Sue had just gone through into the kitchen. He followed her in, she was putting plates into the dishwasher. He walked up behind her, he stood closer to her than he ever had, she turned, and he held her arms, she looked at him "what are you doing"? He held her in the small of her back and pulled her closer in an embrace, he smiled at her and said "for once in your life shut up and listen, I would like it very much if you would be able to come to Salcombe with me....... today!", really Posh? Oh Posh, she melted into this embrace, his strong arms holding her close.

"Yeah really, but you need to get a move on and get the pub closed up, we leave in an hour", she shook her head, her blonde hair swinging, "Im not closing the pub she replied, I have cover" "you're not that special you know Mr Henry - yet any way". Posh smiled and said, "Girl Scout eh?" "you'd better believe it", she said smiling with a coy look, Posh slowly closed in for a kiss, Sue responded warm and tender.

Cox and the crew were assembled on the quay, Posh had arrived with the Landy Oars were strapped to the roof rack, Tony and his wife had Tallet on the back of his pickup truck, Jenny and Blaggs were in another car and already on their way into the 45-minute trip to Salcombe, Jake and Jools arrived, and Tommo and Fish were all loaded up and ready to go. Quentin and Mary turned up last minute, it all was in place.

"A Ditsham convoy here today" said Coxy to Quentin, the weather had improved somewhat, and the warmth of the sun fell upon the crew, the banter was good as always, the mood was better.

at 12.00 midday Coxy said "ok let's go and get that Silver Salva", the Tallet crew en'mass made their way to war "Tallet crew were on their way to ruin some one's day".

The crew gathered outside the Portside Hotel, June had gone inside to allocate rooms and a table and private room for the team meal later that evening, June came out with keys, she handed them out, where is Quentin and Mary called June Sue called over the car park "Quentin and Mary had gone off into Salcombe to view the water!", Posh and Sue, Tommo and Fish found the bar, Jake and Jools helped Cox in with the bags, the weather was good , warm September afternoon, the garden of the hotel was green and overlooked the blue of the sea, the sea was calm and quiet, boats were sailing and motoring in and out of the estuary it was a normal Salcombe day from the view point of the hotel.

Salcombe Town Regatta week is jam packed with activities on land and sea for all ages, from sailing and swimming to fireworks and fancy dress. The name "Regatta" means a series of boat races, either rowing or sailing but for the team Tallet this was the highlight of their year.

The whole crew met in the Hotel and settled into a meal, the ladies sat opposite from the men, the six rowers sat in the order they rowed in, after the meal, Cox said ok crew can I have your attention. So tomorrow is D day, we have one chance to take the salva back home, this is your only chance this year to take a major prize, our key to the success is .....Cox looked around the table,

"Blaggs! our question for Blaggs is he ready?, a cruel question but we have come a long way".

The whole crew and table looked at Blaggs, there was a silence, he put down his napkin, leaned back in his chair and addressed the crew.

"Lads, im sorry for the last 12 months, I've been and asshole and despite the challenges I have been involved in my passion for rowing Tallet has remained at the top of my world, I am fit for tomorrow, I admit, I am in pain, but I know that by the time that gun goes off tomorrow afternoon, I will be in the moment, in the groove and pulling my way to a win".

"So, my question is right back at you guys Tallet Crew, do you want me on board tomorrow?" "if you do im in" 100%, and thankful for a couple of things, one is the support from you guys however small or big I guess some of you are a bit pissed off with me right now, and two thankful my injury wasn't more serious for me, and I mean this when I say for you, I mean the crew Posh, Tommo, Jake, Jools and Fish , im sorry we arrived at wrong time, wrong place that wasn't by my design. So im asking you, Tallet Crew and Coxswain, to make your own decision, it's your race as much as mine."

A silence dropped on the table again, Posh Henry said "can I say something, this is my race but it's not all my effort, its all of us, a team, the Crew Tallet. It is absolutely the case that Blaggs is an asshole, he is a grumpy bastard, he is a twat of the highest qualification, having said that, I Posh Henry couldn't row Tallet with all the verve and aggression needed to win tomorrow, if that twatish grumpy, asshole wasn't sitting next to me pulling in pain for all the might he can muster, and if he was to let us down and then in turn let me down I will after the race hunt him down and sink his boat. "

Tommo put his hand up, "Coxy, I can't row tomorrow, without Blaggs being on seat 2", "Fish raised his hand and said I can't row tomorrow unless he is behind me", "I do want Blaggs hurting behind me," Jake said "I will not row Tallet without my teammate Blaggs earning pints for me with every stroke", Jools said "if I don't have to look at him, I'll row tomorrow with Blaggs in the seat 2."

Quentin arms folded looked across at Coxy, he said "So, Coxy you have the final word", "I do said Cox, "it is clear we have one chance, Salcombe are aggressive fast and we are on their turf, so I need all the good men on Tallet, my men, my team, the Tallet Crew".

For the next hour Cox and Quentin talked about the boat, balance oar position seat positions Cox said here are the seats for tomorrow, Posh Henry seat one, Blaggs Seat 2, Coxy looked at Blags over his reading glasses, Jake seat 3 Jools Seat 4 Tommo seat 5 and Fish in 6 why have odds gone to evens asked Tommo, Quentin said can I answer that Cox, er yes carry on Quent, so the previous pattern gave to problems with leg extension and the balance of the boat in the water.

Tommo and Fish need to let the oars out longer, Blaggs and Posh need to remain as is but Blaggs needs to shorten your oar and lengthen your stroke a little.

Why all this now, the night before the race asked Posh? because the boat was out of trim and balance Quentin explained that he and Cox have been working on the finer point for weeks. Cox ended the meeting with the start line shenanigans he was expecting from Salcombe, they have been accused of interlocking boys, pushing onto our course, so beware and look out shout at me not at them. The start line will be up the estuary and will turn at a location in the mouth of the river on the tide in open water. We will then turn, and the race will finish on a line adjacent to the town quay.

Quentin continued, "Tomorrow morning at 8.30 we will launch Tallet from the Town Quay slipway, we will then explore the area on the water, a simple morning of slow rowing, steady not strenuous, a lunch will be served at 11.45 it will be a cold lunch with tea or coffee served by June and Mary off waterside. Tony and the five girls will follow the race in the observation boat. Quentin will be on the race directors' boat as an umpire.

So, Crew Tallet, it's getting late, we have an early start, any questions? The Crew sat around the table said nothing, ok lads it is bedtime, get some good sleep and we will see you for breakfast 7.00 sharp in the morning. The table emptied with groans about the early start, each man could feel the tingle of excitement in their bellies as the race day was only hours away.

Er lads just before you go, I have some bags here said June rushing to the back of the room, she passed them out each bag was named , Tommo opened his and said wow , Fish and Jake opened their awesome said Fish, in each bag was a rugby shirt, on the from was the word Tallet, on the back the name of the rower , Coxy said these have been done by June and Mary , so hip, hip the crew bust into a hip hip hooray for the girls, then they sang the war cry, "*In the Halls of Valhalla, where our brave sons live forever - Tallet crew has come to ruin your day!!*"

The morning was cool, the weather forecast was misty start then clearing for the rest of the day. Tony had struggled to get the long boat down to the Harbour Quay as the streets were narrow and crowded already with event organisers vans and truck parked everywhere. Tallet came off the trailer without a hitch, she slid into the water looking bright and graceful. Tony tied her up on the harbourside as Tommo and Fish were the first to arrive, both guys looked good in their new shirt and dark sunglasses. Tony left them in charge whilst he moved the pickup truck. Fish had gone off to collect a couple of lattes from the café on the harbourside.

Tommo was on board Tallet wiping the seats down, and generally trying to make Tallet look her best, he heard a voice say hello there, could you tell me when the big race start? Tommo didn't look up, he said Im sure it sets off at 2.00pm this afternoon, ok thanks, then he recognised that Voice, he looked up and there was Charlotte Oh my god said Tommo, hey Charlotte, how are you?

He scrambled off Tallet and gave her a big hug she reciprocated and enthusiastic kisses were exchanged, you are a sight for sore eyes said Charlotte, oh really Tommo replied.

Fish arrived back with hands full of coffee, Hi Fish, Charlotte said as he arrived hey Charlotte how are you, where is Olivia? "well, im really sorry Fish Olivia had a bit of a pantomime getting away from the terrible Margot, Fish's face dropped a look of disappointment crossed his face, Charlotte said "yeah Margot has been a real bitch but as in all good pantomimes there is a happy ending, she winked at Fish and smiled "She's behind yooou!" shouted Charlotte, Tommo burst out laughing "hey Fish you should see your face".

Fish swivelled round and there was Olivia a vision in her shorts and cropped tee shirt long hair and a warm smile and kiss for Fish to sink into. Fish said to Olivia, "it's so nice to see you again", "likewise" Olivia said in her Canadian accent.

They were soon holding hands and sharing laughs and the Latte's, the tow Canadian girls were full of stories of their lucky escape from the clutches of the sea by their two hero sailors and how Margot had not let them out of her sight for days. Slowly the rest of the Tallet Crew and partners arrived, Blaggs and Jenny came onto the quayside, by the Coffee shop was a woman, as Jenny and Blaggs passed her, she had her camera out snapping away, Jenny spotting her making some notes on a note pad, Jenny put on sunglasses and stood in front of Blaggs as he took his waterproof top off.

The woman started to make her way across to the area on the Town Quay where Tallet crew were preparing to push off from, "are you here for the race asked the woman", "we are" said Coxy, oh good are you the team from Dittisham?, "we are that" replied Coxy, Have you come here to watch us?, " I am more interested in your crew member there Mr Blaggs or Baddaforde as he seems to be known in St Margaret's hospital, Blaggs overheard her ,Yeah? said Blaggs "what do you want",? "I wanted to ask what your thoughts were in relation your connection to a woman's body found in Bigbury a few days ago and the report you have been shot, would you like to make a statement Mr Baddaforde? "

Jenny stepped forward cutting off the woman's approach and said "you are not going to ask any questions to Mr Baddaforde today", Jenny produced her ID, "a police matter already said the woman, Interesting!", behind her Tony Walked up to Jenny he too was wearing dark sunglasses, "perhaps I can help you" said Tony, "ah Detective ", "under the terms of Clause 3 of the Editors' Code can I have your name please, " That sounds very official" she said, she put her note pad away in her shoulder handbag she pulled out a card "Judith Hayes" was on the card.

Tony Looked at her and said, "thank you", "I wish I could say the same" Ms Hayes, "why do you say that DC Hansome? I didn't know you were a follower of the rowing fraternity", said Ms Hayes "that just shows your lack of local knowledge and appreciation of the fundamental relationship between the Police and the press Ms Hayes" Tony replied confidently, "you seem very sure of that DC Hansome". "Are you still working for the Plymouth telegraph?" Tony asked, you're very perceptible DC Hansome, Ms Hayes said, Jenny stepped away and dialled on her Mobile phone.

Ms Hayes there will be a good story to be had in relation to your interests right now, and I don't think you will need to worry about getting first grabs on the hot story, but I must warn you now is not the time, Ms Hayes looked around at the masculine assembly before her, these big men getting onto the boat, why is that? Ms Hayes asked, her mobile phone started to ring, she looked at the screen, it was her office in Plymouth, she said to Tony "excuse me DC Hansome", Jenny nodded to Tony, "of course Ms Hayes" he said as She put the phone to her ear.

A gruff voice of her editor in chief was on the other end said the words "Get away from there now"! "Come back to Plymouth now, we have a document you need to see, I want to see you in the office, but, but Ms Hayes tried to interrupt, 1 hour be in my office! The call was ended. Im sorry DC Hansome I ned to go back to my office, it seems someone has tipped my boss off she stared a long stare at PC Fenton who was back-to-back with Blaggs. "so nice of you to drop by" said Jenny, Ms Hayes stormed off through the crowds gathering on the town Quay.

Jenny tapped Blaggs on the shoulder, ok all gone big boy go play in your boat, fucking hell Jenny im all a shake!" Blaggs said, Jesus! where do she get my name from" "doesn't matter right now Blaggs we will take care of that", Jenny re assured him, "you'll be fine just put it out of your mind for today. Ok? Blaggs all is under control." Tony stepped forward, Blaggs go win the fucking race ok! Blaggs said thanks Tony, thank you. Posh beckoned Blaggs to his seat, the crew stood up in the boat and held oars vertical.

On the opposite side of the town Quay were the Salcombe team, all were watching as the sleek and smartly uniformed Tallet and crew were gently pushed off to float out on to the main water, the sun was bright and the reflection off the water was harsh, Cox passed forward two tubes of sunscreen and six baseball caps each with Tallet across the brim, plaster yourselves in this slip slap slop and get your cap on "said Cox.

Tallet drifted for a while, the river there wasn't busy at this time of the day and the water was quiet and still. There was time. each man looked like a pale skinned red Indian with war stripes on their noses and under their eyes, the new red shirts and hats made a smart statement on the water. A marked contrast to Salcombe's team they were a scruffy team.

Tallet was powered into a few slow long stokes of the massive oars, she moved gracefully downstream clearing into the deeper water channel, there the water was softer easier to row, the boat started to float with the water, soon Cox was asking for 30 strokes the boys were warming up nicely, in the midmorning sunshine. They could see that the town was filling up, the regatta attracted many locals and those living in the South Hams areas as well as a swell of tourists and holidaymakers, the sea and estuary was turquoise green the splash of any wave produced a pure white spray which was a fresh and cool contrast to the sun now beating down, the few hours on the water had got the crew comfortable settled, the banter was back to where it was always good and the foundation of friendship and comradeship not found in many other close working team sports.

Coxy knew this, he had learnt his trade following many years of rowing, he first rowed in Tallet at the age of 19 and he was now in his mid-50's his father and uncles had the same sort of history on Tallet.

The core of his teachings was as his father had taught him, was to work together to an end, it may not always result in success every time, or first time, but his deep belief was that one day one of these exceptional men in front of him would aspire to take his place and bring the old girl Tallet to win after win and his legacy would live on.

Time was moving on and the radio crackled, it was Quentin, "Cox, time to meet at waterside, we are here and looking forward to feeding you greedy buggers, over",.......ok replied Cox we will be there in 20 minutes Over. Coxy put the radio down and said to the guys, Right boys if you are hungry make for the Waterside Quay the family is waiting to feed us up before the race. We are 2 hours away from being on the line, so we don't have much time. the boys put a sprint on, and the strokes were well over 40 Coxy was loving the experience of low, flat cruising speed the Tallet again showing her brilliance as a craft able to cut the water with a unique wood on water hull rasp, Coxy looked at Jake and Jools they were looking back at Coxy?

"What's up Cox? said Jools as the noise on Tallet was now deafening, "if this is my end said Coxy "Then Lord Jesus take me now!"

The crew of Tallet laughed, Waterside was now a few hundred yards away, Cox stepped the pace down and Tallet settled into the water, the waterside Quay was secluded but still within easy access of the river and start line, the boat came alongside the quay side, assembled were the Canadian Girls, Jenny, Mary, June, and Tony's wife. The crew raised the oars and one by one got out of the boat stretching their legs. Set out on a table was a spread of food and good things for kings, pasta chicken legs savoury pies and ham and egg pies boiled eggs rice dishes, salad, sandwiches cake lashings of tea this was an unexpected feast said Tommo, all of the ladies had had a hand in preparing the food and putting it out.

It was very much a good lunch the boys looking fabulous in their red and black tops, dark sunglasses finished off the mystery of Tallet crew Sophisticated, yet a fitting set up for a small Dittisham team to take on the Salcombe regatta opposition. The girls were looking good too, this made for a great lead up to the start of the race.

Quentin said ok Tallet crew you have 30 minutes to get on the start line, it is 1.20 pm now we need to be on the line at 2, so, get off to have a piss then be back here in 5.

Quentin got on board Tallet he cleaned her down and bailed out her bilge. Coxy wiped down all the seats and foot hold, he checked all the thole pins and leathers, Tallet was dry light and ready to go.

The crew returned to the Waterside well-watered, fed and fuelled up and ready to do battle. They all looked magnificent strong confident and ready.

They climbed aboard what they knew as the best boat in the South Hams area, each man sat down and raised his oar vertical, the ladies looked on proudly as their men were going into battle.

Kisses were blown by the girls as the Tallet was set free again onto the open water. Quentin had made his way to Town Quay, the ladies were due to board the observation boat, so all was left on the quay where it was and off, they set.

Tallet made a steady trip across the river to Kingsbridge Basin, there the opposition boat "lady" was circling, the crew were big and rowing strong, straight backed and jabbing at their pulls of the oars, the tallet crew could hear the bang as the Salcombe boat shocked the gunwale Pins "look and learn" said Coxy, Blaggs look at the lead oar, yeah I see it said Blaggs they are jabbing a the oars.   Cox asked the boys to stop rowing and let then drift for a while , we still have 10 minutes said Cox, "Take some time to ease your breathing boys, so remember look at me, I am your focus, let me tell you how to win this race, it may get choppy and it might get like a war zone but stay with me, our turns will be good , we know the crack so let's do this boys , it is 45 minutes of hell but I want us , I want you to win! Dig it?" "Yeah!" was the reply "I knew you would" Cox smiled. The radio crackled, it was Quentin, "looking good Cox, tell Tommo to shift in 6 inches he's leaning on the sidewall, tell Blaggs to sit up". "Ok" said Cox, "Tommo move in 6" Blaggs sit the fuck up!".

The radio crackled again, "good afternoon Tallet this is the starter, please approach the start line", Coxy signalled for the crew to slowly paddle to the start line, there opposite was the Salcombe team, their boat was old too, the hull varnished and dull, their oars patched, and leathers worn.

Coxy looked across, their lady Cox looked back, it was eye to eye contact and the war was about to begin, the opposition boat shouted a pathetic Oggy! Oggy! Oggy!! in a vain weak attempt at a war chant.

Coxy nodded his head at their Cox and said guys, "that sounded soggy, soggy, soggy! we need to sing the opposition a song don't we boys?"

"Ok 1,2,3" and the crew growled the Viking war chant across to the other team, *"In the Halls of Valhalla, where our brave sons live forever - Tallet crew has come to ruin your day!!" Huugh!!!* Team Tallet punched the air as their chant rang out across the water, the ladies on the observation boat held hands, as they could hear the boys Viking shout it added to the already high stated of excitement.

There was now just 1 minute until the cannon. Cox shouted to the crew, "Lads thank you for your efforts so far, now im going to ask you for hell on earth, the countdown was now at 15 seconds, enjoy this lad as its going to be a rough ride.

He called out the countdown coming from the radio, at 5 seconds he called oars in" the cannon went boom across the water, Cox's timing was perfect, the first stroke got tallet moving, the second shot them forward in out in out coax shouted, he could hear the Salcombe Cox shouting too.

Cox called out "and give Meee 40 lads I need 40 x 100 Blaggs was pulling well, Posh Henry in time on time and digging deep, oars in oars out and move this bastard ship" Cox called, "now and now and now , Coxy and Tommo made eye contact, Tommo smiled, Cox just stared back half in awe of the effort he was putting in and half making sure he was settled in, Cox admitted to himself it was maybe a harsh and critical look but this was war.

Tallet's speed was increasing she was riding the water well "in -out in -out" he called, looking across, the Salcombe crew were neck and neck there was nothing in it in the first 200 yards, heading down the course the Tallet crew were flying, Jake and Jools were pulling hard, already pain on Jools's face told Cox they were giving it their all.

So were Salcombe, they passed Snapes point coming onto the main run into the Salcombe Harbour, each heave on the heavy oars bought Tallet faster, and smoother, each man grunting as he lifted his oar clear of the water, Cox called out again "watch your oars boys keep them level" the noise coming from Tallet was immense, Cox could hardly hear the cheering and shouting coming from the cavalcade of small boats behind them, Tallet was making noises like she was singing to them, they could feel her silky flow and rasp of the hull across the water, "pull it through boys" Cox encouraged the crew each pull on the oars left 6 perfect marks on the water behind the boat, behind them was the race directors boat and a carnival of other boats turning up the pale green water into a white wash as they followed the race.

Coxy looked across at Salcombe their bow just 6 feet in front of Tallet, the crew on Salcombe's boat were pulling hard, too hard thought Cox, the speed was good, but she was laying bow high, all her weight was in the stern, the bottom of the boat was showing itself as they heaved ho on the oars.

Cox could see his crew pulling harder as they saw Salcombe creep slowly into a small lead. "OK boys let it go, we follow to the turn", Cox steered Tallet just behind Salcombe slipstreaming off their stern, the pressure came off his crew as they rowed with deeper oars than Salcombe, the pace eased but their speed kept on track with Salcombe, Cox could see ahead he could see Salcombe's Cox looking back to see how far off the stern Tallet was, the spray coming from the bow of tallet was minimal but the spray over Salcombe was starting to show.

In a second Blaggs caught a crab, bang! his oar jumped out of the thole pins and his oar dipped and twisted, he was out of time with Tommo and Posh, "Lift it!!" Cox bawled at Blaggs,

Blaggs was gritting his teeth aaaagggh! Blaggs growled as he struggled to maintain his composure and drop his oar back into his pins and get the oar back in time with the rest of the crew. It took two or three strokes to make contact again and join in the cadence. Blaggs looked at Cox fear was on his face, Cox saw his concern and called back "good recovery Blaggs, don't do it again" Blaggs found himself back in time with his fore and aft rowers.

Tallet did not lose any time and were no further back, the estuary opened up into the bay past Starehole bay, this was still a mile and a half away Cox's tactic was to stay where he was and then position himself for a rapid turn on the turning boy under cutting Salcombe's boat and sprinting back , Cox's mind was now on the turning point, there were a large number of boats at the back of the Tallet, so he was mindful of the chaos which might come from a sharp turn at near full speed. They were now passing Fort Charles in a few 100 yards they would be turning with the curve of the river mouth and in sight should be the turning buoy.

Blaggs was starting to feel his shoulder burn, the swelling from the gunshot was stinging he felt he couldn't grit his teeth any more for fear of breaking one, he was rowing eyes closed, his focus was on the end of the race he knew though there was another 20 minutes of agonising pain to get to the finish line.

They had just cleared Fort Charles as the Salcombe boat started to pull away, within 100 yards they were a good length ahead.

All the ladies on the observation boat were screaming at the tops of their voices and waving hard, even to suggest Cox could hear them was farfetched. but they were willing Tallet to catch up.

Coxy sat low in the boat every part of keeping Tallet low and sleek was thought through, the boys were hot sweating but not too over stretched. The marker buoy for the turn was now ahead 500 to 600 yards at least, Salcombe had pulled another length and their Cox shouting at his crew like a man possessed, Posh Henry was almost laughing at him as he at the bow of Tallet was close enough to hear him. The Tallet rowers could see behind Cox and it was a sight to behold, there were 30 or so pleasure boats, motor launches the officials the wake of the following armada was in high spirits and close enough to each other to be a harbour master's nightmare.

Cox looked back, he picked up the radio and called Quentin, Quentin replied "Ok Cox still looking good, we need another half-length on them before the turn... over" "Lads I want 40 for 100 ok go", Tallet sped up and closed the gap, Salcombe saw the advance and sped up themselves, their 6 rowers now feeling the pull and wishing it was over soon. The turning buoy was 500 yards out, they in 12 stokes had it down to 400 another 15 pulls and it was 250.

Cox sat up he eyed up the turning buoy as Salcombe moved across, to block Tallets was, the expectation from the Salcombe boat was that Cox would move over too but he stood firm he shouted "Starboard "! The Salcombe boat didn't move, Cox couldn't see the Buoy, his view was lost by the Salcombe boat blocking his line to sight, the buoy was ahead of the Salcombe boat, their cox slowly moved across, Coxy could Just see the top of the red turning buoy over Posh Henrys head, Cox shouted to Henry "where the fucking buoy?" Posh looked around and they were almost on it ," here, here ; here"! shouted Posh , Cox stood up and saw the buoy just passing the front of Tallet.

"And Turn Noooow Lads!!" the starboard oars dug in, the boat slowed right down, Salcombe went flying on past the buoy, on Tallet the port side raised their oars up clear of the water.

Tallet almost stopped as she swung around the front of the buoy, her stern riding her own wake as was her style it was a graceful manoeuvre.

Cox was shouting "get those fucking oars in Tallet we are going home!". As the oars dropped into the water they rowed as if they had been running in a straight line.

The Salcombe boat had shot forwards and gone on to perform a turn ahead of the buoy and was only half-way through a disorganised paddled turn, the armada of sight-seeing boats were swerving out of Tallets way as the boys got into the pace of the sprint to the finish, Cox was shouting pull on Tallet go, go and go, and go.

Cox shouting forward at the boats coming head on waving them from side to side, the race directors boat captain was agasp as the Tallet slew past him in the opposite direction. As they passed all of the pleasure boats and officials launches Cox could see choppy but clearing water ahead, the water was only choppy after been churned up by the spectator's boats, Cox and Quentin plan was perfect their strategic plan was working, Cox scoffed for further disruption was befalling Salcombe as the spectator boats were turning to catch up with Tallet, There was dozens of pleasure craft all over the place, Salcombe's Cox was finding it hard to navigate through rough white water churned up by the melange of boats. The Race Directors launch was soon in pursuit and the Salcombe boat back on tracking Tallets lead, Tallet was now 20 lengths ahead of Salcombe, the finish line was 2000 yards ahead, the spectator's boat was still in a turn out past Starehole bay the chaos went on for several minutes.

Cox shouted to the Tallet Crew "come on boys fast as you like get me and Tallet across that fucking line," for every 9 strokes the boat covered 100 yards, the boys did the maths in their heads as Coxy gave them the rough yardages to the finish line, Jake and Jools had a clear view to the rear of Tallet, they could see the high bow of Salcombe 200 yards behind, the gap was huge, Jools shouted to Cox "they are closing."

Cox turned and shouted at the crew , "keep that gap boys, its 40 plus till we cross", The radio crackled, Quentin was there observing with binoculars from the race directors boat said "keep to the port side of Fort Charles, keep it as tight as you can it will cut 20 yards off the line", "ok" Cox said, he steered left and kept a tight line , he could see in the distance ethe building in the town and headed the bow for the church steeple 1200 yards away.

"Keep this pace boys, keep it light keep it tight, timing everyone, smooth actions give me plenty of smooth speed", Cox looked at each row of the crew, Jools Tommo and Blaggs on the port side, Jake, Fish and Posh Henry on the other side all pulling like a well-oiled machine, all of them had pain in their faces, thighs were straining , deep stokes meant the oars could sometime unseat them, Cox would make a call if he saw a rower unseated, with his usual "sit the fuck down"!

900 yards to go, the boys still running at 40 strokes, Salcombe boat still closing, Cox sat low in the boat again, he now could hear Tallet singing her vicious victorious hull rasping song, the whole of the boat sang in unison with the water, that familiar rasp told Cox things unwritten, a feeling which words couldn't describe, six men powering a 32 foot long 138 year old elm built pilot gig at speed close to 12 knots Coxy considered it was a privilege to sit in the Coxswains seat.

On the observer boat the two Canadian Girls had made themselves known the June and Mary, Jenny was in the Dittisham ladies huddle too, The Canadian girls Charlotte and Olivia had never seen this spectacle before it was exciting beyond words, Mary was holding on to June hands clasped and Sue and Jenny shouting for Tallet, Sue almost losing her voice.

The observer's boat had caught up behind the Salcombe boat and was holding its point there, the Dittisham huddle wanted to see their boys and shouted to the captain to make his way onwards, he moved over to the right and the armada of boats followed in turn as they passed to the side of the Salcombe boat the wakes from 30 plus boats started to affect Salcombe's water turning it from a wind chaffed sea scape on a sunny Saturday afternoon to a Grand Canyon type rapids.

The Salcombe Cox was complaining to the race officials launch by radio, the cavalcade motored on, The gap between Tallet and Salcombe was now 30 yards, Coxy looked back and in looking ahead to the finish line 400 yards ahead reckoned this was going to be tight, Tallet were still pulling 38 -40 strokes , we need a bit more lads called Cox, they are on our arses , the lads could see the Salcombe boat behind only just in front of the swathe of white water churned up by the following spectator boats official boats and family observer boats.

Cox asked for more, "come on lads they are on your arse, go and go and go" Coxy could hear the Salcombe boat behind, "300 yards to go boys come on pull, pull, pull, pull", he was working them hard, really hard, they hadn't missed a beat apart form Blaggs slippage.

The sweat and pain was clear to see, and smell. All the Dittisham team were in pain, giving their all, not one man slacking, each stroke was in balance with each other and the boat, each man clutching his oar like it was their baby.

The Salcombe boat was making its move with 20 yards behind, their Cox screaming for more speed. "Tallet crew come on!" Cox continued to shout for more steam, Tallet sped up and the gap was maintained, there was a lead of 10 yards the finish line was marked across the town quay to the marker on the opposite side.

Coxy could see the line, "come on Tallet we can smell it now", each of the six Tallet men grunted and pulled and gasped as they push themselves to the limit.

Salcombe were now 10 yards behind starting to move over, Coxy watched his line.

He had a line of sight and he was sticking to it, Salcombe moved over and were now just with in tallets boat length just on Cox's shoulder, this could be a dangerous place to be, going on Salcombe's reputation for an interlocking of oars at any time between now and the finish line Cox was nervous of this, as some research by Quentin had found a little too many interlocking stories with the Salcombe crew and young Cox.

"Look at me!" Cox instructed his team, "Just give me 1% more boys come on stop this lot getting past us, the line is 120 yards a head".

The crowds were shouting whistling and yelling, it was sounding like the wild west, "12 strokes lads and we are home come on! "Cox pleaded with the Tallet crew.

The observers' boat was right behind Tallet, Salcombe had now come along side and starting to close in, Jools and Cox both shouted "starboard" as the Salcombe boat tried to move across, give me full speed Tallet, growled Coxy from the back of his throat, now! now! noooow! give it me now!"

Salcombe were now only 2 yards off the line, in the very last surge of a minute, Tallet sped forward and the last pull on the Tallet Oars took her across the line. She was flying fast sleek and now far beyond the finish line, she continued across the water.

Coxy shouted "Yeaaaah! Welcome to Valhalla"!

The Tallet crew pulled the oars across the boat and collapsed into each other's laps, chests were heaving desperately gasping for breath, legs burning and thighs aching the seats were hot and bum numbing.

Coxy pretended to roll a cigar next to his ear, he congratulated the crew, well done lads, well done, is everyone ok? you did it, we are the champions" yeah came back groans. The boat started to slow down, Cox handed out water bottles, Blaggs just poured it over himself and put his hand out for another, Jools and Jake were panting hard trying to get their breath sweat running off their heads.

Posh Henry completely laid out in the bow of the boat, Blaggs head in his hands, sweat dripping off his nose, Cox steered the boat past the off-set pontoon moorings, Jools and Jake gently rowed her back towards the town quay where the spectator's boats and the observer's boats were letting people off. The town quay was packed, the official race directors' boat was further up the town's other slipway, the race director and his officials and referees were disembarking and in a revelry of straw hats, stripe blazers, box fresh white trainers and clip boards were making their way briskly to the town Quay.

The Dittisham ladies were all together and lined the side of the town quay waiting for their valiant men to arrive. Salcombe's crew had already arrived and were trying to look composed as the losing team in the final of the South Hams tournament.

The applause was loud and constant as the Tallet and its crew came alongside the quayside, all six men looked exhausted. Oars were lifted aloft and each man stepped ashore with pride, smiles from the girls with one or two tears of joy, the applause got louder and yelling and whistles sounded off as Coxy stepped aside the Quay, as he stood up the applause went wild, June couldn't help herself as she rushed to him and gave him a hug and hold "well done Coxy my love," "I love you" she gave him another kiss, he whispered in her ear "that one was for you my love".

Coxy moved over to the crew, they all clapped him, and he clapped them, then it was a team huddle, in which the valiant men sang, "*In the Halls of Valhalla, where our brave sons live forever - Tallet crew has come to ruin your day!!*"

A great cheer went up followed by the usual Huuhggh Skol!

The Chairman of the regatta stepped on to a small stage at the front of a marquee on the town quay, he tapped the mic as it screamed, good after noon ladies and Gentlemen we have had a wonderful regatta this year and the final of the South Hams Pilot Gig Rowing tournament has end, in a very hard-fought battle, the winning team will take away the South Hams trophy Silver Salva which has just been engraved behind the scenes. So, can I ask our lady Lord Mayor to present to the Crew of Tallet from Dittisham the winner's trophy. All seven men made their way to the stage and Cox was shuffled along to accept the silver platter, Coxy thanked the Lady Lord Mayor and spoke.

"This year has been a year of challenges and opportunities; this win today wouldn't have been possible for several thing not least of which is the dedication and determination of the Tallet crew and supporters. We have a wonderful team, and we love our sport. Most of all we show each other we are capable of great things. So, I would like to thank June, Mary, Sue, Jenny, Olivia and Charlotte Quentin and Tony for their help in getting us here today. And of course, the skill and dedication of Crew Tallet who are always the real talent on the water, thank you".

Coxy held up the Silver Salva high above his head and a huge cheer went up. the Crew of tallet were given a medal and the applause lasted for several minutes. The tallet team stepped down to a welcome from the Dittisham and Canadian ladies.

Sue came round to find Posh Henry, hey you big man I am so impressed Posh that was something special, Posh looked at her and said with his cheeky smile "come here you," Fish and Tommo found the Canadian girls, Charlotte said "wow guys that was brilliant" Olivia was speechless but offered a kiss to her hero, Charlotte was soon to join in, Mary and Quentin went to see Coxy still clasping the trophy and June like a limpet was holding on to her man. Blaggs was sat on his own, Jenny Came up to him and said impressive Mr Baddaforde, thanks Jenny, she smiled,

Sue said to Coxy and June, "I don't know if I've done right but the pub in Dittisham has been done out with flags and bunting, there is a spread being put on, and a bit of a hoolie is in the offering, all I need to do is call my guys and its done. "Oh ok Sue that sounds good, said Coxy, well a possibility" " Just give me a minute, lads, lads, listen up !" Cox called the crew together, he explained what Sue had said and the conversation was short, the reply was unanimous, and they wanted to celebrate the win back on home turf at the Ferryman's Inn.

Coxy made his way through he crowds to the Cox and Crew of Salcombe's boat, He said "Hi, we are going back home now, thanks for the race, the young lady Cox just said, "yeah ok thanks", she turned her back on Cox and June. Coxy shook the hands of all the six crew from

Salcombe, they all congratulated the Tallet squad and said "thanks", the young Cox gave Cox and June a nod as they left. June said her attitude is disgusting", " it's called being a bad looser June don't worry".

The Tallet was already out of the water and on her trailer, it had been agreed that they would pull the boat by hand off the town Quay area as the street were full of visitors, the crew were all packed up and lifts were arranged for the two Canadian Girls.

The Tallet visitors were on their way back, they would be at the Ferryman's Inn in an hour.
Blaggs had arrived with Jenny early and helped Tony put the Tallet on show outside the pub. The pub had been decked out in bunting and Union Jack flags, the main lounge of the Pub had been set up and closed for a private party.

Sue had arranged a cake in the shape of Tallet, everyone in the party was amazed at the welcome from villagers and visitors alike as coxy held the Silver Salva aloft.

Food and drink flowed for the rest of the afternoon and into the evening. Posh found himself helping Sue behind the bar, and the others crew and followers enjoyed the success Coxy had bought for them and the village.

"Speech, Speech, Speech!" Cox was hoisted to his feet Come on Coxy speech! "ok, Coxy cleared his voice and coughed, Er, well lads what can we say? What a great win from a sour Salcombe bunch over the hills. Coxy had had a few beers and was well oiled. "I would like to say my sincere thanks to my Team Tallet "Schkol!" all of the crew joined In and raised their glasses, Coxy Continued, "This year has been a challenging year for all of us, some more than others, but we are here we are victorious, and we are one big family, and perhaps that aspect of being a Cox brings to me more joy and satisfaction than any finely finished plaster work, or my wife's cooking!"

"Oiy! shouted June, watch your step mister, or you'll be cooking for me!" "Yes love" said Coxy, the gathered laughed.

Coxy looked around the room, all eyes were on him, a quiet came over the room.

………….."The events of the last few days and last week have bought an element of real world here in our village, unfortunate but that is what can happen, I suppose that we are still, despite the holiday letting nightmare around us remain a small unique independent village, we still operate as a community and it's the sport of pilot gig racing that is, in some little way, is one of the bonds that holds us together, and for that I am thankful of.

"So, without our big crew we would not have that glue and perhaps and really, we might not have been here today. So, can I ask that you raise you glasses and congratulate the Crew of Tallet and the folks of Dittisham who support her.

"I toast you, Tallet and all who row in her.!" The banging of fists on the tables and shouting of Schkol Schkol Schkol!! Commenced.

"Ok Ok Ok Come on!" Coxy called out across the crowded room. The room quietened down.

"One last thing, I have been Cox aboard this wonderful boat Tallet for 10 years next year, this has been a wonderful year for me, culminating in our great victory in South Hams today".

"I've known this boat all my life since I was a boy, and so,…. next year will be my last year as Cox",

The Crowd erupted, "no Coxy" ooh Coxy no! Coxy why?" the room was full of chatter and discussion. Quentin was leaning against the wall at the back of the room near the door with a smile on his face, he raised a glass to Cox and nodded his head at his lifelong friend, he and Cox were in a silent agreement.

Coxy Continued, "ok ok, calm down!

"Quiet !!" Blaggs Shouted "

Coxy tried again above the din. "In order to grow you have to accept change, our boat is as unique as the crew who row her to victory, I am looking to retire from Coxing, I want to spend some time with June, on busty, I need to sort my house out, lots of things."

"Im not running away and want to be part of the rowing club going forward, but its time to appoint a new Cox to take over from me next year, now I have a few names in my hat, but applications need to start to be considered.

"On top of that I want to grow the club, we need a junior team, and junior ladies' team, a winning ladies team. So, from that aspect I'll still be here grumping and moaning, and from that aspect I want the club to change and I want the club to grow. Then we can have more of that wonderful unique Dittisham glue that holds us together."

"Cheers everyone" Coxy raised his glass, the room stood up and raised their glass to Coxy who had been joined by June she hugged him and kissed her hero.

The room rumbled as the deep voices of the Crew and all the assembled men and club members grew in unison in the room started to sing their own Viking War Chant.

"Across seas of monsters and oceans of the

waves we travel to war, let no warrior not see that we come to thee, as mighty as Thor, and that within the walls of Valhalla where our brothers live there forever, the Tallet Crew has come here to ruin your day".

"Schkoll"!!

The End.

- This is BBC South West, here is the news bulletin at Midday.

- Police in Plymouth today have issued a joint statement with the Home Office regarding the discovery of an unidentified woman's body at Bigbury earlier last week.
- Home Office Officials have issued a statement regarding the arrest and detainment of 4 Ukrainian nationals who have been linked to the death and are helping police with their enquiries.

- Two men were taken from a yacht bound for the Azores after coming into difficulties as their yacht's engines failed on Thursday evening whilst attempting to make port at Plymouth.

- The other two men were detained in a London art gallery in the early hours of Friday morning, the police have also linked the discovery of 22 refugees linked to the case and hidden in what police described as disgusting conditions at a farm in South Devon, drugs and drug making equipment were discovered there, along with the details of a drugs distribution network throughout the UK and mainland Europe.

- On board the yacht in Plymouth drugs with an estimated street value of £20 million were discovered in a sophisticated smuggling ring, the Police said in a statement that an 18-month undercover investigation had revealed people trafficking drugs manufacture and distribution and money laundering through art sold at a London gallery.

• In a separate statement an official from the Home Office said it been working closely with other agencies in Europe in a collaboration with the Ukrainian authorities to bring two suspected war criminals to justice.

• It was reported from a written statement that when the British authorities had concluded their investigations the two Ukrainian men would be repatriated for face charges in the Hague and subsequently in The Ukrainian Crimea.

• Other arrests were made in the east of the county at a farm where individuals were involved.

• A third man is being detained thought to be the ringleader and financier of the gang who have been operating throughout Europe for 5 years but have eluded capture.

• Detective Constable Hansome from West Devon and Cornwall Police said in a separate Police statement that this was the conclusion of a long and dangerous investigation, he thanked the local community and undercover personnel involved in the case.

Now more news..................

Printed in Great Britain
by Amazon

15679141R00164